C000075641

A Life Eternal

by
Richard Ayre

Burning Chair Limited, Trading As Burning Chair Publishing
61 Bridge Street, Kington
HR5 3DJ
www.burningchairpublishing.com

By Richard Ayre
Edited by Simon Finnie and Peter Oxley
Cover by Mellie M Designs

First published by Burning Chair Publishing, 2020
Copyright © Richard Ayre, 2020
All rights reserved.
Richard Ayre has asserted his right under the Copyright, Designs
and Patents Act 1988 to be identified as author of this work.

This is a work of fiction. All names, characters, businesses,
places, events, locales, and incidents are either the products of
the author's imagination or used in a fictitious manner. Any
resemblance to actual persons, living or dead, or actual events is
purely coincidental.

This book may not be reproduced in whole or in part, in any
form or by any means, electronic or mechanical, including
photocopying, recording, or by any information storage and
retrieval system now known or hereafter invented, without
written permission from the publisher.

ISBN: 978-1-912946-09-9

Dedication

This book is dedicated to two wonderful women I have never met, but who have helped me so much. Both read the embryo of this story and helped me shape it into what it has become.

Anita Waller, Yorkshire lass and consummate author, and Loretta Paszkat, my Canuck friend. Thank you both for all your help and support over the years. I hope you like the finished product.

Richard Ayre

Part One

Richard Ayre

I

The sudden silence was immense. Its heavy intensity pushed me to my knees in the filthy mud, where I stayed immobile for what seemed like an eternity.

The lack of sound seemed complete, but it wasn't; it was just that the guns had stopped. The fading thunder of the last roars of those now unemployed weapons rolled across the sky and disappeared.

There were still noises. Horses progressed in their lines past me, their harnesses jingling and creaking. Wagons squealed by, full of pinch-faced, rotten-toothed, laughing boys who had behaved as men for far too long. Birds sang. Soldiers talked.

And what did they talk about?

Home, of course. What they were going to do now the war was over.

The shock of survival was painted all over their ugly, wonderful faces. They had lived. They had got through it. In truth, I think most of them were only just coming to terms with this rather than wondering about what was next. They seemed lost, if anything. There were no obvious celebrations I can recall.

As for myself, I just remember that morning as a time of nothing. No thoughts. No feelings of what I had seen, what I had done. Of the men I'd killed or the friends I'd lost. There had been too many.

Even at that early stage of my new life, I was beginning to disregard them, to forget them. I had lived. They had died. War had thrown its fickle dice and they had lost, whereas I had won. It was as simple as that. Fate did not come into it, just luck. Pure, blind luck had seen me through to the end, or so I then believed, and the intense comradeship which warfare brings about had almost instantly disappeared. The only real memory I have of the eleventh of November 1918 was the sudden silence of those guns. And that I was hungry.

I eventually got to my feet and looked about for something to eat.

I spied some smoke in the distance and stepped through the recumbent throngs of khaki-clad, filthy individuals towards a rough fire which some of my lads had got going. The smell of the frying meat made my nostrils twitch as I neared.

There were four soldiers hunched over the fire, poking at it in a desultory manner. One of them noticed me and grinned, showing filthy teeth.

'Alright, Sarge?' he asked. 'Smelled the bacon, eh?'

I nodded. My mouth was watering. The young lad, clad in a motley collection of rags that had once been a uniform, scratched his head vigorously, dislodging lice by the bucket load. We were all covered in the little bastards. He handed me some bacon on a broken plate which had been swiped from the remains of one of the houses in the decimated village around us.

The other soldiers nodded at me as I caught their gaze, but they didn't smile. They didn't want me to stay. They didn't want me near them, I could tell. I didn't blame them.

'Ta, Shanksy,' I said to the young lad and moved away to sit by the road and watch the endless columns rumble by, stuffing the hot bacon into my willing mouth.

The noise of the columns—men, horses, even the occasional bellowing tank—soothed me. I didn't like the missing sounds. The silence of the guns unnerved me; it didn't seem natural.

I watched the columns and it slowly dawned on me that this was my new life. I would now watch, not do. I had become a watcher of life, no longer a dispenser of death. Like the guns, I was unemployed. Surplus to requirement. Pointless.

I polished off my bacon and threw the plate down, where it broke and mingled with the scattered glass and ruptured brickwork.

German POWs were now marching by. Their uniforms were rags, they were like skeletons. They walked towards a future even bleaker than my own: although at the time neither they, nor I, knew this.

It was over.

This single thought began to pound incessantly in my head as I watched the battered Germans shuffle past me. It was over. Four years of my life.

*

'Over!'

The officers' whistles squealed, and we scrambled up the side of the trench. To my left, one of the ladders snapped and two men fell back onto the mud-smeared duckboards. There was hysterical laughter from their comrades as the sergeant kicked and shouted at them until they got to their feet and went up another ladder. I walked forward into a sudden maelstrom.

Three men on my right went down instantly, one of them screaming shrilly. I knew them all: Archie Thompson, Bobby Cooper and George 'Dilly' Dilson. It was Dilly who was screaming.

Half his face had been torn away by the enemy machine gun fire. I remember the one eye left in that horror mask staring at me with a terror I could comprehend only too well. I stepped around his gutted, dying body, ignoring the utterly still forms of the other two. I went on, leaving them on the hard ground.

It was like being surrounded by angry, invisible bees. Bullets tore all around me, the warm air fluttering and buzzing from their intensity. The line of men was being cut down all over; in twos, in threes, or single men falling.

Some of them were flung backwards, some of them crumpled slowly. Some of them screamed like Dilly, some of them made not one sound. It was totally random. The noise of the machine guns and the death they unleashed was overpowering.

Our artillery guns joined in the cacophony, still firing from behind our lines in a blistering barrage even though they were supposed to have stopped by now. I swear some of the shells were no more than five feet above my head. I had to duck more than once. They roared or screamed or thundered forward, smashing and crashing down two hundred yards in front of us.

I kept going, trying to concentrate only on following the orders of the officers and sergeants as they urged us forward.

Ahead of me, I got my first glimpse of the trench we were supposed to take. The yards of twisted barbed wire did not seem at all troubled by the week-long bombardment it had been subjected to. It was a tangled, jagged trap, waiting for us, its prey.

I registered a flash of smoke-laden sunlight on a steaming gun barrel and took one more step. Then someone punched my chest three times in rapid succession, and I was slammed to the artillery-ploughed earth. I lay with the corpses of my comrades.

I stared up at the suddenly clear blue sky. Boots tramped past me, accompanied by harsh, frightened breathing. They were moving forward without me. I tried to speak, to urge them on or to beg for help, I don't now know. They left me. The blasts from the shells moved on.

A swallow flitted above me, still hunting for food over the savage games of the fools below. I coughed and something warm and wet spattered onto my face. A whining sound came to my ears and I thought it must be a shell coming in towards me, even though they were moving away. I felt no pain. I was simply short of breath and tired. I just needed a little nap, that was all. The whining noise grew louder and overcame me.

The sky turned black...

*

A hand on my shoulder brought me back to the village. I looked up and realised Captain Greene had been talking to me, asking me something. I scrambled to my feet.

'Sorry, sir. I was daydreaming there for a second.'

Greene nodded, a smile on his face.

He was, like all of us there, a young man: younger than me and I was only twenty-two. But his eyes held the shadow of what he had seen in his years of war. It had scarred him, even if nothing showed physically.

'That's all right, sergeant. It's nice to have the freedom to do so.'

He looked around the destroyed village, then at the never-ending columns winding slowly past us. Eventually, he turned back to me.

'What are we going to do now, Rob?' he asked, softly. His eyes begged me for an answer I didn't have.

I shrugged. 'God only knows, sir. I don't.'

He eventually nodded. He was a man caught in a sudden void. For two-and-a-half years he had lived in squalor and fear and noise. He had made decisions which meant men died, often in violence and horror. He, like all of us, had shied away from thinking about any sort of future, because that future should not have been allowed. He had lived from day to day; indeed, from minute to minute. Now his future stretched before him in a blinding kaleidoscope of probability. He, like I and everyone around us, was drowning in possibility.

'I was wondering if you had any plans,' he said, eventually. 'Do you have a family to go back to? A wife? Children?'

I squirmed uncomfortably. Greene and I had shared a lot. We had sat on cold, frosty, starlit nights and talked of the day-to-day running of the company. Of the men under his and my command. It was Greene who had recommended me for my sergeant's stripes two years before. He had seen something in me I hadn't seen in myself. But we had never really talked in any sort of personal manner.

I remembered his first day as a lieutenant. I remembered a callow, flush-faced boy whose Adam's apple had bobbed nervously after every word as he had tried to exert his superiority over men who had seen death and carnage to such a degree that their humanity was in danger of being snuffed out forever. I remembered laughing bitterly about him with the lads. I remembered thinking he wouldn't last five minutes. I remembered being wrong.

Jonathon Greene had proven to be a most unlikely warrior. Tall, thin, and aristocratic, but imbued with a steel most uncommon. He had survived, he had learned his trade of death, and he had adapted. Quickly. He had become the best leader I had known in my long war.

I had helped him as much as I was allowed once I realised the type of man he was. As a corporal, promoted through necessity rather than any latent talent, Greene seemed to see in me someone to emulate. He always asked my advice and often acted upon it. He had quickly become a leader his men respected and perhaps even loved in their rough, raw way. They valued him immensely and they followed him unswervingly. Not just because he was their lieutenant and later captain, but because he was a man they wanted to impress. When he made me sergeant he had simply handed me my stripes and smiled his wry, lopsided smile at me. He had said not a word. He didn't have to.

He never barked an order, was never short with any of his men, even in the heat of the bitterest battle. Instead, his commands were given in a soft voice and he was always quick with an encouraging smile and a joke.

When he made me sergeant we began to rely on each other more and more, and this reliance turned into something that made our section of the trench a place where each man felt he had a place and his duty was to his captain and his sergeant. The men lived and died safe in the knowledge they wanted to because of Captain Greene. Not so much me, Sergeant Deakin: I knew full well they all thought there were increasingly strange things about me. But

Captain Greene? They would have followed him into the mouth of Hell itself just for a glimpse of his smile.

'I have a sister,' I replied, eventually. 'Muriel. Back in Northumberland. She's married. Got a young boy. I might visit her, I suppose.' I looked around at the devastation and shrugged. 'I'll need to find a job.'

'No family of your own?' he persisted.

'No. My parents are both gone, and I was only eighteen when all this started. There was a girl once, but she's probably settled down. There's really only Mu.'

Greene nodded again. We stood in silence for a while, just watching the column.

'You worked as a Gillie, is that right?' he continued.

I laughed.

'I worked on the lands around Rothbury. I wasn't a Gillie. My dad was the gamekeeper for the Armstrongs. They own everything around there and he, like almost everyone else, was in their service. I helped out. I mostly worked in the stables, did a bit of beating in grouse season, looked after the dogs, that sort of thing. I thought I'd become a gamekeeper eventually, I suppose. But then the war came along.' I sighed. 'Last time I was back, everything was different. Not much work. All the women were doing the jobs I used to do and doing it a bloody sight better than I ever did.'

I laughed again and Greene joined in.

'When did your parents die?'

'Not long after I joined up. Dad died out in the fields. My mother died a few months later. Mu wrote to me and told me the news.'

I became pensive again. I was a taciturn man in those days. I was worried I might be talking out of turn with my captain, but Greene seemed interested, so I continued.

'My Mam was a lovely woman. I'm not ashamed to say I shed a tear when I heard the news.'

'Your father?' asked Greene, probably already knowing the answer.

I shook my head, briefly.

'We didn't really get on, me and Dad. Mu was always his little girl. I think he mostly just saw me as an extra pair of hands. He didn't want me to join up, that's for sure. He said I was needed to help him work the land. He was a man who talked with his fists a lot of the time. He wasn't a bad sort, but we never really saw eye-to-eye. He couldn't understand why I wanted to go and fight. He never understood why I wanted to leave Rothbury. I think it was because I wanted to be away from him that I joined so early. I wanted to see what sort of man I was, not the sort he thought I was.'

I stared into the distance for a while, not seeing much of that Belgian village. Greene seemed to understand.

'You joined early?'

I returned to the conversation.

'Aye. Two days after the outbreak. August sixth, 1914. My eighteenth birthday. Went down to Morpeth and joined the recruiting parade. Told them I was nineteen.'

I laughed, bitterly. 'My dad was furious. Said I'd abandoned them all. The last time I saw him, he stood at the door and said, "I hope you get killed as soon as you get there." Then he went out. I left that day.'

Greene saw the look on my face and touched my shoulder. A typical response from a man such as him.

'He didn't mean it, Rob. We all say things we regret, at times.'

I nodded, unwilling now to pick at the scabs any longer.

'I'm sure you're right, sir. But he had his heart attack and I never got to speak with him again. It doesn't really matter now, anyway. Not after all this.'

Greene knew what *all this* meant. He seemed to come to a decision.

'After you've been home,' he said. 'After you've seen your sister and your nephew, if you'd like a job, I have some land I need working.'

I looked at him, shocked.

'A job?' I repeated.

He nodded. 'In Hampshire. It's my family estate. Mine now. I'd like someone I know who I can trust as my first employee. Someone I know would do a sterling job.'

I was unsure. From my rudimentary geography, I believed Hampshire was a long way from Rothbury. He smiled at my indecisiveness.

'I'll give you my details,' he said. 'No pressure. Nothing like that. If you want the job, I'll keep it open until the summer. After that, we'll see. Go and see your family. If you stay, I'll understand completely. If not, the job is yours.'

I stared at him. I opened my mouth to say something but, at that moment, Major Graves wandered along and told us to get ready to march.

We were going home.

II

The soil was black, darkened by the drizzle that seeped in dreary sheets from the lowering sky. It reminded me of the trenches. The rain dripped from my nose and soaked my new suit. Six feet below the newly turned soil lay my sister, brother-in-law, and nephew: protected forever from the elements. The graves were still fresh.

A few days beforehand, my men and I had been loaded onto an old tug in Boulogne and, after a short journey across choppy waters, had disembarked at Folkstone, where a train waited to take us to London.

The soon-to-be ex-soldiers, still carrying filthy packs and wearing their ragged uniforms, had stumbled onto the platform to be greeted by flags and trestle tables and old ladies who poured us mugs of tea and gave us sausage rolls. We marched through the streets in watery sunshine, past crowds who cheered us, to a town hall where our uniforms were taken from us to be replaced by trousers, shirts and coats.

When we emerged the rain had started, the crowds had dispersed, and we were civilians once again.

I watched as war comrades bade each other farewell. Nobody spoke to me; it was as if they knew there was something wrong with me. I wandered around the corner and found a pub, where I bought a pint of ale and stared into the mirror behind the bar.

I saw a tall, broad-shouldered man with sandy hair and blue eyes. Young in years, yet strangely old. The face that looked back at me seemed too mature for someone only twenty-two.

The war had done it. It had aged me in strange ways: given me a guarded, enigmatic aspect, an inner reticence. I looked like a man with secrets and, glancing around the bar, I could easily spot the men who had been to war and those who hadn't, for the veterans had the same look about them. They caught my glance and nodded solemnly back at me. They could see it in me, too.

I caught a train to sooty old Newcastle, where I found a landlady who took me in for the night. The next day I caught another service further north to Morpeth, a small market town in South East Northumberland. By the time I got to Rothbury, Mu and her family were dead and buried.

It was the grippe. I had seen it in the trenches over the last few months. It had swept through the filth, striking men down in swathes: although at the beginning some of them had recovered after a few days. I had not succumbed, but many had. They were not calling it grippe now, however, for it had changed and it was deadly. It had a new name: Spanish flu.

It was early December and the flu had already killed more people around the world in four months than the war had managed in four years. Of course nobody knew that at the time as the wartime censors were still keeping a lid on reality. Only triumphant news was allowed.

Almost a quarter-of-a-million people were dead or dying from it in Britain alone. My sister and her family were just three more statistics to add to the legions killed from conflict and disease.

I had loved my sister dearly, but I didn't weep for her at her graveside. I couldn't. At the time I believed this was because I was immured by my experiences in the trenches, that I could not reach inside myself and let the grief out because of the war. That I was simply a burned-out, used-up shell of a man. All this was true. But later in my life I discovered another reason for my stoicism.

What was the point of it all? I had fought for four-and-a-half years in a war that had done nothing except kill and maim millions of innocents. There were no victors, whatever the newspapers trumpeted. Instead the population of Europe had simply been reduced, randomly and horrifically, to become nothing more than a continent of shattered survivors. Instead of anguish, I just felt a cold, stony anger, a sense of unfairness. The belief that nothing—*nothing*—I or anyone else did made any difference to anything. The deaths of the last of my blood kin left me as I'd been for years: morose.

I eventually went back to the cottage where my sister had lived and found it already occupied by new tenants, just like my parents' house. The ragged people in those poor dwellings stared at me suspiciously until I moved on. They too had probably lost more than they could comprehend in the war. Like everyone from all of the countries that had fought, they were stained and defeated by conflict.

I didn't go to the house of Sally Robson, the girl I had spoken of with Captain Greene. I had no wish to find out what had become of her. In all honesty, I didn't care.

I wandered around my home village for the rest of that day, past the shops on the small high street still only half-full of victuals. I sat in the pub for a while, nursing a beer. One or two people recognised me, but they kept their distance. They looked upon me with distaste; they had probably lost sons or brothers or fathers and begrudged my survival.

Eventually, I went down to the river and sat on a bench in the rain, watching the water flow by.

What would I do now?

I had nothing. I had left Rothbury as an immature boy and my adult life had consisted of nothing but battle and fear and noise and filth. The war had changed me and shaped me, forged me into something no longer suited for civilian life. But I needed to do something; anything. I needed a job, and I needed time to come to terms with my survival.

For the first time in my life, I was alone. Before the war I'd had my family, and during the war I'd had my comrades in arms, at least up until the Somme. But now my family was gone, and the men I'd shared the trenches with wouldn't give me the time of day: they knew there was something wrong with me.

The rain turned to sleet and, as night fell, I made my way to the railway station and caught the last train back to Newcastle. I had a little money in my pockets and spent a chunk of it on a cheap room near the railway station.

Sat on the edge of a hard bed in the cold, bare room, I pulled out the letter Captain Greene had given me back in Belgium. He had said a job awaited me if I wanted it.

My family were gone, and I was homeless and almost penniless. It seemed I had little choice.

I dreamed that night, as I sometimes still do, of the Medic. That's how I thought of him, whenever I thought of him at all: the Medic.

*

He had black hair and dark eyes. His nose had been broken at some point in the past and he had a ragged scar on his right cheek. He was aged about thirty.

In my dreams he wandered slowly down the ranks of shredded meat that had once been men. Staring, staring.

The three bullets that had torn into me had ruptured my lungs. The bullets had gone through me but had caused massive damage, and there was little hope of me surviving the night. I had been found and collected by medics on that body-strewn battlefield and they had dumped me onto a hand-pulled cart along with several other men with wounds equal to or worse than mine. One of the men who slumped opposite me on the rickety, bouncing cart stared at me for the whole journey, grinning at me horribly. It was only when a fly landed on his eye that I realised he had been dead the whole time and his grin was the rictus grimace of death.

The cart was unloaded at a field hospital, where I was bandaged and then left to die on a stretcher on the grass, while the men who had a chance of surviving were treated first. As the light began to fade, a man walked through the dead and dying and knelt beside me.

He muttered something to me in French, a question I think, and then sighed. He was a young, blonde man. He looked very tired and his white shirt was black with stiff, dried blood.

I could not answer him, even if I had understood what he had said. My breath bubbled in my chest. I felt as if I were drowning. Drowning on dry land. My burst lungs were filling with blood and the pain of those breaths was abominable. But I clung tenaciously, frantically, to life.

The next thing I remember was being placed into a low bed in a hospital ward. The ward was inside a church and French nuns were administering pain relief in the form of soup and prayers.

It was obviously just somewhere they had found to let the dying expire quietly, providing them with the illusion that they were actually being treated for their injuries. It stank like a butcher's shop. The whole place was lit by candles and gas lamps, while Jesus glared down at me from his cross high above. I stared at the wooden figure and felt his suffering. I knew I would die in that church. I knew I would not see another morning.

A low moaning sound was rising and falling around me like an aural tide as the hideously ruptured men breathed their last in the gloom. Some of them whimpered pathetically, some of them hissed as they stoically kept their enormous pain to themselves. Some of them wept and screamed and called out for their mothers as they felt the cold fingers of eternity touch them. They were boys. Just boys.

I couldn't make a sound, even though pain thumped throughout me, keeping time with my weakening heartbeat.

And in the middle of the night, ignored by the nuns and unseen by most of the patients—they were by now almost all dead—the Medic came to me.

I couldn't move by then. My blood had seeped through the useless bandages and into the thin mattress beneath me and the pain was, thankfully but ominously, lessening.

I was suddenly aware of his presence as he leant over me. I stared up at him, my face no doubt ashen. I was icy cold, yet perversely hot. My head felt as if it were going to burst and my body seemed to be disappearing into the sodden mattress. I was sinking fast and could feel almost nothing. Only that hot ice and the thumping in my brain.

His candlelit face hovered in the blackness above me, his dark eyes stared down at me.

He placed a hand on my chest.

He was smiling.

*

I woke with a start, panting, the dream fading but the memory of those black, smiling eyes still there in my vision.

I sat and wiped a hand across my brow and let out a long, wavering sigh, slowly getting my breath back.

At last I stood and moved over to the small washbasin in the corner of the room, cupping the cold water over my face and head. I looked at myself in the mirror.

I still wore my trousers, but I had stripped off my jacket and shirt before falling asleep the night before. I stared at the three small scars on my chest. They were puckered, white. I knew there were similar, slightly larger, marks on my back where the Maxim had spat its bullets through me. They had torn away huge chunks of muscle and bone and ribs as well as decimating my lungs, and yet all that remained were those small scars. My breathing was untroubled, I felt no pain. Not for the first time since that July morning two years before, I wondered how I had healed so quickly and so completely.

I stood there for a while longer, hands either side of the bowl, then I pushed the thoughts away and shaved. I dressed, went down to my poor breakfast, paid my bill, and walked to the train station.

My rapidly decreasing funds bought me a ticket back to London, where I spent a lonely Christmas day. From there I caught a service to Winchester. The place I wanted was called Longwood Manor, just outside Owelsbury, wherever that was. I had no income, no prospects, and no future. My family was gone and so was my career in the army. I had little choice but to see if my erstwhile captain had told the truth.

I would go and work for Jonathon Greene.

III

The years I spent as Greene's gamekeeper were some of the best of my life. Not the happiest by any means, but some of the best. Upon finding Longwood and introducing myself, I was shown into a huge library by a servant: an old retainer named Brewis, who looked like he'd been part of the household for decades. I mooched idly around the room as I waited for Brewis to get Greene, glancing at the books lining the walls. A lot of them were written in a language I didn't understand (I later found out it was Latin), and there were leather chairs either side of a warming fire.

I stood before the bay windows and looked out onto a rather overgrown but very substantial lawn, with a forest beyond it. Rain had started again, spitting in a desultory manner against the panes. It was very quiet. I paced the room as a log cracked and shifted in the fireplace.

An ancient dog wandered into the room, wagged its tail at me, and allowed itself to be petted for a minute or two before wandering out again. A clock in the hallway outside chimed a resonant note. I stood, staring down into the fire, thinking of my sister.

'Rob!' shouted a happy-sounding voice behind me, and I automatically whirled and drew myself to attention. Greene chuckled.

He was dressed in expensive-looking, perfectly creased trousers, but his shirt was crumpled and oily and his sleeves were rolled-up exposing equally oily arms. He strode across the room, extending his dirty hand towards me.

'At ease, Sergeant.'

Another chuckle.

'It's good to see you, Rob. Good to see you.'

I nodded.

'Thank you, sir. You too.'

It was now early January 1919. Only a couple of months since Greene and myself had talked in that Belgian village, but already a lifetime away. I could see he had changed.

He had grown a little more padding around his frame, although he was still quite spare. But this was not the real change. He now seemed much more at ease with himself, as if being back in his house had rejuvenated him, made him whole again, and had started to erase the thin, tension-filled individual he had been in the trenches. He seemed *better*.

'Sit down, sit down,' he urged and gestured at one of the chairs. He sat in the one opposite and grinned at me.

'So, I'm hoping the reason you're here is to take up my offer?'

I nodded.

'If it's still available, sir. I'd be very grateful.'

Greene waved this away.

'Of course it is. I wouldn't have offered you the post if I hadn't meant it. I take it you went home to see your family. They're well?'

He must have seen the sudden look in my eyes, because he leaned forward, his dirty arms on his knees.

'They are well, aren't they?' he asked, concerned.

I told him what had happened to my sister and her family and he sighed in sympathy. He rang a bell and when the butler came in he ordered a couple of whiskeys. Before long the warming glow of the liquor was in my stomach.

'I'm so sorry, Rob,' Greene said. 'I've heard about the Spanish flu. Deadly stuff. Awful.'

His gaze turned to the fire and he suddenly looked once more like the haunted young man I'd known in the trenches.

'I sometimes wonder what else God has in store for us,' he murmured, almost to himself. 'I sometimes think the war was such an abomination that He has decided humanity must just go. Disappear. What must He think of us?'

He turned to me, looking for answers I was in no position to provide.

'One goes through all that,' he continued. 'One does one's duty. One survives. Then innocents like your family are taken away because of a disease.' He shook his head. 'I'm so sorry, Rob,' he repeated.

I swallowed another mouthful of the whiskey to cover the prickling in my eyes. At the graves of my family I hadn't been able to shed any tears, yet sitting here, with a man who knew what I had been through, what I had experienced, they now seemed to want to flow.

I blinked them back and simply said; 'Thank you, sir.'

Greene contemplated me for a second longer.

'Do you know anything about oil burners?' he suddenly asked.

He showed me his hands.

'The bloody boiler has been playing up. I've been whacking it about the head and neck with a spanner but it hasn't seemed to have worked.'

So we went down to the cellar and, within an hour, I got the boiler working.

Greene was ecstatic.

'Oh, good show!' he cried. 'Oh, jolly well done! I knew I was right to offer you the job. This bloody thing has been the bane of my life since I got back.'

He stuck out his dirty hand again and I gripped it with my own.

'Welcome to Longwood,' he said.

*

I soon settled into the routine of working for Jonathon Greene. To my amazement and pleasure, the job came complete with a gateman's cottage. My very own house. It was a small, stone-built affair, with a simple open fire in the kitchen / sitting area, a separate bedroom and an outside privy. The privy even had a flushing toilet! It was heaven.

My job evolved over the years into a sort of gardener-cum-handyman role, as well as the responsibilities of a gamekeeper, and it was a role I cherished. Whilst at Longwood, I believe I started to live again, started thinking about my future and enjoying my present. It was as if my blasted soul, battered by the horrors and deprivations of the war, began to wake up and started to learn how to smile again. The work was hard but it kept me in shape and I had my little cottage to sit in at night by the fire.

One of the Labradors at the Big House had a batch of puppies and I chose a stout male to train. I named him Hector. During the day he would come with me on my rounds and at night he would lie beside me in front of the fire and listen to my stories. Every now and then Greene would visit, often arriving in the dead of night, clutching a bottle of some sort under his arm and grinning conspiratorially. On those nights, Hector would hear more stories and memories shared. He would hear the laughter of friends. As I have said, those years were good.

But they didn't last. Nothing ever does. It was on my twenty-sixth birthday when things changed forever. Sixth of August, 1922.

The night-time visits from Greene had begun to lessen over the last year-and-a-half, and I was more than aware that the reason for this was because of the appearance of a certain Miss Jane Godley.

She was a beauty, I'll give her that. Small and slim with huge, baby blue eyes and golden hair. She was the daughter of a local businessman and, although I obviously never said anything, I guessed that her wealthy background was as big a pull for Greene as her appearance.

Like all the landed gentry in those days, Greene was seeing a huge adjustment in his fortunes. The war had changed a lot of things, not least the balance of power in the country. Commerce and trade had replaced title, and Longwood was expensive to run. Jane Godley must have seemed like manna from heaven for my captain and employer.

She didn't like me. That was made clear from the first time we met. One evening, in early June of that year, I was finishing my rounds, and the sun was setting as Hector and I made our way back towards the cottage.

I was thinking of supper. I'd bagged a hare out on the back fields and it would go nicely with some of the vegetables I grew in the small garden by the cottage. Hector, as usual, was bounding along ahead of me, and he'd disappeared around a bend in the leafy lane. I heard him bark and then I heard a woman's shrill shriek.

I pelted around the corner to find Hector jumping up and wagging his tail at a pretty young woman dressed in a pale blue dress that was now caked in mud at the front where Hector had pawed at her. He was a friendly dog, but over exuberant at times. He shouldn't have jumped up to be petted, I'd told him off enough times about it. But he didn't deserve the clout he received from the young woman's parasol. He yelped and scuttled backwards away from her as she advanced, the parasol brandished threateningly in her hand.

'Hector!' I bellowed. 'Come!'

He immediately ran to me and slunk around my legs, sitting to heel. He looked up at me and regarded me balefully for a second. I could see he was upset.

But as I looked back at the woman, I also saw he wasn't half as upset as she was.

'That beast needs destroying!' she shouted at me. 'He tried to bite me!'

I stepped forward, shaking my head.

'Hector would never do anything like that, Miss. He's just over friendly. Please accept my apologies.'

'Look at my dress!' she shrieked at me. There were two red spots on her pale cheeks. She was furious. She wailed when she followed her own advice and looked at the dress. It had paw prints all over it.

'It's ruined!' she screamed.

'I'll gladly pay for the dress to be cleaned, Miss…' I started, but she broke me off.

'Who are you? Why are you skulking around on my land? Are you a poacher? Is that what you are? I'll have the police onto you, you rogue. Come along, explain yourself, you impertinent ruffian!'

I didn't know what the hell she was talking about.

'Your land?' I asked. 'This is Jonathon Greene's land, Miss. Perhaps you're lost? I can show you back to the main road.'

'I know whose land this is!' she bellowed at me, making Hector cower. 'Do you take me for a complete fool?'

I have to admit, I was starting to think that very thought. I opened my mouth to ask her what she was talking about, when Greene appeared through the trees.

'Hello! What's all the ballyhoo?' he asked. 'Is everyone alright? I heard shouting.'

The woman turned to him, her demeanour changing instantly from dragon to damsel-in-distress.

'Oh, Jonathon. Thank goodness you're here. This man's dog attacked me. I think he may be a poacher or some other such villain. Look what the beast did to my dress.' She clung to his arm and showed him her dress.

Greene shook his head.

'No, no, my dear. This is Deakin. He's my gamekeeper. And that's Hector. Hector wouldn't hurt a fly, would you, old thing?' He patted his knee and Hector ran forward to be petted.

The woman squealed and Hector stopped mid-track, nervously eyeing the parasol.

'He works for you?' she asked.

Greene nodded. 'Jane, Rob Deakin. Rob, Miss Jane Godley.'

I nodded and touched my cap at her, but she just gave me a

venomous look and then turned back to Greene. 'Can we go back to the house, Jonathon? I feel rather unwell.'

Greene immediately looked concerned and took a firmer grip on her arm.

'Of course, dear. We shall go and have lemonade. That will make you feel better.' He turned to me. 'Thank you, Deakin. That will be all.'

That in itself was strange. Greene had every right to speak to me like a servant, but he had never done so in the past. It had always been 'Rob' or 'Sergeant.' I touched my cap again and simply said, 'Sir.'

As they turned away, I said, 'I'm very sorry about Hector and your dress, Miss. My offer is still there to have it cleaned for you.'

And Jane Godley looked at me. A look I've rarely seen in my life, and I've lived a very long time. The look she gave me was of utter hatred. There were actually tears of anger in her eyes.

'The very thought,' she whispered, harshly.

They turned and walked away.

I pursed my lips and looked down at Hector, who stared up at me like a victim. 'Trouble's coming, Hec,' I told him.

His eyes told me he knew I was right.

*

And trouble she was.

Brewis, the old butler, told me he'd overheard her and Greene talking that evening over their lemonade. Brewis and I often chatted when we bumped into each other around the grounds and he said that Miss Godley had virtually demanded my sacking for my "impertinence". On that occasion, Greene had talked her down, saying I was a good man and we had just got off to a bumpy start. Brewis also told me that she would not let it go. She was pouring poison into Greene's ear at every opportunity and his protestations were getting weaker. He needed her and her money more than he needed me.

On that August evening, as Hector and I celebrated my birthday with a nip of best scotch for me and a bone for him, a groom knocked on my door and told me Greene wanted to have a word with me. When I got to the house, Brewis's face told me everything I needed to know. He squeezed my arm in sympathy as he showed me into the library.

Greene was standing with a rather large glass of whiskey in his hand, staring out across the lawn that was now wonderfully manicured thanks to my work over the years. He turned when Brewis introduced me and sighed.

Strangely, I felt sorry for him. The padding I had first noticed when I came to Longwood back in 1919 had grown. Greene was becoming podgy and flaccid. His dark hair was thinning. The whip-thin, iron-willed individual was no more; murdered by a slim, blonde weapon named Jane Godley. I waited for him to speak.

'I'm afraid I have some rather bad news, Rob,' he started as an opening gambit, but then stopped, unsure of where to go next. As I looked at him, I tried to remember the man he had once been before he had been eviscerated by that bloody woman.

'Bad news, sir?' I asked. I was not going to make it easy for him.

Greene turned back to the window. He seemed unwilling to look me in the eye.

'I'm afraid I've had to do some, erm, shuffling. Yes, shuffling.' He turned again and tried to look at me, but his eyes flickered constantly around the room.

'Of resources, I mean,' he continued. He nodded at me, as if what he had said made sense.

'Resources, sir?'

'Personnel,' he finished.

I stared just past his right ear as I had always done when talking to an officer. I remained silent.

'Oh, come along, Rob,' he said, testily. 'You know the situation. She don't like you, man. She don't like you for whatever reason and she won't stop harping on about it. She complains endlessly.

Deakin this and Deakin that.' He gulped at his whiskey and looked at me like a boy who has been whipped. 'She wants you gone.'

I let the silence hang for a second longer before saying, 'I see.'

The silence grew again until Greene drew himself up. It seemed as if he was going to say something else, but then he slumped once more and just looked at me.

We had shared so much, him and me. In two years of battle we had shared more than most people share in a lifetime. And he was turning away from that for a woman. For the first time in my life, but certainly not the last, I felt something turn and heave within me. Something raw and elemental. Something furious. It seemed to swell inside me before quickly fading away.

'You want me to leave, sir?' I asked, keeping my voice calm, ignoring whatever that strange feeling had been.

Greene sighed, about to refute it, perhaps to say it was not him who wanted me gone, but he seemed to realise how that would make him look. He nodded.

And that was that. My time at Longwood was over. Greene gave me a decent parting payment, which was nice of him, I suppose. We shook hands like men, but I couldn't help thinking that his grip had become soft. War had not defeated him, not for one second. But Jane Godley had.

I packed my bag and left the Gatehouse the next day, taking Hector with me. I wasn't leaving him there to the tender mercies of that malicious bitch. She'd probably poison him.

We walked out the gate and strode down the lane towards the train station, neither of us quite sure of what would happen next. When we got there, however, the last train had left and so, as it was a warm evening, we spent a comfortable enough night in a hedgerow.

I stroked Hector's flank as he slept beside me and wondered what that strange feeling had been when Greene had dismissed me. It was like nothing I had felt before, a savage and disturbing wrench within me. For a moment, standing there in Greene's study, I had felt a surging hatred, previously alien to me. I searched myself for an answer but found nothing and I soon forgot about it. I had obviously just been disappointed by my sacking, that's all. I sighed, wondering what I was going to do now. I was once more adrift.

Something will come up, I told myself, uncertainly.

Eventually I slipped into slumber.

IV

The docks at Southampton were rammed. The noise of the cranes and of the stevedores shouting and swearing at each other reminded me of the trenches. The huge bulk of the steamer *St Agnes* blocked the sun.

The money I'd saved from Longwood and the final payment from Greene had kept me going long enough until I found myself a job at a local farm where Hector and I had slept in a barn and I worked the fields until the winter came.

At first I didn't know what to do with my life, but on a visit to the local town I'd seen an advertisement in a shop window showing a steamer under the watchful gaze of the Statue of Liberty in New York. As I sweated and toiled in the fields that image stayed with me and I eventually made my decision.

I would try my luck in the Land of Opportunity. I would go to America.

Hector couldn't come, of course. The voyage would be too much for him, even if they had allowed him on the ship, which they didn't. The farm owner was a good sort, however, and said he'd take him in as he was a well-trained dog, so, when I'd got the money together in early January 1923, I gave Hector a final pat on the head and told him to be a good boy.

Twice I almost turned back on the country lane that led to the train station, but I knew he was better off on the farm where he could grow old in peace with the other working dogs. I missed him though, old Hector, and I often thought about him in the years that followed. He was always a good friend.

The voyage took just over a week. I was way down in the bowels of the ship, in steerage where my sort belonged, bunked up with a couple of Irish lads who had been in the war too. We had plenty to talk about and, being Irish, they always knew where the parties and the beer was. The crossing was quite pleasant.

The day dawned when we slid past that statue and we docked on Ellis Island where I went through customs and exchanged my few pounds for a few dollars at a kiosk outside. I wrapped my thin coat around me and walked out onto the cold streets of New York.

I still remember the awe in which I beheld that city. After the years of rural England and the close and frugal comforts of the *St Agnes*, New York was like another world.

The freezing streets were full of noisy cars and electric trams that rattled and clanged and juddered. The pavements, or sidewalks as they called them, were packed with people wrapped in topcoats and furs, all hurrying to and fro, seemingly all in a rush to get somewhere fast. My breath was clear in the cold air and I walked the streets of Manhattan in a daze, gawping up in astonishment at the skyscrapers and brownstone buildings. The city was like a glittering prize, wrapped up in noise and smoke and hope. It was as if I had stepped into a future world, a world of machines and metal and carefree decadence. I loved New York as soon as I saw it.

Priorities soon took over, however. I needed a job and I needed it fast. I had won a little money on the ship playing poker with the Irish lads and I probably had enough to see me in lodgings for a week, maybe two if I could find something cheap enough, but I needed to ensure I had some money coming in or I would quickly starve. It suddenly struck me how stupid I had been. I had left Britain on a whim, seduced by the idea of a foreign city, and now reality was raising its ugly head. A job. I needed to get a job.

I bought a newspaper and went into a diner and had a cup of coffee, which was very agreeable. I scoured the ads at the back of the paper. It began to dawn on me that all my past working experience was going to mean very little in this sprawling metropolis. I was used to hunting, fishing and farming; New York had no need for any of this. The shops were full of goods and the only animals I saw were pets. I thought of Hector, sleeping in the barn we'd shared, and began to fret again about having made a horrible mistake.

A bang on the diner window jolted me from my worries. It was Sean, one of the lads I'd shared a berth with on the *Agnes*. I waved him in and he entered with a flourish, pulling his cap from his head and rubbing his hands briskly.

'Have you seen the size of the streets here?' he shouted at me, grinning. 'They're bloody huge. What a place!'

I grinned back at him and he helped himself to a gulp of my coffee. A pretty young waitress came over and refilled the cup, smiling professionally at Sean as he tried to give her some of his supposed Irish charm. Sean was small and almost toothless, with a pockmarked face. I didn't think he was going to get too far.

We talked amiably for a while until, after a glance at the clock on the wall, Sean got up to leave.

'Where are you going?' I asked him.

'My uncle's. He has a small business here. That's why I came over: to help him out.'

My interest was aroused.

'You've got a job lined up?'

'Of course I have. I wouldn't be so stupid as to come all the way to America without having something to do when I got here now, would I?'

I grinned, uncomfortably. 'No, of course not.'

Sean looked down at me.

'Hang on,' he said, understanding spreading slowly on his monkey-like face. 'You're not telling me you've got nothing promised, are you? A man who plays cards like your good self would never be so stupid as to sail all the way across the Atlantic and have nowhere to go when he got here now, would he?'

I said nothing, then shrugged.

Sean laughed.

'Jesus, but you're one mad bastard Englishman!' He laughed again, louder. 'Christ Alive, I thought the Irish were supposed to be stupid. But you, my friend. You're not right in the head!'

I sipped my coffee in embarrassment. Sean was right: I was a bloody fool. What the hell had I thought I was doing? My predicament washed through me like an ice flow. I was suddenly very frightened of what my future held.

Sean must have seen the look on my face and recognised it for what it was. He sat down again.

'Tell you what,' he said, eventually. 'My uncle has a few irons in the fire, so he has. Maybe he'll have a job for you? We could ask him.'

I looked up at him in sudden hope. 'You'd do that for me? Sean, that would be wonderful.'

He held up a hand. 'I'm promising nothing, but there's no harm in asking, is there.'

He suddenly looked unsure.

'What's up?' I asked, thinking he'd changed his mind.

'My uncle,' he said. 'He hates the bloody English. His brother, another uncle, was part of the Easter Rising. Been cold in his grave these past seven years. He wouldn't give an Englishman the smell off his shite.'

He suddenly brightened.

'However, that accent of yours, it's no English accent I've ever heard and I think he'll be the same. We could say you're Scottish. He doesn't mind the Scottish.'

With that he stood up.

'Come on then. Let's get going.'

'Where does your uncle live?' I asked, standing and putting down some change on the table. I followed him out onto the icy streets.

'When he came here, he said he'd seen the place where he lives now and thought it was perfect for a poor Irish renegade who'd had nothing but shite for most of his life. He said the name of it appealed to the devil inside him.'

We stepped outside the café and started walking further into Manhattan.

Sean turned, walking backwards. The massive panorama of that amazing city was behind him as he spread his arms wide and grinned at me. Snow began to fall from a leaden sky.

'Rob, me friend. We're off to Hell's Kitchen!'

V

Mickey 'Irish' Donovan was a strangely mixed man. He stood at only five feet five inches or so, but he was almost as wide as he was tall. His shoulders extended a good ten inches either side of his braces and his head seemed to sink straight down into them, untroubled by anything so frivolous as a neck.

His face was only roughly sketched, with a large blob for a nose and two fleshy slugs instead of lips. He had the remnants of many bar room brawls drawn on that face, and his hands were like a bunch of bananas. Yet his suit trousers were of the best quality and his shirt was silk.

His hair was slicked back straight from his ploughed forehead and a thin, delicate, well-tended moustache decorated the space between the blob and the slugs. His ice-blue eyes regarded me like the fox regarded the gingerbread man.

'Scottish, you say?' he asked, suspiciously.

We had found his storefront easily enough and we had no sooner been shown into Mickey's back office before Sean was almost crushed in a bearhug of an embrace.

'Well now!' Mickey had cried, releasing the gasping Sean and holding him at arm's length. 'If it's not my little brother's boy. God save us, Sean, but you haven't grown much since I saw you last.'

Sean grinned. 'It's a poor diet we have back in the auld country, Uncle Mick. I've had no chance to grow.'

Mickey laughed and hugged him again, noticing me for the first time over the boy's shoulder.

'And who's this one?' he asked, releasing Sean.

'Uncle Mick, this is Rob Deakin. We met during the war. Rob, this is my uncle, Mickey Donovan.'

Mickey stuck out his hand.

'Any friend of young Sean here is a friend of mine, even if you both met fighting for the bastard English. Where are you from? Deakin doesn't sound like an Irish name to me.'

I glanced at Sean and he nodded imperceptibly.

'It's Scottish,' I said.

Mickey, as I have said, sounded suspicious.

'Whereabouts in Scotland? I've been there a few times. Glasgow and such like.'

'I'm from the Lowlands, near the Borders. A place called Eyemouth. It's on the East coast, just north of Berwick.' I'd decided on Eyemouth on the way to Mickey's as I'd been there on a few occasions and didn't think the East coast was somewhere he would know much about.

Mickey nodded a couple of times, then went back to his desk and sat down behind it, lighting a cigar.

'What's in Eyemouth, then?' He still didn't believe me. He was a naturally cunning man, was old Mickey Donovan, as I would find out to my detriment a few years later.

'Fish and seals and flat-chested women,' I said. 'That's why I got the hell out of there and came to America.'

Mickey stared at me for a second. Then he roared with laughter and the two big men who flanked him, joined in a moment later. They all seemed to relax.

'Well, Mr Deakin of Eyemouth,' Mickey said. 'Welcome to the USA.'

He then turned to business. I was to find out quickly that Mickey's moods were mercurial.

'We've got you all lined up, Sean,' he said to his nephew. 'I didn't realise there would be two of you, though.'

'I'm sorry, Mickey,' said Sean. 'Rob and me met on the boat and he hasn't got anything sorted, jobwise. I was wondering if there was anything he could do, even if it's only until he gets himself a permanent job sorted.'

'I thought you knew each other from the army,' said Mickey, quick as a snake.

Sean didn't miss a heartbeat. He could lie as good as any man I have ever met.

'We did. Imagine our surprise when we found ourselves on the *St Agnes* together!'

Mickey stared at him suspiciously before relenting. 'I'll sort you out with something, Rob,' he said. 'But for now, I want to spend a bit of time with my nephew. This calls for a drink.'

With that, he got up and nodded to one of his men, who disappeared out the door. Mickey picked up his coat and hat and then indicated for us to follow him and we went out to find a car waiting. We got in and coasted along Central Park until we got to West 67th Street. Here the car pulled up outside an innocuous-looking brownstone building.

We got out and Mickey and his men made their way up the steps. One of the men pressed a buzzer. I noticed a policeman standing on the corner and I watched him turn and walk away when Mickey glanced at him.

The door opened to reveal an old woman who smiled and held the door open when she saw Mickey. We went in and marched down a corridor towards the back of the building. As we did so, I began to notice the muted sound of music playing from somewhere.

We got to another door and another buzzer was pressed. There was a darkened window set into the door and I got the impression someone was staring at us from the other side. The door opened and the sound of the music got louder. We stepped into a small foyer-like room, with a padded door at the far end. The goon who had opened up nodded at us and then opened the far door.

And we stepped into paradise.

The Prohibition years were something I have never forgotten. It was such a grand time to be alive. It was freedom, it was hedonism, it was wonderful. Of course, it was also a time of murder, chaos and heartache but in that moment, at that point in time, it was the best thing that had happened to me in my, so far, short life.

The room was ablaze with light. Tables were laid out all around the floor, and waiters moved between them smoothly, filling the glasses of the raucous people who sat at them. Brightly coloured ticker-tape ribbons flew everywhere. At the side of the huge room was a bar doing a very healthy trade, and at the far end was a small stage where a band played lively jazz behind some dancing girls whose costumes left very little to the imagination. In front of the stage, couples danced enthusiastically. The noise was incredible.

A waiter scuttled over as soon as he saw who had come in and showed Mickey and the rest of us to a table set aside from the others. Champagne was poured and Sean looked at me in disbelief, laughing as he saw the same look on my own face. The waiter brought us menus and we chose food. I ordered steak as Mickey said to get what I wanted. I was starving because I hadn't eaten since the previous day.

We ate our meals, drank illicit booze, and got chatted up by the girls paid to do just that.

I had encountered my first prostitutes in the cafes and bars of Belgium and France during the war and, like all the other virginal boys there, was at first shocked and dismayed by what we considered to be the loose morals of those exotic girls. However, daily life and death in the trenches soon made us realise that we had to take everything we could before we were obliterated, and we had all became enthusiastic students of their teachings.

Some of those prostitutes had been beautiful, some of them pug ugly, but the hookers in Drew's Bar were something else. They wore their hair in short bobs, as was the fashion of the day, and draped their long legs and uncovered arms all over the willing customers, blowing smoke into their faces from their ebony cigarette holders.

Sean and I got plastered that night, as did Mickey. His goons stayed sober, however: eternally vigilant for any danger that might present itself to their boss.

I'd quickly come to the understanding that Mickey's 'business' was not what one could exactly call legitimate. He was obviously involved in bootlegging, as well as prostitution and illegal gambling if the roulette wheel over in a far corner was anything to go by.

I didn't care. I was a young man on an adventure. At the time, it all seemed to make sense. What harm was it doing to allow people to let their hair down once in a while?

The *Volstead Act* of 1920 had banned the manufacturing, transportation and selling of alcohol. It never banned the consuming of it and that had maybe been its mistake. The gangsters moved in to fill the hole the government had left, and to them it was just a business. As I laughed and caroused with Mickey and Sean on that, my first night in New York, I had no idea of the ugliness and murder and brutality behind the smooth facades of the criminals who ran the various activities.

I would soon find out.

*

Mickey got me a job on the wharfs of Manhattan.

The duties were simple enough: I unloaded the carefully blank boxes from the ships when they came in and transported them via truck to the various illicit drinking holes situated all over New York. It was easy money, well paid, and it meant I got to know the city very well. I was received enthusiastically wherever I went— as long as I kept away from the territory of the other gangsters littering the mean streets of the city—as it was generally known who both I, and Mickey, worked for.

William 'Big Bill' Dwyer owned the docks where the supplies came in. Whiskey from Canada and rum from the Caribbean were brought in on a regular basis and dispersed throughout the city by me and men like me, very much ignored by the police who were well recompensed for their inattentiveness.

We never got to meet Dwyer. He just owned everything. It was Mickey, his commander on the docks, who was our boss. We heard the stories about him, however. Tales of people ending up floating in the Hudson with their throat cut, or simply disappearing mysteriously if they got in his way. I don't think I really believed all the accounts at the beginning, I thought them little more than tall stories concocted out of boredom or jealousy. And anyway, what did I care if some other bootlegger got chopped off at the knees, or a rival Italian ended up wearing a concrete overcoat? They were all villains so they all probably got what they deserved.

As long as I had a little money in my pockets and was not involved in any of the darker elements, I could live with the thought that it wasn't all fun and laughter. I was already a cold man back then. The scars of the war ran deep, but there also seemed to be a dark, brooding miasma inside me that had first reared its head when Greene had sacked me back at Longwood and had never really disappeared. At the time I simply thought it was just a trait of my character. I know better now, of course. I simply enjoyed what I did and didn't care all that much about the consequences of the work.

I liked the people at the Speakeasies, I liked making good money just driving trucks around and I enjoyed the fact that the local coppers kept out of my way. I enjoyed New York.

And there was one more reason I was pleased I got a job working for Mickey Donovan.

It made me rich beyond my wildest dreams.

*

I had been in America for just over a year when, whilst delivering my illicit goods around the city one afternoon, I met a young Bostonian named Percy Drebham. And he changed my life.

Percy was the manager of one of the Speakeasies on my rounds.

It happened to be that first one I had visited with Sean and Mickey when I first got off the ship: Drew's Bar on West 67th.

I was trolleying in the goods when Percy came outside to stand in the sun for a smoke. He nodded at me and I nodded back. We knew each other a little by this time, but had only really talked about where I had to drop off the booze.

It was July 1924, and it was a warm day. I stopped for a rest in the shade of the porch and wiped the back of my neck with a handkerchief. Percy and I watched the cars and trams clattering by, listening to the chatter of the people on the sidewalks and the sound of bright jazz music coming from an open window somewhere. He offered me a cigarette and we smoked companionably for a while. He was reading a newspaper.

'Electric irons,' he murmured.

'Sorry?'

He smiled up at me from the paper. 'Electric irons. In fact, electrical goods of all shapes and sizes. That's what I'm investing in.' He returned to the paper and did some mental calculations. 'I believe I have made just over $2,000 this morning.'

I was mightily impressed. It was a king's ransom.

'How?' I asked, interested.

'Stock market, my friend. Stocks and shares are the new future. Anyone can make a fortune if they invest in the right things. And electricals are the right things. They're only going to go up.'

I didn't know what he was talking about. I'd heard of the stock market but had assumed it was something for bored highfliers and millionaires to play with on their time off. I knew nothing about it, and I said as much to Percy.

'You don't have to understand it, friend; you just have to play it.' He smiled, secretively.

Percy was a dapper young fellow. He wore a finely tailored suit, Homburg hat, and spats on his perfectly polished shoes. His cigarette case was gold, and his cufflinks and tie stud were glittering diamonds. Maybe he was on to something.

I asked more about the ins-and-outs of stocks and bonds,

and he gave me a quick rundown of what he thought might be worth investing a little money in. He seemed eager to share his knowledge.

It would have to be only a little money for me. I made a decent amount working for Mickey Donovan as I was employed, in essence, in an illegal trade but I didn't have a lot of disposable cash. However, after questioning Percy a little more I found out what I had to do and he put me in touch with his stockbroker. I put my few dollars down to see what would happen.

It's incredible to think now, how much money I made in the next couple of years. As Percy said, it seemed everyone was at it. Shoeshine boys, barbers, shopkeepers. They were all indulging in the glories of Wall Street.

Once I became more knowledgeable, I learned that a lot of people were buying their shares on what was called the "margin". This meant they only had to stump up about ten percent of the worth of the shares they bought, the other ninety percent being funded by banks as a type of loan. It seemed there was no real downside to the stock market, but a cautious part of my nature baulked at doing this and I made sure I only bought shares I could afford myself. What if something went wrong?

It didn't seem to be going wrong though. My investments went up and enabled me to invest more and more. Within a year-and-a-half I had made enough money to move out of the shared apartment I had been renting and into a very nice place of my own in Greenwich Village, not far from Washington Square.

I became a minor expert, and even began to give tips myself, like Percy had done for me. Sean made a little extra cash from my advice, although I think he spent most of it in Drew's. Still, he seemed happy enough with it.

Apart from the new apartment, I kept my dabbling to myself. I didn't start wearing flashy clothes or buying cars or diamond cufflinks or anything stupid like that. I invested, I sold, and I banked. By 1927 I had almost $120,000 in my account, an enormous sum of money in those days. And by 1927, I needed it.

Because by then I was a marked man.

VI

The apartment in Greenwich was owned by a certain Mrs Molly O'Brian. She was aged about forty or so, with a thick mane of jet-black hair that the grey had yet to mar. Her eyes were huge and dark, in a face that was careworn but seemingly carefree too, and her smile was warm and wide and welcoming.

I found her instantly alluring and, before too long, I also found out that the body beneath those rather staid clothes was firm and smooth and voluptuous. She was a rare beauty, was Molly O'Brian.

Donovan himself had put me on to the apartment. He knew I'd been making some money and he also knew it was not a threat to his own, much more lucrative, business. I think he even admired me a little for making my own way, and he never had any cause to complain about my work. I enjoyed what I did. The stock market was simply something I participated in on my time off. It was a sort of perverse version of the American dream.

When he heard I was looking to upgrade my housing situation he called me into his office in Hell's Kitchen. He asked me how much I was willing to spend on rent and then told me about the apartment block Molly owned.

Of course, what he didn't tell me at the time was that he and Molly were lovers. If he had then things may not have got out of hand; although even if I knew I probably would have done what I did anyway. I was getting cocky by then.

I found the apartment and rang the bell, and Molly answered. I was attracted to her immediately, despite the fact she was about ten years older than me. I think that was actually part of the attraction; she was all woman.

When the door opened I was confronted with a vision of dark, wild beauty. She was so different to the Flappers of the time, with their short hair and ironing-board figures. She wore a simple, ankle-length skirt and white blouse, and her thick black hair was piled on her head in what had been the height of fashion a decade or so before. I don't think she wore any make-up on that first meeting. Then again, she didn't need to.

'Mrs O'Brian?' I asked, taking off my hat.

'You must be Mr Deakin,' she answered in a thick Irish brogue, smiling a smile that made my heart jump. 'Michael said you would be stopping by.' She pronounced his name *'Moichael'*.

She opened the door wider and showed me in.

'You've come to look at the apartment, is that right?'

I nodded and she smiled again.

'Please, come upstairs.'

She turned away and I grinned to myself as I closed the door. It sounded like a very good idea.

She showed me the apartment and it was very nice, as I knew it would be, but to be honest I'd have taken it even if it had been infested with trench rats. Mickey had said Molly lived in the apartment block on the ground floor. Any chance to catch a daily glimpse of her was enough of an incentive for me to take it.

After showing me around the apartment—I lingered in the bedroom with her for far too long—we came to a mutual understanding. I paid the deposit then and there and arranged for my belongings to be moved over.

A week later I was sitting in a comfy chair, listening to Whispering Jack Smith singing *Gimme a little kiss, will ya? Huh?* on a gramophone, smoking a cigar and sipping an illegal whiskey while gazing out of the window over Washington Square.

I loved it there in my apartment on Bleecker Street. The place was a haunt for Flappers, and there were plenty of Dwyer's Speakeasies within easy reach.

A picture palace was only a twenty-minute walk away and I often visited it to watch Harold Lloyd or Mary Pickford. I particularly enjoyed Charlie Chaplin films and it was at The Roxy I first saw *The Gold Rush* one of my favourite movies ever. I've seen it many times since and it always brings back memories of my time in New York. They're bittersweet memories now: fading, but somehow still relevant.

I had only been there a couple of months when things went, as I thought at the time, unexpectedly well but, in reality, terribly bad.

I'd been out. It was a Saturday, and Sean and I had been to Drew's. We'd danced to the Black Bottom and the Charleston with some of the girls there and had drank our fair share of booze.

Sean had a little spare cash, earned with one of my market tips, and had decided to take up the offer of the attentions of one of the working girls. He asked me if I was doing the same, but I politely declined. I had looked upon the faces of some of those girls when they thought no one was looking, and they always seemed to exude a melancholy that killed any ardour in me. They all looked so incredibly sad. Tired and sad. I just felt sorry for them.

Anyway, I'd had enough for one night. My head was swimming and I just wanted to go to bed. I hailed a taxicab and it dropped me outside the apartment.

I opened the front door and started up the stairs, but stopped when I heard a noise coming from Molly's apartment. I frowned, listening. There it was again.

Sobbing. Someone in the room was sobbing. I slowly went back down the couple of stairs I'd taken and put my head near her door. She was breaking her heart in there.

For a moment, I almost left it. Who knows how my life might have turned out if I had? Maybe I would never have found out about the Medic. Maybe I would never have gone to war again. Maybe I would never have met Madeleine. Or Pearl.

But I didn't leave it. Our lives are made on the decisions we make at every moment. Fate does not exist; I am as sure of this as of anything. There is no overriding guiding force to our existence, no guardian angels moving us down some pre-ordained destiny. Life is simply a clutter of lines, moving in every direction. We take the ones we take and we deal with the consequences, good or bad. I knocked on Molly's door.

The sobbing stopped. She was listening now.

'Who is it?' she called, a catch in her voice.

'It's Rob. Mr Deakin. From upstairs. Is everything all right?'

For a while there was only silence from her room. I thought she must want me to go away so I moved back towards the stairs, but then I heard the turning of a lock and the door opened enough for her to poke her head around it. I pulled my hat from my head.

She had definitely been crying. Her eyes were red-rimmed and bleary, although they were still as gorgeous and as mournful as ever. Her hair was loose and cascaded over her shoulders. Her blouse had been undone a couple of buttons and I willed myself to keep my eyes on her face and not on the ample cleavage which I could see in my peripheral vision. Even so, she seemed to read my mind and her hand clasped the blouse at her throat.

'I'm sorry,' I said. 'It's just, I heard crying. I don't mean to pry. I was only wondering if you were all right.'

She swallowed and then nodded. 'I'm fine, thank you. I've just had a little bad news, that's all. I'm sorry I caused you to stop. Thank you for your concern.'

It sounded as if she was finished, and she should have closed the door after we had both said goodnight. But she didn't. She just stood there and stared at me, as if willing me to understand something I could not.

'Is there anything I can do?' I asked, lamely.

She shook her head again, but her face crumpled and the brimming tears trickled down her cheeks. She stared at me like a child.

Without thinking too much more about it, I stepped closer and pushed gently at the door. She didn't stop me. We stared at each other for a second longer, and then I opened my arms and she came to me, weeping into my chest and soaking my shirt. After a while I closed the door and led her to a settee near the fire. We sat down and I continued to hold her as she cried her heart out.

I didn't say anything, I just held her warm body close until she had cried herself out. She clung to me like she was drowning and I was a life raft.

Eventually she pulled herself away and went over to stand in front of the mirror above the fireplace, dabbing at her eyes with a handkerchief. I saw her reflection close its eyes and shake its head slightly. She took a deep breath and then turned towards me.

'I'm so sorry, Mr Deakin. Heaven knows what you must think of me. I appreciate your help, I really do.'

'Is there anything I can do?' I asked once again. 'Can I help in any way?'

She shook her head again and smiled at me. 'No. I've had some news from home, that's all. Bad news. My mother, she…' She swallowed and seemed to fight back more tears. 'My mother has died. She had been ill for a long time, but still it was unexpected…'

Again she stopped and indicated limply to a letter lying on the occasional table by the door. 'You always expect your parents to be around forever, don't you,' she said. 'Even though you know they won't be.'

I sighed. I understood her sorrow, but I had seen so much death it seemed more natural to me than life. Still, I felt sorry for her. I could see she was devastated.

'When is the funeral?' I asked, softly.

'Two weeks ago. It takes a while for letters to get here.' She seemed to stare into nothing for a second, perhaps seeing a cold, fresh grave bereft of flowers from a daughter to a mother.

She wiped her eyes again with the soggy handkerchief and sighed, long and low. I stood up, taking the sigh as a dismissal.

'I'm so sorry for your loss,' I said. 'Please, if there's anything I can do to help, don't hesitate to ask.'

She nodded once more.

I smiled at her and made my way to the door, but she laid a light hand on my shoulder.

'Wait.'

She suddenly seemed unsure what she wanted. She started again. 'Will you have a drink with me? A toast to her? I'm all alone here. I'd like to share a toast with someone.'

'Of course.'

She smiled at me, thankfully, and went through to her kitchen, returning with a bottle of Dwyer's best hooch and two glasses. She filled them and we stood in front of each other. I lifted my glass.

'To your mam,' I said and she laughed, sadly.

'In Ireland, we say 'Ma.'

I smiled back. 'We sometimes say that where I come from too. To your Ma.'

We drank and she closed her eyes as the whiskey warmed its way through her.

We finished those drinks and then had another. And another.

Molly told me of her childhood in Cork. It was the usual thing: grinding poverty, hunger and heartache, but ensconced in an envelope of love from a big-hearted Irish family. I asked her how she ended up in New York but she became a bit evasive, pouring us more whiskey instead. I was already floating from the drinks before I got there, and I could see she was starting to feel it as well as she spilled some whiskey as she poured it.

'Whoops,' was all she said.

It was after one in the morning when I stood to leave again. By that time my jacket was laid on the arm of the sofa and my collar was undone. I picked up the jacket and my hat, and she stood with me and walked me to the door.

'Thank you again for your sympathy, Mr Deakin,' she whispered.

'Please, call me Rob. All my friends do.'

'Am I your friend?' she asked, moving closer, and I smiled down at her.

'Of course you are.'

She nodded. Then she reached up and gently grasped the back of my head, pulling it towards her. Our faces were just inches apart when she stopped and looked deep into my eyes. What she was looking for, I don't know. But she seemed to find it, because she pulled gently again on my head and kissed me.

Her lips were as warm and soft as I had imagined. She tasted of a sultry mix of whiskey and cigarettes, and I felt myself becoming instantly aroused. She seemed to understand this, and she seemed to like it. She drew herself closer to me, pushing her body against mine, and she groaned softly as she felt my want for her press against her stomach.

Eventually, she pulled away and stared into my eyes once again. She didn't need to say anything else. She silently took me by the hand and led me into the bedroom.

I let my hat and jacket fall to the floor and closed the door carefully behind me.

VII

I left Molly sleeping in the early hours of the morning. Something told me she wouldn't want me there when she woke up. I closed the door to my apartment softly and climbed into bed.

I couldn't sleep. For some reason my night with Molly had dredged up more memories of my past, and they haunted me. Eventually, I climbed out of bed and pulled on a robe, sitting in my chair by the window, smoking a cigarette and watching the city wake up.

*

I awoke from as deep and refreshing a sleep as I have ever known, to the sounds of muted talking and the squeak of wheels from a trolley. I opened my eyes and saw that the trolley was a gurney, and it was taking out the body of one of the men who had died in the night.

Other trolleys were depositing more bodies from the Somme Offensive onto the still warm beds of their previous occupants. The smell of blood and shit and vomit stained the dank air.

Sunlight streamed through the church's stained-glass windows. Jesus was still up on his cross, but I noticed he now seemed to be smiling at me. I swallowed and took a deep breath. I could breathe again! It hurt quite a lot to do so, but not half as much as the previous night. Nothing like it in fact.

My mind flickered back to the previous night.

I remembered the Medic's dark, swarthy face staring down at me, but my memory of what happened after that was almost non-existent. He had placed his hand on my shattered chest and I had seen his lips move, but what he had said escaped me. I recalled nothing else after that until I woke up, feeling immensely better than I had when I had fallen asleep.

I plucked feebly at the thin, dirty sheet covering me and saw the crusted, brown bandages around my chest.

I frowned. How was I still alive? Why was the pain so much less than it had been the night before? I peeked under the bandages, the hairs on my chest snapping and sticking, and stared down at my wounds.

The holes were still there as far as I could see, so it hadn't been a dream. I had definitely been shot.

But there seemed to be pinkish scar tissue covering those holes now, scabs forming on the wounds. I took another, tentative breath. My chest was sore, but that was all. It felt like I had a healing bruise rather than ruptured bones and muscles.

A shadow fell over me and I looked up into the eyes of an old nun. She was frowning at me in disbelief. As I watched, she sketched the sign of the cross over her own chest.

'Comment allez-vous?' she asked, sounding shocked. I shrugged; I didn't understand French then.

'How are you feeling?' she translated in broken English.

'I don't know,' I replied. 'I'm feeling better than yesterday.' I was surprised at how strong my voice was. Twelve hours earlier I couldn't speak at all, couldn't even move. Now, the pain in my chest was diminishing with every second.

'What's happening to me?' I asked her, seeing the alarm and fear in her eyes, but she just shook her head. She took a step back and hurried away, and I watched as she disappeared into a sort of chantry. She returned a few minutes later with another nun.

51

The second nun stood over me, with the first standing behind her, clutching at a crucifix around her neck.

'I am Sister Agnetha,' said the second nun. 'Sister Clara has asked me to speak with you as her English is not so good. Do you know where you are? Do you know why you came to this place?'

'I was wounded,' I replied. 'I was brought here. I think I nearly died.'

'Mais oui!' she said. 'You should be dead! Your wounds are big. Too big.' She frowned down at me. 'How are you alive?'

I had no answer to a question like that. We stared at each other for a while, until she turned to Sister Clara and fired off something at her in rapid French. Clara nodded and scuttled away. Another gurney was trundled past us; another dead soldier being taken to his final resting place.

Agnetha bent down beside me. She pulled back the sheet and inspected my chest, drawing in a shocked breath as she did so. She straightened and crossed herself as her companion had done. I was getting worried about their reactions now.

'What is it?' I asked her. 'What's wrong with me?'

She looked as if she was going to say something, but approaching footsteps ringing on the stone floor cut her off. An old man appeared, stared down at me, and smiled. He was quite short and portly, with pince-nez spectacles and a fringe of white hair encircling an otherwise bald head. Only his stained doctor's coat stopped him looking like a monk.

'I am Doctor Artigue. Sister Clara asked me to come and have a look at you. Is it all right if I check your wounds?'

I nodded and, with a final crossing of their chests, the two nuns left.

Artigue pulled down the sheet once again and carefully cut away the crusted bandages. He took some clinical-smelling liquid from a tray by the bed and cleaned around the wounds with a cloth, frowning as he did so.

'Can you sit?' he asked.

I nodded again and he helped me up, cleaning the wounds on my back too. I heard him mutter something in French. I don't know what *it was, but he sounded as shocked as the two nuns.*

He laid me back down, staring into my face.

Eventually, he shook his head. 'I don't know how, but it seems you are healing. Your wounds, they… You should be dead!'

He said these last words in a rather accusatory manner, as if I had done something to upset him. I stayed quiet. His demeanour was disturbing me a lot now.

Eventually, he straightened.

'I don't know how you are still alive, young man. But you are. And you need to be somewhere else other than here. You need a hospital. This is a place only for the dead, and I don't think you belong to that category. Not anymore.'

'I'm going to live?' I asked, hope fluttering through my heart.

'Yes. Yes, I believe you are.' His words should have been spoken with a smile of congratulations. But they weren't.

And so I was taken away from the church of Saint Theresa Marie. A military ambulance was called to come and collect me and, as I was being loaded into it, I grasped Doctor Artigue's arm.

'The other doctor,' I said. 'Where is the other doctor? The man who came to me last night?'

Artigue frowned down at me for a long time before shaking his head.

'I am the only doctor here,' he said. 'I'm retired, you see. I only help out, doing what I can for the men who come here. There is no other doctor.'

For some reason, a shiver ran through me at his words. An errant gust of wind brought to my ears the distant grumble of the never-ending artillery fire from the Front.

The last time I saw Doctor Artigue was as the ambulance doors were closed with a bang. He had on his face a look of utter terror.

*

Over the next few weeks and months, my nightly visits to Molly O'Brian's apartment continued.

I noticed she started wearing a little make-up, and that she was often 'accidentally' down in the foyer when I got in from work. We would smile and chat in a friendly way for a while and then she would offer me a cup of coffee or tea.

I would accept and we'd go inside, and she would unveil her wonderful body to me and we would make love, sometimes right there in her sitting room on the carpet or using the settee as an improvised bed. I began to look forward to finishing my shifts.

I asked her to step out with me on more than one occasion, but she always declined. I assumed it was perhaps because she was ashamed of the age difference between us; but whatever it was she didn't want to be seen in public with me, and she made me promise never to mention our affair to anyone, especially to anyone at work.

It was about three months after our first night together that I found out why.

I had just driven into the docks to drop off the truck at the end of my shift when I saw Sean leaning beside the warehouse door, smoking a cigarette. He was staring appreciatively at a couple coming out of the office.

My breath stopped when I saw who they were.

Mickey was smiling at the woman on his arm. She laughed at something he said and kissed him lightly on the cheek, tenderly touching his face.

It was Molly.

They climbed into the back of the shining Buick Model 24, and I saw Molly lean over to Mickey and kiss him again as they left the wharf.

Sean saw me staring from the cab of the van and sauntered over, flicking the butt of his smoke.

'She's a looker all right, ain't she?' he said. Sean had started to pick up some Americanisms during his time in New York.

I managed to nod and parked the truck up, tossing the keys to one of the goons who guarded the place. Sean and I wandered out of the docks and he offered me a lift home in his own car.

'You'll know her, I think?' he asked as he drove.

'Who?' I tried to act as normal as possible, even though the image of Molly laughing and kissing Mickey was branded into my mind.

'Mickey's piece of skirt,' replied Sean, and I felt that darkness inside me rear up once more. I had to restrain myself from punching him in the mouth, traffic accidents be damned.

I nodded. 'My landlady, I think. Seen her a couple of times.'

Sean grinned through the windshield. 'I know she's an old woman, but by God, Mickey can pick 'em. She's got a hell of a rack on her. I'd love to know what she looks like underneath that dress.'

He chuckled and I took a deep breath. I knew exactly what she looked like under her dress and I had been looking forward to seeing more of it that very evening. I shook my head. It all made sense now.

Molly had always been a little cagey about how she came to New York, and how she had managed to set herself up as the owner of a very nice apartment block. Now I knew. Mickey had helped her with his illicit money. And she was obviously repaying him in the same way as with our own relationship. I was upset and jealous at first; but by the time Sean dropped me off outside the apartment, I was furious.

Her door was closed as I walked into the foyer. I stopped and listened but there was no sound coming from the other side. She was obviously still out. I was just about to go upstairs to change when the front door opened and two of Mickey's goons appeared, Mickey and Molly following them in. They stopped when they saw me; I had bent down and was pretending to fasten a bootlace.

'Rob!' cried Mickey. He seemed to be in a very good mood. 'How you doing, me auld mucka.'

I smiled at him. 'Evening, Mr Donovan.' I touched a finger to my cap. 'Good evening, Mrs O'Brian.'

She seemed very pale, but she managed a wan smile. 'Good evening, Mr Deakin.'

'I didn't know you knew Mr Donovan,' I said, sticking the knife in.

She managed to nod. 'Yes, I know Mr Donovan.'

We stared at each other, then she turned and kissed Donovan on the cheek. 'Thank you for looking after me, Michael,' she whispered. 'And for seeing me home safe.'

Donovan seemed a little disappointed that he wasn't going to get shown into her apartment, as he well might, but he smiled gallantly, took off his hat and kissed her hand. 'Any time, Molly my sweet. Any time.'

He nodded at me and then turned away, his goons trailing him.

Molly turned back to me. She sighed into the long silence.

'Well,' I said eventually.

'Rob…' she started, but I just turned away and walked up to my apartment, leaving her standing forlornly in the foyer.

*

Molly caught up with me a day or so later as I was going out.

She must have been waiting for me at her door, and she asked me to come inside to talk. I hesitated for a minute but then relented. She closed the door behind us and sat me down on the same settee where we had explored each other's bodies so often.

She told me how she came to New York eight years previously, penniless and broken by a marriage to an alcoholic husband. She had escaped Cork, taking her young son with her, looking for a future brighter than her blasted past. And she had found, instead, Mickey Donovan.

When prohibition kicked in, and Mickey had started to make some real money, he had taken her on as a working girl. She had prostituted herself to feed her and her son, only to have the boy die of Spanish Flu, the same disease that had killed my sister.

They had been in America only a few years. She took out and showed me a photograph of a dark-haired, handsome little chap. She stroked the face in the picture briefly before putting it back in the drawer.

Donovan had seemed to take pity on her and had taken her out of the clubs and into his own household as a servant, only for her to quickly become his lover.

She had succumbed to his advances. Still numb from the death of her boy, she looked upon Donovan's affections as something good. He had always been nice to her, she said. He had never forced himself upon her at any point, had never been violent, but had simply stated that if she gave him what he wanted, he would set her up. She would be safe and secure and, for a woman who had known only heartache, she had grasped at this false happiness with both hands.

She knew Donovan was only using her and that, very soon, he would tire of her. She was getting older and Donovan already had another, younger woman on the go too. She didn't mind. All she had to do was keep him happy while he wanted her and then she would be left alone to get on with her life running the apartment.

She knew all she had to look forward to was becoming an old, grey spinster, but at least she would have food in her stomach and somewhere to live. It was the most a woman like her could hope for.

But then she had met me. And she had felt something she hadn't felt for a long time: affection for another human being. She said she had started to live again, not just survive. She hadn't wanted me to know about her and Mickey because she knew it would have been the end of our relationship. She had been happy when she was with me and now, she knew, that was gone.

For my part I felt only sympathy for her. Any anger I had towards her disappeared. She was a broken woman, a haunted beauty with nothing but pain in her past. She had grasped the opportunity of happiness with me, a last hurrah if you will, before age caught up with her and she would simply retire into herself, running the apartment block until she could run it no longer. To have a roof over her head, to have food on her table and some ready cash in her purse: those were the height of Molly O'Brian's dreams. Her relationship with me had spoiled this and I knew she must have felt some genuine love for me, otherwise why would she put all that at risk?

We talked long into the night. Molly was the first person I told about my experiences in the war. She had seen the scars of course and, without going into too much detail, I told her about the church and the Medic and how close to death I had come. She made the same sign of the cross over her chest I remembered from the two nuns. The Catholic upbringing still ran deep, even in a washed-up prostitute.

She asked me, begged me even, if we could remain friends. She knew our secret affair was over. She accepted it, even though she said our relationship was the one good thing in her life. She just wanted me to like her, I suppose.

I promised her we would. I said I understood, which I did, although I hated her for it even so. I said I would always be there for her.

Which was a lie. Because when she did need me, when she really needed my help, I failed her.

Molly O'Brian died because of me.

VIII

The winter of 1926 was awful. It was so cold the wharfs had to close because the river had frozen. Ice coated everything in fangs of white and then, in December, it snowed for six days solid, covering the city in snow metres thick.

I had been unemployed for a while. My job was erratic at the best of times but, with the booze unable to come in, Mickey had closed down operations until the weather warmed.

I didn't mind. The stock market still functioned, and I continued to make money. I spent most of my days at home, listening to the radio or the gramophone and watching the snow fall outside, or having sex with Molly O'Brian.

We had started again. As I've said, I understood her position and now I knew the truth, I didn't blame her for her actions. I didn't ask where she'd been or what she'd been doing, and decided to simply enjoy the time I had with her. For Christmas I bought her a small gift: a gold bracelet. On the inside of it I had it engraved, *'From R'*. She was overjoyed and gazed at it on her wrist admiringly.

It was that bracelet, *my* bracelet, that got her killed.

I never found out what happened exactly. I just know what the result of it was. I can only assume Mickey had discovered the bracelet and demanded to know who *'R'* was. I don't think Molly told him straight away, because when I saw her body she had been tortured abysmally.

For all his smooth exterior, for all his joviality and his talk of his work as just 'business', Mickey Donovan was nothing more than a cold-hearted monster. He enjoyed hurting others and, when it came to his pride, he would let nothing and no one stand in his way.

He—and I think it was him, not his goons—had tied Molly to a chair in her apartment. She must have held out for quite some time, because he had ripped out most of her fingernails and sliced open her face before she gave him my name. I think Molly died from shock more than anything else. But she tried to stop him coming after me. She tried to stop him murdering me and she paid the price for it.

And not one person in that whole apartment block came to her rescue. They knew who was dealing out her pain, and they closed their doors and turned up their radios as she screamed in agony. Such was the power of the gangsters of New York, the 'Robin Hood' lies which were torn away in the sadistic torture of a woman who was one of the most genuine and lovely people I have ever met in my life.

Sometimes, even after all these years, when I allow myself to get drunk I weep over Molly O'Brian, and I hope she was reunited with her little boy. I hope she is now happy, and I hope to meet her again someday.

His goons found me quickly enough as at that time I had no idea what had happened to Molly. The snow had eased off by then and two of his men nabbed me as I parked the truck up at the docks. They dragged me into their car and took me to the apartment to look upon the still and bloody corpse of the woman Mickey had owned, and I had adored.

Mickey was still there, the knife he had used on her face still sticky with her blood. The goons held me as Mickey advanced towards me. He was in his shirt sleeves and his hair was sticking up in clumps. He was white with anger, the smooth imposter ripped away, the look of a demon upon his face.

I couldn't tear my eyes from Molly. I couldn't believe what he had done to her; I couldn't believe she was dead. I don't remember feeling any fear: just shock and a rising anger at the bastard for what he had done.

Mickey grabbed me by the throat, brandishing the knife. 'My nephew,' he hissed. 'Did he know anything about this?'

I knew he was asking if Sean knew anything about me and Molly. I shook my head.

Mickey nodded to himself. 'Just as I thought. The little fucker's too stupid to know anything.' His Irish accent was very thick in his fury.

He looked at the corpse of Molly before turning back to me. 'How could you do it?' he asked. 'How could you stab me in the back like this? After everything I've done for you?'

He seemed genuinely hurt. As if it was *me* who had done the dirty on *him*. I said nothing for a second but, as I stared at Molly, that strange blackness within me suddenly heaved and surged, bringing with it an anger the likes of which I have known all too often. It has defined my life, this anger. It is dark. It is powerful. It is all-consuming.

It was close to the battle frenzy I had experienced during the war, when terror suddenly enveloped everything in a red mist and I just killed, killed, killed, until there was no one left to kill anymore. But it was stronger, so much stronger. I felt that red mist descend upon me as the reality of Molly's death battered against my brain. Mickey seemed to somehow sense the change in me and he licked his lips, suddenly unsure of what was standing in front of him.

'Everything you've done?' I shouted at him. 'What about her? She did everything you ever asked her to do and you carve her up like this? She didn't deserve this. She didn't deserve you. I owe you nothing, you bastard. Nothing!'

The uncertainty in Mickey vanished. He had a new look in his eyes, and it was the real Mickey Donovan. Not the cool, jazz-loving philanthropist businessman, but the evil, black-souled devil he really was.

He screamed incoherently at me and stabbed the knife into me in a frenzy. Again and again the blade sliced into my stomach. I felt my flesh burst with each thrust, my blood pouring from me in a welter of agony, soaking the carpet that Mickey Donovan had paid for.

His enraged face, splattered with both my own and Molly's blood, began to recede from my vision and the pain from the stabbings faded away. I slowly crumpled to the floor.

*

I've led a very strange life, and it was in New York in the January of 1927 when it began to dawn on me just how strange it would be.

Whenever I've found myself in a situation like the one that day, and there have been a few times, my memory never really brings back to me what happens. It was the same as when I first came across the Medic. Only fractured pieces remained.

I remember being stabbed to death by Mickey Donovan, but the next thing I knew I was lying on the frozen riverbank of the Hudson, spewing up cold, filthy water. I was face down on the riverbank: slime-smeared, shivering with cold, a strange feeling of tightness hugging my stomach.

It was now daytime. Mickey had dragged me to the apartment block in the evening, so presumably it was now the next day.

I hauled myself completely out of the river and pulled at my torn shirt. There were very small, pinkish scars on my stomach: new looking, about eight of them. The water had washed away whatever blood there had been, but that was it. I had been stabbed multiple times and then thrown into a half-frozen river, and all I had to show for it was a few marks and a slight feeling of bruising.

That night in the church, over ten years before, swam into my memories again. *What had he done to me?*

Whatever had happened, my survival instinct soon took over and I stumbled to my feet, crunching up the ice and shingle and climbing over a low balustrade.

There were only a few people about and I guessed it was still early morning. I was soaked and freezing and, if Mickey found out I was still alive, I was a marked man.

The thought of Mickey and the sudden remembrance of what he had done to Molly made me groan in anger. The red mist had gone now, replaced by a cold, stony fury. I was out of control, but it was a calm madness; I knew exactly what I was going to do and I couldn't wait. He had it coming to him. I put my survival from his attack out of my mind and made my plan.

When the banks opened I took out some cash, ignoring the look the cashier gave my soaked and crumpled chequebook, and went and bought a new, off-the-rail, suit and overcoat. Heavy boots and a pullover helped warm me from the freezing wind. I then went and bought a revolver from one of the people at the speakeasies I had come to know over the years. He didn't yet know of Molly's fate, so he didn't ask too many questions about it. Such was the company Mickey Donovan kept. It would be his undoing.

I hailed a cab and went to Hell's Kitchen.

It was still relatively early, and I knew Mickey was in the habit of sleeping in. I didn't think one more killing would disturb his rest. I knocked on the door and one of Mickey's boys opened it. I was pleased to recognise him as one of the men who had been at the apartment the night before. One of the men who had held me tight while Mickey had driven the knife into me again and again. One of the men who had stood by and watched as Mickey tortured and murdered Molly. He gaped at me in utter disbelief and I shot him in the face.

I jumped over his twitching corpse and sprinted up the stairs to where I knew Mickey had his apartment. Another goon came from a side room beside Mickey's, half-dressed and rubbing his eyes, alerted by the sound of the shot. He got the second bullet in the head. Four left.

I kicked open Mickey's door and found him and a young woman struggling upright in bed. He primly clutched a sheet to his chest as the woman screamed. I indicated to her with the gun and she ran, naked, from the room. Mickey stared in astonishment and horror when he saw who his executioner was.

'It can't be,' he whispered. 'It can't be you.'

'Oh, it can,' I said, grinning at him in a way that drained his face of colour. 'It is me, Mickey. You thought you were rid of me. You thought you'd killed me. But you can't, because I'm the Devil himself and the Devil can't be killed. I'm here to take you to hell where you belong.'

I levelled the gun at him and he held out a hand in supplication.

'No…' he started.

'Goodbye, Mickey,' I said, and emptied the revolver into his chest and stomach. He was dead before I turned to leave the room.

I made it to the bottom of the stairs before my luck changed.

There was no sign of the woman, but another of Mickey's men came out of a room near the front door and shot at me wildly, hitting me in the thigh, holing my leg and my brand-new trousers. My revolver was empty so I just screamed madly and ran at him, ignoring the pain in my leg. His mouth fell open when he saw who I was. It was the second man who had been at Molly's the night before.

I covered the space between us swiftly and head-butted him in the face as hard as I could, snatching the gun from his fingers and immediately shooting him in the chest. I scarpered before he fell. I've no idea whether he lived or died, and I'm still not bothered one way or the other. This may sound cold-hearted but he, like Mickey and Dwyer and the more famous gangsters like Al Capone, deserved everything they got. They worked in an industry of death, and they all got their comeuppance in the end. People usually do, in my experience.

I caught another cab to my apartment and quickly packed a few essentials, changing my trousers at the same time. And it was then the true reality of my survival from the stabbings hit me as I saw how quickly, and how strangely, my body seemed to recover from trauma.

When I pulled off the ruined trousers, I saw that the hole the bullet had made in my thigh was blocked by something. I frowned when I realised it was the slug from the gun. As I watched, my body literally pushed the bullet out in a series of small spasms. It reminded me of watching calves being born when I was a kid, each spasm pushing the bullet from my leg. With one more heave and a last trickle of blood, the slug fell to the carpet. The hole immediately began to knit together, a scab forming. The bleeding had completely stopped. In the twenty minutes it had taken to get from Hell's Kitchen to Bleecker Street, my body had healed itself.

I stared at my leg in disbelief. My thoughts returned to the Medic; whatever he had done to me in the church had changed me, I was sure of it. His touch had made me immune to death. This thought whirled in my fevered brain like a Catherine Wheel.

I was immune to death!

I needed to find out who he was; I needed to know what he had done to me. And there was only one place to start.

I left the apartment, glancing at Molly's closed door, wondering if her body was still in there. I hoped I had avenged her. It was all I could have done, and I had no remorse for the murders I had committed. I still don't; as I've said, they deserved it.

But Mickey's remaining men would soon be coming after me and, although I now believed they couldn't kill me, I wanted to get the hell out of New York. There was nothing there for me anymore.

I went to the bank again and transferred all my money by wire to a French account. The bank manager wasn't very happy about this, but there was little he could do. I knew a ship was due to leave the next day as the ice was receding and the lanes were open again. I bought my ticket, first class this time, and the next day boarded the ship.

The last time I had seen the Medic was in France.

So to France I would now go.

IX

Paris. Tuesday the fourteenth of February, 1928. St Valentine's Day.

In a year's time, back in the USA, gangsters of Mickey's ilk would gun down their opponents in an atrocity that would come to be called the St Valentine's Day Massacre. It would be the catalyst to begin to curb the power of those hoodlums.

But that was in the future. On that chilly evening in 1928 I was returning from a restaurant I had come to know.

I breathed in the cold air. Not as cold as New York had been in winter, but cold enough. The smell of roasting chestnuts from the sellers on the Boulevard de Clichy came to my nostrils as I walked the tightly packed, brightly lit streets.

I had been in Paris for over a year but was still no further forward in my quest to find out about the Medic and what, if anything, he had done to me during the war.

I had travelled to the hospital in Amiens where I had spent time after leaving the church all those years ago and, after a few days of filling out forms and waiting around, I was granted access to my records. They told a bizarre story indeed.

My recovery from the machine gun wounds had been nothing if not miraculous. They had healed within days of arriving at the hospital and my muscles and ribs were undamaged. It was as if I hadn't been shot at all, apart from the scars on my chest and back. But however interesting my records were, they showed me nothing of the man who would come to mean so much to me.

I found the church of Saint Theresa's. It was near Abbeville and, on a warm spring morning, I took the train there.

I didn't recognise the area. That didn't surprise me, as most of my time in France had been in the front line, and I had been unconscious until I woke in the church with the Medic staring down at me. I entered the quiet church and located the area where my bed had been. It was now just a space occupied by pews and I sat quietly, thinking of the night I now believed had changed my life. And of the man who changed it.

I spoke to the priest there, mostly in sign language and broken French, and showed him the name of Doctor Artigue, but he couldn't help me. He hadn't heard of either Sister Clara or Sister Agnetha.

I wandered into Abbeville.

I knew it had never fallen to the Germans during the war, so it was not as knocked about as other places near the front line. I asked about Artigue around the cafes and bars, and eventually an old woman pointed me in the direction of the local cemetery. I searched for hours, and finally came across his grave. He had died in 1925. So no help there, then.

There was another, newer cemetery in Abbeville for the fallen of the Great War, and I wandered around it aimlessly for a while, thinking of men I had known who had never made it home. Thinking that they were so different from me. Finally, as the sun set, I caught the train back to Paris, empty-handed.

I had rented a small, top floor apartment in Montmartre and, on that February evening as I made my way home, I watched young lovers strolling hand-in-hand, smiling into each other's eyes. Marriages would be proposed that night, futures stitched together. Lives would be planned.

I now knew that I was different from them. The Medic had

made me different; I was sure of it. I was a man apart. Those young people around me would marry, have children, and grow old. They would all one day die, that was for sure, and I wondered how that would happen to me. How could a person who seemed to be immune from death die? Would I just keep going, clinging on to life? Would I grow older and older and simply continue to exist, becoming a wizened, dried-up, mummified horror show?

It was a sobering thought, and the chill that swept through me as I reached for my key was not entirely because of the cold Parisian wind that whistled down the darkening street. I needed to find the Medic. I needed to know what I was but, for a year now, he had eluded me.

That year in Paris was not entirely useless, however. I learned enough French to get me by and, on that February night in 1928, I finally got some indication that the Medic had survived the war and of where he may have gone.

There was a letter waiting for me on the floor when I opened the apartment door. It was written in a precise hand and it came from a Doctor Ducos, who worked at the hospital I had been asking questions at months before.

In the letter, Ducos said that he had heard about my inquires and he believed the man I had been looking for was named Francois Valin, someone he had met briefly during the war.

Apparently, Ducos had been a medic at that time, and Valin had worked at a field hospital alongside him. He had only been there for a few days but my description of him, his swarthy face and the scar on his cheek, struck a chord with Ducos. He said that if I wanted to meet up to discuss more about this, he would be in Paris the following week, visiting family. He would be pleased to meet me then.

He had left a return address and with shaking hands I replied, saying I would be most grateful if we could indeed meet and suggested a café bar I knew, near the cathedral of Notre Dame.

I couldn't sleep at all that night and I spent the days in between our appointment in a frenzy of thought. Was I finally to come face-to-face with the man I had dreamed about constantly for years?

Eventually, the day of our meeting arrived and I took a taxi to the café, ordering a bottle of Beaujolais to keep me company until Ducos arrived. I recognised him as soon as I saw him.

He was the blonde man who had knelt by my stretcher at the field hospital when I had been wounded in 1916. The man who seemed surprised to find me still alive. The man who had sent me to the church of St Theresa Marie to die.

He looked older, obviously: it had been twelve years. As I stood to greet him he didn't seem to recognise me, though, which made perfect sense. This man had seen thousands of torn and mutilated soldiers, both dead and near death. Why would he have remembered one out of so many?

We introduced ourselves and I offered him a glass of wine. I took out my cigarettes and we smoked in silence for a time, until I prompted him to tell me about Francois Valin.

'I was a medic, as I said in the letter,' he began. 'It was a British Field Hospital, but mostly staffed by French medics. Valin worked there for only a few days but I remembered him from your description to the other doctors at the hospital. The broken nose, the scar on his cheek, but most of all his eyes. The term you used in your description was "black". I remember those black eyes.'

He seemed pensive for a second or two and sipped his wine before continuing.

'There was something not quite right with that man. I have seen what war can do to people. I've seen shellshock. I even worked in a mental asylum for a few years. I have seen all the different manifestations madness can take. The screaming, the hallucinations, the usual things one connects with poor mental health. But I've also seen quiet madness, a creeping darkness that can be seen on certain individuals as they sit and think their twisted thoughts.'

Again, he became quiet, thinking back to the past.

'There is no doubt in my mind that Francois Valin was mad. A quiet mad. In the few days he was posted at the field hospital, I saw it on occasions. I saw him smiling as he watched men die in the most awful agony. He enjoyed it. No, that's not right. He…' He paused, searching for the right words. 'He *required* it.'

I felt a shiver run through me at these words.

'Do you know where he went?' I asked him. 'After his time at the field hospital with you?'

I already knew part of this answer, of course. He had gone to St Theresa's. He had crouched by my bed and he had touched me. I believed he had healed me somehow. Changed me. But where had he gone after that?

Ducos delved into his pocket and brought out a crumpled telegram

'I found this the day after he disappeared,' he muttered, handing me the telegram. I read it quickly.

'URGENT: FROM: MAJOR GENERAL I.E.J HAWDON STOP TO: LIEUTENANT COLONEL R.T. FOREST, ACTING COMMANDER, FIELD HOSPITAL 422, ABBEVILLE STOP CC MAJOR F. VALIN STOP MAJOR VALIN TO BE APPREHENDED AT ONCE STOP HE IS TO BE TAKEN UNDER GUARD TO ARMY HQ AMIENS STOP THIS IS AN URGENT REPEAT URGENT ORDER STOP IF MAJOR VALIN RESISTS YOU ARE AUTHORISED TO USE DEADLY REPEAT DEADLY FORCE STOP'

I frowned and looked up at Ducos.

'Turn it over,' he said.

I did as he asked and saw a hand-written address, along with the date of '*July 1, 1916*'. The day I was shot. My frowned deepened.

'I found that in Colonel Forest's room,' he said. 'We had to evacuate the day after it was sent and I stuffed this and other papers in my pack as we were de-camping. Forest never got to read it, though. He was killed before he could do so.'

'The hospital was attacked?'

Ducos shook his head, grimly.

'No. He had his throat cut. I believe Valin did it and I believe that's Valin's handwriting on the telegram.'

I looked at the address.

'This is in Berlin,' I said.

Ducos nodded again.

'Valin was a German spy. It's the only thing I can think of. That's why we were to apprehend him. He must have found out about the telegram first, murdered Forest, and disappeared into the night. I sent a telegram to HQ letting them know what had happened once we were back in operation, but I never got anything back from them. The war rumbled on and the telegram lay forgotten with the rest of my things. I'd forgotten all about it myself until I heard you were looking for him.'

I stared at the address again, taking in the neat, flowery handwriting. The Medic had cut a man's throat to stop him finding out about him and had then written a forwarding address on the incriminating evidence and left it to be found. Then he calmly came to the church where I lay dying and had healed me. Changed me. Maybe.

It made no sense at all.

'This address is almost twelve years old,' I said. 'Chances are he doesn't live there anymore, if it's even his real address.'

Ducos nodded and finished his wine, standing and putting on his hat.

'Indeed,' he said. 'But I thought you would like to know about it. What you do with the information is up to you.'

I stood too and he told me to keep the telegram.

'I don't want it,' he said. 'It was a bad time. A very bad time.'

I stuck the telegram in my pocket and shook his hand.

'Thank you for giving me this. I believe I need to meet this Major Valin.'

Ducos seemed to scrutinise me for a second.

'You have the same look in your eyes as he did,' he said, finally. 'So I would be very careful, and very sure that you do want to meet him. I believe you would be better off burning that telegram now and forgetting all about him.'

He hesitated, as if to see whether or not I would do that. When I didn't, he seemed to shrug to himself.

'I believe he may be the death of you,' he said. He then gave me a nod and walked out of the brasserie, disappearing into the crowds.

I should have heeded his warning, but of course I didn't. Instead of burning the telegram, I burned with impatience. Berlin! The Medic had gone to Berlin after he had knelt by my side in that church.

I drained my glass, paid the bill, and walked out into the streets.

The address was old so he perhaps wouldn't be there now, but someone might know where he was. And I had to find him. I had to know what he had done to me.

I needed to go to Berlin.

X

I arrived in the German capital a few days later, after an overnight train journey from Paris.

The address Ducos had given me was on a street just off Friedrichstraße, still a wealthy area in those days. It turned out to be an apartment block.

It was an old, formidable-looking building made of stone. The address was one of the apartments above a large restaurant that covered the ground floor. I entered the foyer and went upstairs to the door.

There was an ornate bell on the wall, but I hesitated before using it. What would happen if the door opened and that swarthy, sardonic face appeared? What would I say to him? It seemed ridiculous now, standing at the door, that he had done anything to me at all in 1916. I had just been lucky, that was all.

I once met a soldier in the war, like myself from Northumberland, who told me he had been in a line of men hit by shrapnel from a shell. All around him, his mates had been eviscerated, but the chunk of metal that flung itself at him had instead slammed into the Lee Enfield rifle he had been holding in front of him. The rifle had snapped completely in half, but it had saved him from any injury. He had been totally unmarked. I believe he made it to the end of the conflict. Luck. That was all it was. Luck.

But then Mickey Donovan's enraged face came back to me as he stabbed me again and again, and then finding myself a few hours later alive and well. Those marks from his knife were almost totally invisible now.

How was it even possible? How could I have recovered so quickly and so completely, both from the stabbing as well as the massive wounds from the machine gun, the catalyst for my quest?

I had no answers and I desperately craved some so, eventually and with a quivering finger, I pressed the doorbell.

I heard it echo inside what sounded like an empty room. The building was completely quiet. I pressed it again. Nothing. Nobody in.

I sighed. I would have to come back later. I turned to leave, perhaps to grab a coffee from the restaurant downstairs, when a door opposite me opened. An old, elegant-looking lady stuck her head out and smiled at me, asking me something in German.

'I'm sorry,' I said. 'Sprechen Sie Englisch?'

The old woman's smile faded a little and she shook her head.

'Franzosich?'

She brightened. 'Yes, a little,' she replied in French.

I indicated to the door. 'Do you know the man who lives here? Is it a man? With a broken nose and a scar on his face?'

She seemed to recoil at the barrage of words, trying to work out what I was saying. She shook her head.

'No one lives there,' she said, eventually. 'The apartment is empty. For a year now.'

I slumped against the wall. Although it had always been a long shot, I hadn't realised how much I had pinned my hopes on finding the Medic still here. I nodded at her.

'There was a young family,' she went on, helpfully, 'but they moved out in twenty-three when all the money disappeared. Then Frau Weber took over, but she left last year.'

'Have you lived here long?' I asked her.

'Ja. Since 1909.'

'You were here in 1916?'

'Ja.'

'Do you remember a man who lived here then? As I've described. Dark hair, scar on his right cheek?'

The old woman thought for a long time before shaking her head.

'I do not know anyone who fits that description.'

'Who was here in 1916?'

'Can I ask what this is about?'

'I'm just looking for someone I met in 1916. I was hoping he could help me with something.'

'1916?'

'Yes.'

'And you are English?'

I knew what she was getting at, but I simply nodded again.

'This man was a German?' she insisted.

'I don't know. Possibly, but he may have been French.'

She stared at me for a long time.

'My grandson was killed in the war. Fighting the English. Were you in the war?'

My silence told her all she needed to know, and her lips tightened. She started to close the door.

'Wait,' I called. 'Look. The war was terrible for everyone on both sides. God knows I wish I hadn't been involved in it; but I was, just like your grandson. He died for no reason at all. But I survived, and the man I'm trying to find may have had something to do with that. Are you sure you don't recognise his description?'

The woman stared at me from the doorway, a grimace of old pain on her face. She shook her head and closed the door softly.

I eventually turned away, leaving her with the memories of her dead grandson. I by-passed the restaurant and instead found a beer hall. I used the rest of the day to try and drink the memory of the Medic from my mind.

*

I decided to stay in Berlin. I had no idea for how long, so I kept the apartment in Paris but rented a small house near the apartment block on Friedrichstraße where I could keep an eye on the comings and goings from that building. I spent my days spying on it, hoping for a glimpse of a dark, scarred face, and my nights tasting the wild and exotic club scene of the 'Golden Years' of post-war Germany.

Following its defeat in the war, Germany had been a disaster zone: its people starving and its economy wrecked. The swingeing orders of the Treaty of Versailles had created nothing but failed revolutions and political catastrophe.

The French invasion of the Ruhr Valley, after Germany's failure to pay the huge reparations foisted upon it by the Allies, had led to an incredible period of hyperinflation. This was what the old woman had meant when she said all the money had disappeared. Millions were unemployed, money was worthless, and it looked as though Germany would never recover.

However, Stresemann, the new Chancellor and now Foreign Secretary, had seemed to have saved the country—to a degree. Because of various treaties he had organised, Germany was no longer seen as a pariah state on the world stage and had been rescued with American money under the Dawes Plan. Stresemann had invested this money into industry and Germany had not only recovered but, by 1928, was revelling in its new-found prosperity.

This revelling went a lot further than the economy.

My apartment in Montmartre had been close enough to iconic clubs such as the Moulin Rouge, where the can-can girls and easily available prostitutes who prowled the brightly lit streets had been something to behold. But they were as nothing compared to the nightlife in Berlin. I saw all sorts of things. I visited clubs where women dressed like men and men dressed like women. I watched people dancing as naked as the day they were born, accompanied on some nights by patrons who thought it might be nice to join in. Sodom and Gomorrah could not hold a candle to some of the things I witnessed. I viewed vice and hedonism on a scale I would not have believed possible only a few years before, and I wryly mused that I had come a long way from the innocent farm hand who had first set off to war fourteen years earlier.

But it all meant less than nothing to me. I was fixated only on finding the Medic and I searched incessantly, picking up clues and leads here and there which all turned out to be false.

I only watched the debauchery. I was immune to the charms of the prostitutes, both male and female, and I gazed forlornly at the sex shows from the back of the rooms. I drank alone and lived alone.

I was different. That thought always came to me when a girl caught my eye or offered to buy me a drink. I was as different to every single person around me as a horse was to a fish, and it was in Berlin in 1928 when I first began to look upon other people with distaste.

I started to think of them as polluted, unclean. An inkling began within me that they were somehow *less* than me. They were not as I was, and I began to dislike them. Nothing like the hatred I would hold them in later in my life, but it was in Berlin when those feelings started.

Still, I must have enjoyed their distant company, because I ended up staying in Berlin for nearly six years. I learned the language and I learned the customs. I became used to the German lifestyle and it started to feel like home. A vague, lonely home: but a home nonetheless.

Of course, over those years, between 1928 and 1934, a lot of the bars and clubs I visited began to close down as the Wall Street Crash came along and Germany once again slipped into desperation.

Only to be saved by a new monster on the scene.

1929's 'Black Thursday' was only the start of Germany's economic problems. America, that great and sleeping giant, suddenly woke up and realised that everything it thought it had been was nothing but the Emperor's New Clothes. It heaved a death rattle of colossal proportions and drowned the entire world.

Along with most other countries, Germany sank rapidly into the Great Depression, and I wondered vaguely as I read about the shares collapsing like a house of cards, how Percy Drebham had got on. Did he survive the collapse of the stock market, or was he one of the many who fell by the wayside? Plenty of people killed themselves when the reality of what they had lost became so horribly obvious, and I remembered Percy and his secret smile and his diamonds and gold. Even though he'd worked for Dwyer he had always seemed a decent enough man. I hoped he'd made it through.

For all his skills, Stresemann could have done nothing about his own country's demise. Thankfully for him, however, he died before the Crash happened and so he never saw his country tumble into the volcano on whose edge he had once said they were dancing.

The American banks recalled their loans and the German economy ground to a halt once more. The German people, veterans of a lost war and two lost economies, howled at their political masters for revenge.

And their saviour came to them in the form of Adolf Hitler.

I had only vaguely heard of him in 1928, but by 1930 he was becoming the most recognised man in Germany.

I'd seen some of the running battles between his so-called 'Brown Shirts' and the communists, of course, but I never thought that wonderful country I had lived in for six years would turn into the monster it did.

Those fights between the right and the left became more commonplace, spilling onto every street corner around the capital.

I was out one dull, misty afternoon in early 1931, walking along the street minding my own business. I had been grocery shopping and I'd just transferred one of the bags to my teeth as I fiddled with the lock of my front door when there was an almighty crash behind me.

I dropped the bag and span around, just in time to witness a man being thrown through a bar room window opposite me. He landed in a tangle of arms and legs, his body sliced all over by the broken glass.

The door to the bar burst open and several young men, dressed in their Nazi regalia, fell upon the fellow in the street, belting into his already cut body with their truncheons.

I made to go to his aid. I don't know why, I wasn't really that bothered about him, and the disdain I felt for my fellow man was only getting worse. Perhaps it was just instinct. But before I could move a hand caught my arm and I turned to find an old woman who lived next door shaking her head at me.

'Don't,' she said. 'They'll take you, too.'

I turned back to the fracas in the street, but it seemed to be all but over now.

The Brown Shirts dragged the young man to his feet and threw him into the back of a truck that had squealed to a stop beside them. They climbed in, slammed the doors, and disappeared in a cloud of diesel smoke.

Other figures slowly emerged from the bar, some of them bleeding and one of them holding an arm that was obviously broken. They all wore the red armbands of the Communist Party. They stood around, muttering desultorily for a while before they dispersed. The whole episode had taken only seconds.

I turned back to the old woman and I saw the fear in her eyes.

'This is not right,' she whispered, shaking her head at me. 'This is not right. It is only going to get worse.'

She turned away from me and shuffled off into her house.

There were other occasions. Sometimes the Brown Shirts came out on top, sometimes the Communists did, but to be honest, it didn't seem to make much difference to anyone else's life.

When Germany had been doing well, most people just carried on voting for the centrist politicians, but after the Wall Street Crash more and more people began to take Hitler and his young thugs more seriously and their membership grew.

The Nazi Party's popularity dipped and swelled over the next couple of years, until, in January 1933, Hitler became Chancellor. Things really began to change after that.

The vulgar, bellowing, strutting young men of the Nazi Brownshirts—the SA—seemed everywhere now, and swastikas began to fly from windows and balconies.

I watched distantly as they attempted to stop people buying from Jewish shops—seemingly with little effect at the beginning—and I watched as they opened what they called a 'concentration' camp near Dachau, to house the Communists and anyone else who did not agree with the way they were running Germany. It was, of course, the first of many. Not that a lot of Germans seemed to care.

For myself, I viewed it all with a dark, growing disinterest. The machinations of funny little men with strange moustaches did not excite any concern in me. I was beginning to now believe the workings of human beings as pointless. I think I thought at the time that, once Germany got herself back on her feet, other politicians would come along, and the world would progress as it had done before. It's strange to think now, how wrong I was.

My money was fairly safe, still in the French bank, but I did move some to a British bank to be even safer. It was worth a lot less than it had been, but I at least had some sort of income and a roof over my head: which is a lot more than most people had at that time.

I continued to search, half-heartedly now, for the Medic. One time, I thought I had caught up with him in Munich but found nothing there except more shouting Nazis, emboldened in their heartland. In late 1933 I travelled to Denmark after seeing a photograph that may or may not have been him. Again, my trip was wasted.

I spent more and more time alone in my small house, listening on the radio to Goebbels and his insane propaganda, wondering how the German public could have been so stupid as to vote in these people who seemed little more than jokes to me. I still don't really understand it now.

Then in June 1934, I belatedly came to the conclusion that I should perhaps leave Germany. What came to be known as the

'Night of the Long Knives' changed everything. Hitler and his new favourites, the SS, took out the brown-shirted SA who had helped him gain the power he now possessed and who had been so happy to beat up the communists in the streets for him. It seemed they were no longer needed.

When Hindenburg—the old, reliable President—died in August of that year, I knew it was time to go. Hitler combined the role of President and Chancellor and became the sole leader, or Führer, of Germany. And the public seemed to lap it up.

I at last realised what this man was capable of doing, and I remember my first little frisson of fear for the future as I climbed aboard the train to leave Berlin for what I thought would be the last time. I went back to Paris, cancelled my tenancy on the apartment in Montmartre and, for the first time in years, I tried to forget about the Medic and went back to England.

I went home.

XI

I didn't return to Northumberland as there was nothing there for me anymore. Instead I found a little house in Aylesford, Kent: near enough to London to be useful, but far enough away to be rural. It had a small garden in which I grew vegetables, and I would sit by the fire at night, thinking about Molly and Mickey and my little cottage at Longwood with Hector by my side. Hec would have been dead by then, I suppose, his life expectancy only a little shorter than the humans I shared the planet with, the humans I kept out of the way of.

I continued to live alone, because the realisation that I was more different to them than I had first thought was now something I could not escape. It was on my fortieth birthday that I belatedly acknowledged the truth I had been ignoring for years now. That morning, I stared into the shaving mirror at the face of what, to me, seemed like a boy's. It appeared the Medic's touch had done more than just make me indestructible.

I wasn't ageing. My hair was still thick and full, and held no grey in it. My body was as lean and as powerful as it had been when I was twenty, even though the only exercise I really did was digging in the garden and taking long, lonely walks around the vicinity. I looked exactly the same as I had on the morning of the first of July,

1916. Twenty years ago, now.

I wondered how this was possible. How could the touch of a man *do* this to me? How could someone change my physicality, make me so different to what I had been?

Or maybe I had always been that way? Had I been born only to stop ageing at some pre-ordained time? Had that *always* been in me?

I didn't know and, to be honest, I was beginning not to care. I was just different; cursed. My previous insatiable quest for the Medic seemed like such a waste of time now. Especially with everything else that was going on in the world.

By 1936, the news coming from Germany was becoming more and more frantic. The Olympics held in Berlin that year only confirmed the power Hitler held over his people.

He had taken step after step to take control, and the world had just watched him do it, including the rearmament of Germany and the reoccupation of the Rhineland. It seemed no other country was bothered too much by the concentration camps, and the growing aggression towards the Jews and the disabled and anyone else who did not fit in with the Nazi ideas of perfection.

Those other countries were still too wrapped up in their own economic plights to become involved in what was happening in Germany. They could not afford to do anything about it. And more, of course, was to come. Much more. Hitler's malignance and hatred would soon sweep across the world and cause a conflict that in terms of casualties and destruction, would dwarf even the Great War I had fought in.

I thought about my time in the trenches a lot during 1936. Although I tried to forget about him, my inability to discover the whereabouts of the Medic hung heavy on me for most of that year and the next. I remembered when I returned to my battalion after being wounded.

*

It was Captain Greene I first recognised when I returned, and I was very pleased he had survived. Most of the other soldiers in our company were new faces, so heavy had our casualties been in the Somme Offensive. The battle had descended into a farce that would have been amusing if the toll had not been so high.

Day after day, for months, the men of our battalion and others had tried to take and re-take the same stretch of useless, mud-strewn, blasted land. Rotting corpses were clearly identifiable, either lying where they had fallen, or dispersed all over by the weeks of artillery fire, never to be returned to their families or even to a Christian grave. The smell was abominable. It was sickening.

The few men who had survived from my time were not as pleased to see me as Greene seemed to be. They appeared to find my presence unsettling. They wondered how I had survived no doubt, and how I had recovered so quickly. They began to see me as a sign of bad luck. They began to see me as a Jonah.

The hospital in Amiens had quickly assessed my condition and passed me fit for service. The nurses and doctors were suspicious when they saw the scars on my chest and read the report that came with me from Doctor Artigue at St Theresa's. There was no way the wounds they saw had occurred only a few days ago; whatever had caused the scars must have happened a long time before.

They x-rayed me and discovered marks on my ribs: the signs of old breaks, healed completely along with my flesh and muscle. They probably thought I was pretending to be ill. They probably thought me a coward.

It was Captain Greene I had to thank for not being arrested for cowardice. Because of the pristine condition of my body, they wrote to him, and he confirmed that Corporal Deakin had indeed been wounded on the first day of the Somme Offensive. He stated in very strong terms his high opinion of me, calling me an exemplary soldier and that, whatever the reason for my quick recovery, it was nothing to do with a lack of bravery and fortitude. The doctor read the letter out to me and I swallowed hard when I heard what Greene thought of me and how he was standing by me.

As there was nothing really wrong with me, I was released from hospital after just a week, and given two weeks' leave to 'recover' even though I felt as fit as a fiddle. I think the hospital just wanted me gone.

I went back home and spent the two weeks with Mu and her family: the last time I would see them alive. Mu's husband, Arthur, had lost most of the fingers on his right hand in a farming accident years before, so had been classed as unfit for service. He tilled the land for the nation instead, helped by his wife and his young son.

The girls from the village were by that time working in the fields too and, when I went back down to London for debarkation to France, I saw more of them walking to their shifts at the factories, some of them with hair and skin the yellowish colour of sulphur from the chemicals of the munitions. 'Canaries', they were nick-named. Times were indeed changing.

I got back to the Front and the rolling thunder of the guns grew louder, the countryside becoming more and more stricken and bare. The bodies of men and horses started to decorate the vicinity in horrible tableaus.

Greene, as I said, greeted me warmly, and I thanked him for his letter. He waved the thanks away with his customary nonchalance and handed me the sergeant's stripes I have already described. I immediately sewed them onto my jacket, pleased more about the few extra pence a week than the new responsibility.

The veterans said hello, but none of them shook my hand. They glanced at me warily if they ever looked at me at all, as if I was a mistrustful dog who would bite them as soon as they turned their backs on me. I heard them talking about me too, for whispers carry a long way in the trenches during lulls in the fighting: especially on the frosty, starlit nights.

There were occasions when I would come around a corner and conversation would suddenly stop, all of them guiltily pretending to be busy doing something else until I had stepped around them. I would hear the conversation strike up again as I passed them by.

It's strange; I thought I had only been truly alone in those bars and clubs of Berlin but, in reality, my singular existence actually started *much earlier, only a few weeks after the Medic got involved in my life.*

The rest of the war came and went: more battles were enacted across the same few miles of blasted ground, more men's lives were wasted, until the day came when I found myself standing with Captain Greene in that ruined Belgian village on the eleventh of November, 1918. And in all that time I never got close to another soldier as the others all seemed to do. I was an outsider, I was different.

I was indeed cursed.

*

It was in April 1937 when I realised I was cursed in other ways, too. I was cursed by ill luck. That year, I met a girl called Grace and she set me on a new path of destruction.

I never wanted a relationship with her, or with anyone for that matter, and I wish to God I had never come across her. But I did. The lines of my life converged and I chose the wrong one. Again.

To be honest though, I doubt any man would have been able to resist her, and of course I had the body of a twenty-year-old. Although my mind was older, my physical wants and needs remained that of a young man and, when I saw Grace Yeo, I was spell-bound: totally and immediately.

She was twenty-five and the daughter of the new parson who had recently taken over the parish. I first laid eyes on her as I was sauntering past the church on my usual walk. It was a clear, bright, early spring morning. The trees were just starting to recover from the long winter and daffodils were nodding cheerily at me as I passed. Rabbits jumped and ran in the distant fields and the sun was a golden disc in a bright blue sky.

As I passed the church I saw people coming out, dressed in their finest. I slowly realised that it was Easter and the congregation were emerging from the special service by the new vicar, Thomas Yeo.

It was the colour of the clothes against the backdrop of the grey-stoned church that made me halt at first. They made a fine sight, the epitome of a sunny English day.

I certainly didn't pause in my walk because of any sort of religious conformity. I had stopped going to church long ago, even before my wounding. The war had killed any sort of spiritual belief in me as I could not understand why a being as forgiving and as charitable as the Christian God was supposed to be, could ever have allowed a thing like that to happen. An abomination, Greene had called it when I talked to him in the library at Longwood. I couldn't help thinking he was right.

However, my belief in a God perhaps ratcheted up a notch or two when I caught sight of Grace Yeo, for only a God could have made something so perfect.

She wore a blue, knee-length dress and an open coat. Her hat was wide-brimmed and matched the dress. Her gloves were white and she carried a small purse. Even from a distance I could see that she was an extraordinarily beautiful woman. Her hair was chestnut brown, freshly curled and falling to a level just below her jaw. Her face was delicate, with large, brown eyes, and her figure was slim and athletic. She was standing with her father, greeting the people who were coming out, but she seemed to feel someone scrutinising her and turned to look at me. From my position at the church gate I nodded and touched my hat, and she smiled at me before turning away to take the hand of an old woman from the congregation.

I carried on with my walk, trying to put her out of my mind, but she stayed with me all the rest of the way and so, cursing myself for my stupidity, the following Sunday I pulled on my best suit and headed off to church.

There were less people there than had attended the Easter service, but space was still tight. A lot more people went to church in those days. I sat at the back and went through the motions of the service. It all meant less than nothing to me.

Grace was there again, sitting at the front. She wore the same blue dress but without the coat covering her I saw more details, of a figure a man would climb over hot coals to get to. I knew I was being stupid but I couldn't help myself. I think I perhaps craved something after my years of enforced solitude, some sort of contact. Even just someone to talk to. It's all well and good tearing yourself away from the rest of humanity, but in reality it is a very difficult thing to do. Whatever was wrong with me, however different I was, I was still a man. The last woman I had held was Molly and that had been ten years ago.

I briefly thought back to my time in New York and what had happened to that lovely woman, and then I wondered about Sean, my old companion from the *Agnes*. What had happened to him? I marvelled at how quickly time seemed to go by.

I was broken from my reverie by the sudden awareness of someone standing beside me. I looked up and saw the woman in the blue dress smiling down at me.

I stood immediately and smiled back at her. She held out a gloved hand and I took it in mine, feeling the warmth of her through it.

'Good morning,' she said. 'I hope you enjoyed the service. I'm Grace Yeo, Mr…?'

'Deakin,' I said. 'Robert Deakin. I live just down the road.'

She smiled at me. 'You don't sound like you come from around here. Somewhere in the north?'

'Originally, yes. Northumberland. Although I've lived in a few places since.'

She indicated towards the doors of the church and we walked down the aisle and outside together. Most of the congregation had already left.

'Where else?' she asked.

'Sorry?'

'Where else have you lived?'

'Oh, all over. New York, Paris, Berlin. I seem to have become an accidental wanderer.'

She gave me a look that seemed to let me know she was in on a joke. I forget sometimes how young I look. She must have thought me a liar.

We were outside by now. She gave me her hand again.

'I hope we'll see you again next Sunday?' she asked, her eyebrows raised in a question.

I nodded, non-committedly. 'We'll see. But it's been very nice talking with you, Miss Yeo. Good day.'

'Goodbye, Mr Deakin.'

I tipped my hat and turned away. And, like a fool, I was smiling to myself.

I began to call on Miss Grace Yeo. I wouldn't say her father was pleased, but he would have heard the gossip in the town and realised I had a bit of money in the bank. I wasn't really what you could call gregarious with the population of Aylesford, but people looked at my house and my clothes and the MG PA Four-Seat Tourer I drove and they saw a young, wealthy, man about town. Father Yeo must have been seeing pound signs every time I knocked on the vicarage door. Like any father, I suppose he worried about his daughter's future and who was going to look after her when he was gone.

I found out quite early on that he really did need to worry about her.

We had been walking out for a few months. It was now June 1937 and the future, if not secure, certainly seemed better than it had a couple of years back. Britain, like just about every other country in the world, was still in trouble financially, but for me that spring and summer was like a warm, golden haze. It was topped off when Grace made it clear one night that she was more than willing to take things a little further than just holding hands.

We had been out in the car, touring around the locale, and had stopped off for lunch and drinks at a nice country pub. I asked her if she wanted a night cap at mine before I took her home and she nodded agreeably.

It was still quite early when we got to my cottage. I poured her a glass of the French wine I imported over every now and then and we sat on the sofa. She giggled.

'What is it?' I asked.

'You,' she said. 'When we first met, you told me you had lived in New York and France and Germany. You mustn't have been there very long.'

'You don't believe me?'

She smirked at me. 'I don't have a problem with handsome young men telling me tales every now and then. I quite like it that you were trying to impress me.'

'I wasn't trying to impress you,' I protested. I had been, but it didn't make it less true.

'How old are you? she scoffed. 'Twenty-two, twenty-three? If you were in those places you must have been just a child. Either that or you were only there for a short while.'

I laughed.

'You wouldn't believe how old I am.'

I don't know why I brought it up. I think I *was* trying to impress her. With what, I don't know.

'Come on, then.'

'I'm almost forty-one.'

She looked at me for a second, and then laughed. She clearly didn't believe me, and it was the closest I've come to ever telling anyone the truth, apart from Madeleine. And Pearl, of course. I forced myself to laugh along.

'It's true,' I insisted. 'I lived in Montmartre in Paris, in Berlin, and before that I worked for a gangster in New York, delivering illicit alcohol to Speakeasies all over the city.'

Grace laughed even harder at this. The idea seemed completely preposterous to her. Prohibition had ended four years earlier, and the movies based on that time were very popular. I frowned at her, slightly annoyed by her attitude. I got up and went into my study, returning with a photograph. I handed it to her.

It was a picture someone had taken one day outside Mickey's in Hell's Kitchen. It showed me and Sean frowning menacingly beside Mickey's car.

Grace looked hard at it, taking in the fashion of the dresses two women were wearing as they walked past.

'When was this taken?'

'About 1924, 25. Something like that.'

She stared at the image of me. I looked exactly the same as I did now. She eventually shook her head and put the photo down.

She had dismissed it. It just wasn't important to a person like Grace Yeo. She didn't really care about anyone but herself, as I was to find out soon.

'Well, I don't care if you're forty-one or twenty-one, Mr Deakin. I like you just the way you are.'

She put her head onto my chest and slipped off her shoes, curling her legs onto the sofa. I put my wine down carefully—it was expensive—and turned her face towards me.

I gently unfastened the buttons of her dress and stripped it from her. Her slip came next and I gazed at her naked, magnificent body. She smiled at me, and I smiled back, unfastening my own shirt.

For the first time in almost a decade, I made love to a woman.

XII

1937 turned to 1938 and things really began to deteriorate over in Germany.

In March, the Nazis formed the *Anschluss* with Austria, tearing up another page of the Versailles peace treaty. Once again the rest of the world, devoid of American strength, let Hitler get away with it. I listened to the radio and worried that things would soon be getting out of hand; but Grace Yeo was constantly taking my mind off world events, and I was happy to let her.

Having sex with Grace was now a very regular, and very enjoyable, event. We would tootle around the countryside, go for lunch, take bracing walks along the river, and then retire to my house to make love in all sorts of weird and wonderful positions. Grace, much to my surprise and pleasure, bought me an illicit copy of the *Karma Sutra*, and I have to say that book is the one book in my long life which I have studied the most. For a vicar's daughter she was very experimental.

I was completely happy. I hadn't thought about the Medic in any meaningful way for the best part of a year and I was satiated almost every night. Grace made me content, damn her, and soon the time came when I took her hand, went down on one knee, and asked her to be my wife.

It was a stupid thing to do. I knew it, even then. I was a man unlike any other she would ever meet. Even if it had worked out, how could we have lived out our lives with her getting older and bitterer and me staying young and healthy? It was an impossible dream.

But I was desperate; desperate for a connection to the world. I wanted to be normal; I wanted to be like everyone else. I craved the wonderful ordinariness of marriage and children and hearth and home.

She said yes. We went straight to the vicarage and her father, who had lost his own wife eight years previously, was happy that his daughter would have someone to take over from him once he went off to join his God. He never liked me, Thomas Yeo: he must have known there was something not right with me, but his love for his daughter and his need for her to be protected overrode his feelings. He said he would be honoured to do the wedding ceremony himself.

We went back to my house and celebrated with champagne and the *Karma Sutra*. I went to sleep that night believing I was a happy man.

But I never married Grace. The war got in the way.

In October of that year, the German army marched into the Sudetenland of Czechoslovakia. The land had been annexed from Germany after the war and it was another way for Hitler to bring about his promise of unifying the country. War loomed.

Grace was all for it. She had become an avid listener of the news and, when Chamberlain came back from Munich with his piece of paper, she was livid.

'Hitler must be stopped!' she shouted at me. 'He can't be trusted.'

She was right of course, because in March 1939, the Germans took over the rest of Czechoslovakia. Chamberlain gave Hitler the ultimatum that if he invaded Poland, as everyone now knew he would, then war would begin. But by then it was too late; Hitler simply did not believe him.

Grace and I listened to the broadcast in September as Chamberlain, in a voice as weary as I have ever heard, announced that, once again, Britain was at war with Germany.

I turned the radio off when the broadcast ended, thinking about how different it was to the triumphant, cheering excitement the outbreak of the Great War had brought about. Nobody wanted this. The country couldn't afford it. It was a total and utter disaster.

Grace turned to me.

'You have to join up,' she enthused.

I stared at her. 'What?'

'Join up. You have to join up and fight those beastly Nazis. It's your duty!'

I shook my head, totally bewildered. 'Grace, I'm forty-three years old. I'm not joining the army for God's sake.'

She pulled herself away from me, a look of utter loathing on her face. In that face I saw a strange reflection of Jane Godley, and I got my first inkling of what lay beneath her beautiful exterior.

'Stop saying that! It's ridiculous. You're not *forty-three*. You're barely twenty-three! Why do you insist on telling me lies?'

'I'm not telling you lies, Grace. I was born in 1896. I fought in the Great War. I've done my bit. I've seen one war; I don't intend to see another.'

Grace stood up, glaring down at me. She exuded loathing. 'You coward!' she hissed.

I stared at her in astonishment.

'You've just heard what that madman is doing. Marching his army everywhere he wants. It's every Englishman's duty to join up and fight. And here you are telling me you won't. Telling me you'd let a German Paratrooper come into this very house and have his wicked way with me. Telling me lies so you don't have to defend me. Coward!'

She screamed this word at me. I stood up and grabbed her arms.

'Grace, stop it, you're being ridiculous. You don't know what you're saying.'

She yanked her arms free. 'I know exactly what I'm saying. You

94

are a coward. There. I've said it again and I mean it. You won't fight for your king and country and you won't fight for me. Well. If you won't do your duty, I'll find someone who will!'

With this, she pulled at the engagement ring on her finger and threw it at me. It hit my chest and fell to the floor. I shook my head, dumbfounded by the sudden change in her demeanour and the hatred she now showed me.

I opened my mouth to speak, but she turned and grabbed her coat, storming out of the cottage. The *Karma Sutra*, which I had carefully turned to my favourite page in expectation of the coming night, fell to the floor beside the ring. The door slammed behind her.

I stood there for a long time, various different emotions raging through me, before slowly sinking to the settee. I picked up my wine and sipped it.

She didn't have a clue. She had been raised in quiet comfort by wealthy parents and had seen nothing of the reality of war. I had been dragged up in a Northumberland croft and war had forged my very character. It had changed me completely. I suddenly realised the size of the void between us.

The ring winked at me, as if it were laughing at my predicament. And laughing at the choice it knew I was going to take.

I was besotted, you see. I thought I loved Grace Yeo and, if going back to war would mean keeping her close, then that's what I would have to do. I ran out of the house and down the lane until I caught up with her, telling her what she wanted to hear and pressing the ring back into her unwilling hand. Eventually, she returned to the cottage with me and rewarded me.

As she slept beside me later that evening, I stared at her profile in the moonlight. A terrible reality told me I had made the wrong choice.

*

There were thousands of us crammed onto the beach. We waited;

it was all we could do.

The British Expeditionary Force, to which I now belonged, had been sent to France in May 1940. Churchill had become Prime Minister with the fall of Chamberlain and had immediately put things into motion after months of *"Phoney War"*. I had found myself sent to defend the Maginot Line: a series of huge, concrete fortifications built along the French / German border. However the Germans, with typical Teutonic efficiency, had simply gone around it through a forest to the north and cut us off.

We had been forced to blindly retreat before the massed ranks of tanks and Stukas, finally ending up herded onto the beach at Dunkirk, caught literally between the devil and the deep blue sea. It was, as one young soldier muttered to me as we marched, 'A complete fuck-up.'

After making up, and making love, with Grace, I had travelled to London to join up. Conscription was already under way, but volunteers were still smiled upon.

I gave a false name to hide my true age, the first of many I would use in my long life. One of the women in the village had a son who had died in childhood twenty years ago, so I simply assumed his identity. No one looked too closely at my story. You have to remember that records then were not as precise as they became later on, and any able-bodied man was not going to be turned away. All I had to do was stay alive so the woman would not get a telegram telling her how sorry the army was for the death of her son, years after he had actually died.

So, it was a twenty-two-year-old named William Taylor who was reluctantly sworn into His Majesty's Army and took his place on the ship to France.

Up until then the only things the Germans had thrown at us were leaflets, although there were rumours that the SS had machine-gunned a bunch of unarmed prisoners from a Norfolk regiment to death. But in the army there are always rumours; no one really believed it at the time. The Germans wouldn't do that sort of thing to Englishmen, would they?

I remembered my time in Berlin and the bullying, abusive young men of the SA, pushing and shoving Jewish civilians around, and I wasn't so sure.

The leaflets had a map, showing us surrounded on the beach head, with the words: *'British soldiers! Look at the map: it gives your true situation! Your troops are entirely surrounded—stop fighting!'* written on them.

'Complete and utter fuck-up,' muttered the young lad beside me again.

I had to agree. But I reckoned the Germans had fucked up too.

We had been on the beach for a full night and day now, and still they had not come in and wiped us out: which was well within their power to do so as we had no real defences left. I still don't really know why they halted their advance, and I certainly didn't know then.

However, we were in a precarious position. If we couldn't get off that beach, the Germans would eventually move. We would be lucky if we made it to a POW camp and the war would be over for Britain before it had really begun. As I looked around the khaki masses on the sand, I remember believing most of them would soon be dead.

I wondered what would happen to me. Would I be killed too? *Could* I be killed? What if I was hit by a bomb? What if my body was scattered to the four winds to lay in bloody clumps on the clinging sand? Would I still live, continuing to exist in several hundred pieces of raw meat, or would such a huge trauma end my life?

It had to, surely. I thought about it a lot and I'm not ashamed to say I was frightened by the concept. Not of being killed, but what it might actually take to kill me. As I remembered the terrified face of Doctor Artigue and the wild fury of Mickey Donovan, the thoughts repeated themselves around my brain again and again and again.

Would I die? *Could* I?

And then the next morning, like a gift from the gods, ships

began to appear on the horizon. Troop carriers, yes, but also trawlers, schooners, yachts and ferries, all sorts of different vessels. They came to our rescue, rallied by frantic requests for help at home, and the men around me cheered, waving their helmets over their heads at the approaching armada.

But it seemed they may have come too late.

Some German General somewhere finally made a decision and the Stukas came in, screaming their hellish war cries as they belted down at us like carriages on a roller coaster. Christ, they were terrifying machines and, because of our massed ranks, they couldn't miss. They came in again and again and it felt like every single one of them was aiming its nose just at me.

Explosions rocked the beach, and sand and ragged chunks of bodies were scattered all around me and over me.

The men around me ran blindly and I was caught up with them, the blood-drenched sand sticking to me, grinding against the skin of my neck. I've never liked the feel of sand since then, and don't go to the beach very often now if I can help it.

We were in a total panic. We pushed and shoved at each other in our desperation to escape the death coming from above. The noise was like the bells of hell. It was carnage. Spitfires and Hurricanes did their best to protect us from their bases on the South Coast of England, but it took days of noise and chaos before we were eventually evacuated.

I was near the sea, waiting my turn, eagerly watching a trawler crawl inexorably towards us, when I saw one man blown backwards from the blast of a bomb. He lay spread-eagled on the sand. He must have been thrown ten yards or more.

I saw him move so I ran across to him through the surf, the bombs blasting all around me; I still had some feelings towards humanity at that time. He was semi-conscious, but I frowned as I saw he seemed to be completely unmarked. His entire uniform however, had been shredded. The massive concussion of air from the blast had knocked him out, and it had also ripped his clothes from him. He was bollock-naked apart from his boots.

He stirred and blinked up at me with unfocussed eyes.

'Here,' he muttered weakly. 'Whossagame?' It was the young lad who had said everything was a fuck-up.

Luck, I thought madly. Pure luck.

I grabbed him and waded out to the trawler that had come as close to the shore as it dared. Explosions rocked the sand and ploughed up the water around us. Hundreds of us half-swam, half-waded out to that trawler. Oil from another stricken ship coated all of us. It got into my mouth and I gagged at its foul, burnt taste. I prayed it wouldn't catch fire.

Arms reached down from the trawler and the young lad was hauled over the side. I reached up, shouting to the men on board, and strong, calloused hands gripped my own, heaving me upwards. I was black and slick with the oil.

I found myself slipping and sliding onto the boards of a deck I could barely see for the ranks of wide-eyed, white-faced soldiers packed onto it. The young lad I'd rescued was given a fisherman's jacket to cover his shrunken dignity.

Amazingly, the trawler was not hit. It backed up as rapidly as it could away from the shore, turning when it had enough space, and from the stern I watched the burning beach, scattered with the lost hardware of a defeated army and the crumpled bodies of men who would never be rescued. The beach slowly receded as we made our way back to Britain.

We didn't know it at the time, but we owed a lot of our ignominious escape to the French soldiers who had fought on for us as we scrambled to safety. Our generals had not told them we were planning to escape but they had fought for us anyway, along with thousands of British soldiers who hadn't made it to the beach. Churchill ordered ships to go back and get French survivors, and over 26,000 were rescued. But something like 30,000 were captured and 16,000 of them lost their lives, along with thousands of our own men.

However, the amazing grit and courage shown by the ordinary people of the British Isles got me and 338,000 men off that beach.

We all cheered when we saw the shores of Britain appearing again on the horizon. We were safe for now. But the war in France was over and Germany was in complete control of Western Europe.

It was only a matter of time before Hitler decided to invade Britain.

XIII

I returned to my cottage on the sixth of June, 1940. That date would become very important to me four years later, but at that moment I was simply pleased to have a little time for rest and recuperation.

I had been gone for over four months, what with my initial training and my brief, if disastrous, sojourn in France. I only had a few days' leave, as the survivors from Dunkirk were to be re-equipped and re-organised for the future but, before returning to the barracks, I wanted to see Grace.

I dumped what little equipment I had in the dusty cottage and strolled along the lane, a cigarette keeping me company, thinking about what might happen now.

It was only twenty-odd miles from France to the south east coast, and the rumours were rife about when the Germans would come. London was sand-bagged to the hilt and bejewelled with ack-ack guns and barrage balloons. The enemy was coming and all anyone could do was wait.

I didn't have any answers; I think I was still in shock. Even though I was probably the only man on that beach who had been under fire before, that had been over twenty years ago. It does not get any easier, believe me. The noise and death and destruction is just as shocking, just as frightening, no matter how many times it has been experienced. Even now I sometimes dream of the wars I went through and the things I experienced. Those nightmares still make me scream myself awake.

I got to the vicarage and rang the doorbell. A woman answered the door. She was aged about fifty, attractive in an upper-class, aloof sort of way, and she looked a little like Grace. I guessed she must have been an aunt. She glanced at my lowly Private's uniform and smiled coldly.

'Yes?' she asked.

'Good afternoon,' I said. 'My name is Robert Deakin. I was wondering if Miss Yeo was available.'

She frowned at this but, before she could say anything else, Father Yeo himself came to the door. He looked at me sternly.

'I'm afraid Grace is not in,' he said. 'She's away at the moment. However, she did ask that if you called, I was to give you this.'

He handed me a sealed envelope. I could feel something small and hard inside it and my heart sank.

Yeo seemed to soften slightly at the look on my face.

'It's for the best, old boy. Grace is happier now then I have ever seen her. Surely that is worth a little lingering sadness on your part. We both want what's best for her, eh?'

I lifted my eyes from the envelope and the look I gave them both caused them to simultaneously take a step back in fear, the woman's hand reaching for her throat, protectively. I kept my gaze upon them a moment longer, that strange, dark hatred emanating from me in waves, then I turned away, walking back to the cottage. Once there, I poured a whiskey. I had a feeling I would need it.

The engagement ring fell to the floor as I opened the letter, almost in the same place it had lain when she threw it at me. I didn't pick it up. As far as I know it's still there, for I never set foot in Aylesford again after that day. I read what she had written.

Dear Robert,
If you are reading this then it must mean you have survived. Allow

me to express how happy I am about this. Things have changed in such a short time that I hardly know where to start.

Shortly after you left for France, I received a letter from a childhood friend of mine, Roger Bellews (we knew each other when Father was the vicar of Basingstoke and he is from a very well-to-do family.) He wrote to tell me he was in the area and would very much like to meet me for tea. I naturally agreed as we had been such good friends when we were eighteen or nineteen. Imagine my surprise when we met and I found out that he is now a Commander in the Royal Navy. A Commander! And soon to be Captain, no doubt!

I'm afraid I realised that my affections for Roger have never really disappeared. He looked so smart in his uniform. So dominant! I am afraid he turned my head, Robert, dear. One cannot fight one's base emotions, as we both know. Our relationship was lovely, Rob, really lovely. But that night, when you showed me you would rather break off our understanding than fight for my safety, I'm afraid that night played on my mind a lot.

So, dearest Robert, I am writing this letter to inform you I have decided to break off our engagement. It is in both our best interests as I'm sure you will understand one day. (I have enclosed the ring back to your keeping.)

Goodbye, Robert. I wish you all the best for your future as I'm sure you will wish me the best for mine.

Kind regards,

Grace.

I slowly crumpled the letter into a ball and dropped it beside the engagement ring. I lit a cigarette, swallowed a mouthful of whiskey, and then had another.

Wish her all the best? At that moment I hoped the bitch would burn in hell, along with her *Commander* Bellews. I had a sudden image of Grace writhing, naked, under the body of some faceless man with a copy of the *Karma Sutra* lying beside them open at my favourite page, and a dark, furious jealousy seared through me. It was as if there was something inside me, something somehow different and detached from me, screaming in hatred and spite. I poured another drink and forced myself to calm down, eventually succeeding to a certain degree. It is quite remarkable how quickly that screeching vindictiveness disappeared and the old cold nothingness came back to me. At the time I supposed it was my natural state, although I was to find out I was wrong about that many years later.

I had several more whiskeys that night and, in the morning, I was no further forward. Instead I was only sick in heart and sour of stomach, my head pounding from the most aggressive hangover I had ever known.

I lay in bed all morning, just staring up at the ceiling I would never see again, but in the afternoon I got up and packed my kit bag with a few odds and ends.

I wrote a letter to my solicitor, telling him to make arrangements for the sale of the cottage and also saying that, if anything happened to me, he was to make provisions for all my worldly assets to be transferred to one William Taylor, address to be confirmed soon. I sealed the envelope and took one more look around my house. Grace seemed to be ingrained in that place and I could not face going back there again.

I walked out and closed the door behind me. I posted the letter then went straight to the train station and caught a service to London, where I spent my final few days of leave getting blind drunk.

I heard later that Commander Bellews—he never made captain—was killed when his ship was torpedoed in 1942. Grace Yeo ended up marrying a politician who gave her all the money and status she wanted but who eventually left her penniless and destitute for another woman. There was some vindication for my rapidly hardening heart in that, at least.

I had no idea at the time that our paths would cross again, briefly and disastrously, in the future. But even if I had known I doubt I would have cared.

There was only one thing I wanted to do at that point and that was to disgorge the terrible, ice-cold rage I felt pulsing and heaving within myself.

I wanted to kill. And thankfully, I was in just the right position to do that.

*

The months went on. I re-joined my battalion. Shortly after the narrowly won Battle of Britain we were sent to Africa, where I fought in most of the action there. Once more my life became consumed by warfare.

I didn't think of Grace much in those years; I didn't really have the time. I fought and killed and survived. I became little more than a machine. I was unthinking, unmoved, without any sense of pity or empathy. My cold-hearted professionalism earned me a sergeant's stripes once more, and the last thing many a German saw was my impassive, utterly uncompassionate face. We moved inexorably forward, through the dust and the heat and the blood.

I was shot a couple of times but both were light wounds, scratches really, so I didn't know if the strange magic was still inside me. But in December 1943 I found myself back on leave in London and something happened that seemed to confirm it was.

God, I was an empty man back then. Empty and dark and unthinking and uncaring. The blackness that seemed to have consumed my soul emanated from me in a dark aura, and I was always left unmolested wherever I wandered in the city. I visited various different pubs in the capital and drank the watered-down beer, not even bothering to move from my bar stool when the occasional air raid warnings went off.

There had been few attacks on the capital since late 1941, nothing like at the height of the Blitz, but they still happened now and then and, one night, a bomb went off without warning right outside the pub I was in. The alarms had sounded but the bombing seemed to be miles away, so a lot of the war-worn Londoners had done the same as I and simply ignored it.

The bomb smashed into the side of the pub, blowing bricks and wood into the interior in a sudden maelstrom of crashing orange fire and blasting debris.

I was blown off my stool, thrown right over the bar, where I collapsed in a heap. Rubble rained down around me and onto me. I cowered until the tearing explosions moved on, and then slowly pulled myself free from the wreckage.

It was only then that I discovered the foot-long shard of glass from the fractured bar mirror embedded in my side. The pain cut through my alcohol-dulled body, but I just grimaced and pulled the glass out. The blood gushed from the huge wound but I ignored it, squinting through the dust around the blasted room.

The front of the bar was gone, a jagged hole showing the shattered street outside. Half the roof had come down, leaving a mound of rubble and bricks from which a low moaning now began. Water sprayed mindlessly from a ruptured main.

Rescue teams soon arrived. I was just going to leave them to it; I'm afraid to say that by that point I hardly cared what happened to the survivors. But they asked me for help and so I begrudgingly stayed long enough to help them drag the shattered bodies, both dead and alive, from the ruined building and, when we had got as many out as we could, I disappeared into the night and found another pub.

There, I went into the toilets and inspected my side.

The gash was massive: at least ten inches long and very deep. It must have pierced internal organs but, as I washed away some of the blood, I could see my skin was already beginning to knit together.

I closed my torn tunic over it as best I could and stared into the mirror for a long time, my face blank but my mind in a whirling turmoil of fear and wonder. Then I exited the toilets, sat on a stool, and ordered another pint. I was a bloodied, filthy mess but I ignored the astonished stares from the other customers in the bar as, underneath my uniform, my body healed itself again.

I believe I had become almost totally dehumanised by then. Not quite as bad as I became later in my life, but even so I was a strange, dangerous figure. I was avoided by anyone who encountered me. They all seemed to sense something wrong about me.

Which was fine with me because I despised everyone I met: British or German.

I gazed blearily at myself in the bar room mirror and saw the same, unchanging face staring back at me that I'd seen in the pub when I was de-mobbed back in 1918. By that December of 1943, I was on my way to being forty-eight years old. I was a miserable, ageing man trapped inside the body of a youth.

When I got back from leave I learned that I was not going back to re-join my battalion, which was by now forcing its way into Italy, but instead I was to be part of another group of men who began training for some sort of secret mission. All we were told was that invasion was being planned and my new battalion was going to be part of it. We trained in the wilds of Inveraray in Scotland whilst American troops constantly raided the village of Woolacombe on the North Devon coast.

Something big was coming.

*

The sixth of June, 1944, dawned clear and bright, but quite windy at sea. My first glimpse of France in four years showed me the long, flat beaches of Normandy. The beach we were to take was codenamed "Gold".

The months of military exercises had culminated in this: Operation *Neptune*, the Allies' attempt to re-take France and defeat Germany once and for all. The invasion of Normandy, which we were involved in was codenamed *Overlord*. Not that anybody cared about names at the time.

Our orders were simple enough on paper. We were to establish a beachhead and then take Arromanches, joining up with the American forces who would land at Omaha beach down the coast, before moving inland and taking Bayeux. From there we would start pushing the Germans back to their homeland.

It didn't quite work out like that.

Before we landed, we witnessed huge explosions and heard the booming crackle of heavy artillery on the beach. The tide was running incredibly fast and had stopped the engineers in their mission to destroy the anti-tank defences on the beach, although we didn't know this at the time. We had all been throwing up constantly because of the queasy motion of the landing craft we couched in. As frightened as the mortals around me were, I think they were pleased to get onto dry land.

At 7:26 exactly, we landed.

Me and the men under my command rushed forward, bullets spitting all around us. It reminded me for a moment of the Somme.

I just ran, once again working on impulse and instinct, men falling and twisting to the sand around me, the noise of their screams and the roar of the machine guns ringing in my ears. I dropped down behind the dubious safety of a sand dune as my remaining men caught up with me. We struggled through the sharp Marram grass and I found myself staring up at a house where Germans could be seen firing down onto the beach.

There were a few of these houses dotted along the top of the beach, with the road behind them. Once well-to-do beach homes, they had all been fortified with sandbags and concrete and they were spitting their machine gun fire down onto the men still struggling from the landing crafts at the water's edge. The sea was red already and bodies littered the beach.

My captain, a man named Johnson, slammed down beside me. He gave us brief orders, but in fact we all knew what we had to do. Before we could move anywhere, we had to take these fortifications, and the house we were lying in the lee of was ours. Other units had their own targets.

We split into a pincer shape, me and half-a-dozen men on one side, Johnson and his men on the other. We jumped up and ran towards the house. A couple of Germans popped up as we closed down the distance, but they were thrown backwards instantly from the fire from myself and my men. I don't think either of them got a shot off.

I sprinted to the side of the house and slammed into the wall, glancing around the corner to see Johnson and his men in position. So far so good.

The doorway beside me suddenly burst open and sprouted grey-jacketed infantry followed by a crackle of fire. One of the Germans went down but the other snapped off a shot that rebounded off the wall and hit me in the calf.

Ignoring the sudden pain I limped on, firing at the German until he crumpled in the doorway. We rushed it when we heard the crack of grenades from inside as Johnson and his men chucked them through the embrasure at the front of the house.

Smoke billowed as we entered and we shot at anything that moved in the murk, shadowy bodies throwing up their arms and going down. One of them screamed loudly and then choked into silence.

And that was it. It was over before it had really started. It was suddenly very quiet, although we could still hear firing coming from the other houses that lined the beach as more soldiers fought on.

As the smoke cleared, we checked that all of the Germans inside were dead. Their glazed eyes stared at us while we swept the interior for any more danger.

Johnson and his men came in, Johnson asking me something in a strangely muted voice.

I frowned as I couldn't really hear him. The noise from the explosions had temporarily deafened me.

'I asked how your leg is?' he shouted.

I glanced down and saw blood was soaking the bottom of the left leg of my uniform trousers.

'It'll be fine by tomorrow, sir,' I yelled back at him, moderating my voice as he winced. He frowned at my words.

One of the men knelt down beside my leg and sliced at the material, applying a field dressing to the wound.

Johnson was saying something about getting me to safety, but I ignored him.

'I'm fine, sir, honestly. I want to go on.'

He shrugged and patted me on the shoulder. There wasn't really anywhere safe to put me anyway. We moved on.

The fortifications fell one by one. Men died on both sides. Johnson himself was shot in the head ten minutes after our brief conversation and his brains were scattered bright and red across the road as we crouched and ran and shot.

He was a decent sort, was Johnson. A bit remote, but a good officer. He was left lying in the street with the other dead bodies as we moved rapidly forward.

We pressed on, my leg healing by the minute. By evening, although we had not joined up with the Yanks as planned because the carnage at Omaha was abysmal, we had joined forces with some Canadian troops from Juno beach and we rolled into Arromanches in the early evening. We spent the night re-grouping and trying to rest, for the next day we would be attempting to take Bayeux.

During this brief respite, in the middle of the night I took myself around a corner away from prying eyes and removed the field dressing from my leg. The bullet from the German rifle fell with a tinkle to the road.

The wound had completely healed.

We took Bayeux the next day. The day after that we took another town. And another. We slowly pushed at the Germans from the West as the Russians pushed at them from the East.

Men were losing their lives every day.

But the Germans were on the run.

XIV

It was on the twenty-seventh of June when my luck changed and I have to say, even with what I went through, it changed in the most wonderful way. It was a day that truly showed me what my strange body could do, and a day that was the harbinger of pain like I had never imagined. But ultimately it also led me to Madeleine, which was worth everything I suffered. On the twenty-seventh of June, 1944, I was shot in the head.

I never saw the man who shot me. One rarely does. We had entered Cherbourg: pushing, pushing, pushing. We'd had barely any time for sleep and my men and I were battle weary, stinking and bearded.

I was standing in what I thought was a decently defended position, at the end of a road behind the corner of a house. We knew the main German force was holed up in the buildings at the far end of the road and the junction down there was protected by a Panzer tank. Its barrel glared down the road at us malevolently. My men were lined up behind me, awaiting my orders as I peered carefully around the corner at the Panzer. We could hear small arms fire echoing around the town.

I had just turned back to Connors, my corporal, to give him my thoughts when my vision erupted in a white flash and the most immense pain I have ever felt seared through my head. Then the world disappeared.

My memory of that time is very broken, even more so than when I was shot in World War One and after being stabbed by Mickey Donovan. Everything was fractured. Nothing made any sense. The past and present were mixed together in a maelstrom of images and feelings and smells and it seemed to go on forever.

I saw Molly, lying naked and ready on her settee in New York, whilst Mickey kissed Grace in the corner before plunging his knife into her stomach. Hector appeared at various times, jumping up at Jane Godley and ruining her dress. Greene then turned up and she stuck a knife into *him*. The Medic stood in the background and laughed. Nothing made sense.

My thoughts did not connect properly. I dreamed and hallucinated. Bright sparks and strobing lights flashed on and off in an incessant, jumbled kaleidoscope of feelings and images, and I knew there was something very wrong with me but I didn't know what it was or even what *wrong* really meant.

I would worry about it for a while and then forget it. I would start along a train of thought before it wobbled and faded, and I would forget it until the thread was picked up minutes or days or weeks later. I was in a purgatorial state: never resting but never awake, always aware of something but not knowing what that something was.

I heard sounds that made no sense. Saw images I could not explain. I was going mad and I screamed, but I couldn't move my mouth. The threads of my thoughts would not complete the circuit. They were too short. It was as if I didn't have all the parts I needed to connect them together. As if something was missing.

But slowly those threads seemed to start making more sense. My vision, which had been black to the world, began to work once more: blurry at first but slowly coming back into focus. Pain seared through me again and again, then slowly faded away. My ears began to pick up sounds. My fingers and toes began to heed the commands my strengthening mind gave them. I began to think again.

My eyes snapped open.

She was the first thing I saw. The reason why getting shot in the head was such a good thing.

My angel. My one true love. My Madeleine.

She jumped back when she saw me gazing at her. But then she smiled at me and it was as if the sun had come out.

'Hello,' I whispered in French, because I knew she was French. I'd heard her talking to me at some point, telling me what the day had brought. I remembered it now although I had not understood the noises before as I'd slept. As I had recovered.

She frowned in disbelief, swallowing hard, as if she were frightened by my words. Her reaction reminded me of Sister Clara at the church of St Theresa Marie.

'Hello,' she eventually answered. She stared at me in wonder. 'Do you feel alright?'

I nodded. The movement caused a little pain, like a receding hangover, but that was all.

'Where am I?' I asked.

'You are still in Cherbourg. You were wounded. Can you remember?'

I nodded again. 'I was hit in the head, I think.'

She frowned again. 'I'll fetch the doctor. I think he'll want to see you.'

She smiled again and then left. I was in some sort of hospital room: white walls, equipped only with the bed I lay in and a wash basin near the window. I tried to see what lay outside the window but could make out nothing but grey sky from the bed, so I pulled back the covers.

I swung my legs to the floor and paused as the room swayed around me. When it stopped, and after a couple of attempts, I pushed myself to my feet. The room swayed again and I placed a hand on the wall. Soon, though, I felt strong enough to try and walk to the window.

My left leg felt numb and it dragged slightly, as if it were not fully connected to my brain's commands, but I managed to limp to the window and looked out.

I was standing above a town square. It looked cold and rainy outside. Across from the building I was in was another, more ornate, building that looked like a town hall. American and British flags hung limply from a large balcony.

I turned back and went across to the sink on the wall. I looked into the mirror, frowning at what I saw.

My lips were cracked and chapped, as if they had not had enough moisture, and a bandage was wrapped around my head. My face seemed very thin and my beard seemed very thick. I had no idea how long it would have taken me to grow that beard for the simple fact that I had always been clean-shaven, but it looked like it would have taken a while.

The sound of a door opening made me turn and I was confronted by a young man in a doctor's coat. He stared at me in astonishment.

'My God, he muttered. He had an American accent. After a moment he roused himself from his shock. 'What the hell are you playing at?' he all but shouted at me. 'What the hell are you doing out of bed?'

The woman I had first seen was behind him and I now realised she wore a white nurse's uniform. They both came to me and led me back to the bed. The doctor stared.

'Where am I?' I asked. 'Where is this place?'

The doctor seemed lost for words still, but he finally moved and pulled a stool from beneath the bed and sat beside me. 'What do you remember?' he finally asked.

I frowned, trying to come up with the information he required.

'I remember being in the street. There was a tank. I remember a white light and a pain in my head. Then nothing until I woke up here. How long have I been here?'

The doctor seemed to wonder where to start, then shrugged to himself. 'You were shot,' he explained, ignoring my request. 'In the head. You were brought to us on the evening of the 27th of June, after the town was liberated.'

I opened my mouth to ask a question, but he held up a hand and continued.

'Your wound was... bad. The bullet entered your head, here.' He indicated to his temple. 'And exited here.' He pointed to the top of his head. 'Your skull was blown apart. Half your brains were missing. We know this because we tried to operate on it. You were still alive, you see, when you should have been dead. That's why your men waited until the evening to bring you here. They only went back to you after the town had been cleared, to collect your body. They naturally thought you were gone.'

He stood up and went to the window I had just been gazing out of. 'It's now November twenty-first. You've been unconscious for almost five months.'

I stared at him. Five months!

Of course I knew what had happened, although I could barely believe the truth of it. My brain had been destroyed by the bullet, my skull blasted away. It had taken five months to recover because it was such a huge wound.

I remembered the flashing, disjointed images and sounds that had flitted through my mind as I lay unconscious. Time had meant nothing and the broken thoughts must have been the result of my brain mending itself, knitting itself back together. Rebuilding itself.

I thought back to my fears on the beach at Dunkirk about what it would take to make me die and the old realisation came back, magnified a million times over. I could not be killed!

'We want to take more x-rays,' the doctor continued. 'I want to know how you've survived something that should have killed you, or at the very least should have left you little more than a vegetable.'

I nodded, knowing that, as I was still in the army and that this must have been a military hospital, I had no choice. But I also believed all they would find was a few marks that looked like old wounds. I believed my brain would be completely normal.

The doctor then gently unwound the bandages, nodding to himself as if he knew what he would find.

'We've changed the bandages regularly, of course,' he muttered as he did so. 'We've seen your bone and the flesh healing. We just didn't know how your brain would be affected. As you're so keen to be out of bed, why don't you take a look?' He indicated for me to stand and look in the mirror.

My hair had grown back a little where they had obviously shaved it, and the only thing I could see was a small scar at my right temple. I rubbed the crown of my head and felt a small ridge, about four inches long. I tapped my skull with a forefinger and the doctor winced.

'What's going on in the war?' I asked him.

He shook his head in mute disbelief. 'I hear you speak French?' he asked in return.

I nodded and he indicated the young woman.

'Nurse Besson will fill you in on the details.'

He looked at me once more, shook his head again, then left.

'Please,' I said to the nurse. 'How is the war going?'

Hesitantly at first, she filled me in. Paris had been liberated, as had the whole of Belgium, and the Allied forces were now massed at the Rhine. She had no other real news. The Germans were being tenacious. It would take a long time to finish the job. So, it was still not over. My work was still not completed.

'I need to find my battalion,' I told her. I looked around the room. 'Where's my uniform?'

She stared at me as if I were mad.

*

But I never returned to the fighting. The young American doctor, Bennett, would hear none of it. He wrote to Allied Command, telling them of my survival but also making it clear that the wounds I had received meant I could not return to active service. I don't know if Mrs Taylor back in Aylesford ever heard anything about it or not.

Over the next few months—as well as dispensing with the slight limp, one of the last remnants of my wound—I received an honourable discharge from His Majesty's Armed Forces. It was in the name of William Taylor, of course, but it meant my second and hopefully final war was over.

As well as I felt, I was still not back to full strength. I was thin from intravenous feeding and my muscles were weak. I still suffered from the odd blinding headache as my brain continued to get better. It seemed this wound was one that would take time to heal completely. I couldn't rush it.

However, by late January 1945 I was completely back to normal. Bennett conducted test after test on my skull and brain functions but found nothing out of the ordinary. He said he would have to call in experts to find out why I had recovered so completely. I wasn't that bothered. I spent a lot of time with Nurse Madeleine Besson and, as my body healed itself, she somehow began to heal my soul from the raging black hate that had filled it for years. She began to cure me. She began to make me human again.

Over our time together at the hospital, as we became closer, she eventually told me about her past and it was a terrible story to hear.

She was from Caen and had worked as a nurse. She had been married for four years when the Germans invaded. Her husband, unable to contain his hatred for his enemies, had joined the Resistance, leaving Madeleine with her family. She had only recently found out that he had died under interrogation by the Gestapo three years before and so she never even got to bury his body. She and her mother and younger brother had watched the German tanks and infantry march through the streets of Caen, and those years had been hard as the rationing and occupation took effect. Madeleine said she was pleased her husband was already gone by then, because she believed he would have done something stupid like attacking the tanks with a spade or something. She smiled sadly as she remembered him.

Her mother had died during those years. Never a healthy

woman, she had succumbed to an unknown disease and not even Madeleine's nursing skills could save her. Maybe if they'd had access to the latest drugs and treatments she would have survived, but of course they didn't. They only had their rations and whatever Madeleine could beg or borrow from her neighbours.

Madeleine and her brother had buried her and then lived on the reduced rations allowed by the Germans. One night, a group of drunken Waffen SS men from a tank battalion had broken into their house. They had raped Madeleine and beaten her teenage brother to such an extent that he had died of his wounds.

After that, Madeleine began to give up. She was never molested again physically but her life was ruptured, as was her spirit. She worked like an automaton in the hospital in Caen, saving the lives of the Germans she now hated, until the Allied forces had liberated it. It was Doctor Bennett who had asked her to come to Cherbourg, as they needed trained nurses there, and she had gone as there was nothing left for her in her home town. She really had no choice.

At only thirty-three Madeleine was a broken woman: widowed, orphaned, and alone. Her cheerful demeanour at work hid her inner despair. But, perversely, she told me that her duties at the military hospital helped her to at least begin to come to terms with what had happened to her family and her country.

I closed my eyes in desperation as she told me of her life, emotions I hadn't known for years surfacing. Her presence brought me a peace I had never really known before, and it extinguished and nullified the feelings of hate that had pulsed through me for so long. Madeleine made me smile. She made me feel again, and she at first soothed then quenched my selfish anger. Madeleine made me better. She fixed me.

This didn't happen all at once, of course. It came about over many months and many meetings. I don't think she ever told anyone else about her past. Maybe she thought of me as different because I had survived something that should have killed me, just like her. We were both totally alone and had both been through hell in our different ways.

We were about to go through even more.

XV

In that January of 1945, a man with the unusual name of Herbert Pfumpf came into my life and proceeded to haunt and hurt me for years to come.

It was Doctor Bennett who brought him to see me. Outside the hospital, a frost had covered the square. The war rumbled on without me. In Poland, Auschwitz was liberated and the horrors of the Holocaust began to be unveiled. The fighting went on day after day, and good men continued to die as the Germans were pushed to their inevitable defeat.

One day, Bennett came into my room accompanied by a man of about forty-five years of age: a tall, cadaverous-looking man, with black-rimmed glasses and a waxed moustache. Pfumpf eyed me like a predator as the introductions were made.

'I'm Head of Neuroscience at Carville University, Washington,' explained Pfumpf. He was an American, and his voice was as slick as his moustache. 'Doctor Bennett here alerted me of your remarkable recovery. I wanted to come and see you for myself.' His mouth stretched into a brief grin, like he was testing an elastic band.

'I thought an expert should be able to examine you,' said Bennett. 'You already know how unusual your case is. Professor

Pfumpf is the leading scientist on brain damage and recovery. You should be honoured he's so interested in you.'

'Should I?' I asked, smiling to take the sting out of my words. This man had flown across a Europe which was still a war zone, with all the dangers this entailed. I didn't think I liked the implications of that.

'I'd like to make you an offer,' said Pfumpf, taking off his hat and revealing a domed pate.

'What would that be?'

'I'd like you to work with me. I've brought with me all the latest equipment available to check you out thoroughly. From top to bottom. Get to the nitty gritty, eh?' He flexed his mouth again in his imitation smile.

I looked back to Bennett for some real answers.

'Professor Pfumpf wants to run some checks on you,' he explained. 'Your wounds were massive, as you know. You should have died. And yet you recovered in no time at all. If we can find out why, think of the possibilities. There are men lying around in hospitals all over Europe with head trauma, with no chance of ever living a normal life again. Think what we would have accomplished if we can find out why you recovered and help them do the same thing.'

I remained silent, thinking. I knew that, whatever the reason was for my recovery, the ability to mend like I could did not exist in any other person I knew of.

'I'm just lucky,' I said, eventually. 'You said it yourself, Doctor. I've been prodded and probed ever since I've been here. What good will more checks do?'

'I have access to equipment which has never been used before,' interjected Pfumpf. 'New equipment. We could help so many men afflicted with head trauma, Sergeant Taylor. You could help the Allies win the war!'

'I was trying to do that when I got shot,' I said, flatly.

Pfumpf seemed to get suddenly bored with the conversation and straightened. His face became expressionless. I realised later that this was the real man behind the smiling façade. He reached into his pocket, handing me an official-looking letter.

'This is a reminder that, although you have been discharged from the army, you still have the duties of a British soldier and a member of the Allied Forces. It also has authority from both the British and American governments for you to be taken into my care. You will help me in my inquiries, Sergeant Taylor. It's an order.'

I read the letter and it seemed to be as he'd said, although I found out later it wasn't. It looked like I didn't have much choice, but still I hesitated.

'You'll be in a different part of the hospital,' urged Bennett. 'It's just been set up. Nicer than this military wing. We could even have Nurse Besson moved there to help out. I've noticed you seem to have become friendly with her?'

He leered at me knowingly, and I had to stop myself from standing up and belting him. Did he have even one inkling of what she'd been through? Did he care?

Pfumpf seemed to take my silence as acquiescence. He turned to go.

'We'll start tomorrow,' he said over his shoulder, and walked out the room without a backward glance.

*

I was taken to a part of the hospital far away from the raucous swearing and shouting of the GIs in the military section. Madeleine came with me.

As Bennet had said, this part of the hospital seemed like a new addition. There were armed guards at a gate and the complex inside was packed with Nissen huts and tents where hard-faced American MP's mooched around, staring suspiciously. It obviously belonged to the US army although, according to the sign over the door, it had once been a library.

The car we were in went through the gates and stopped outside the main building. It wasn't actually another wing, as Bennett had said, but was instead a completely separate building, a few blocks from the hospital where I'd spent so many months.

'It's an annex,' said Bennett when I questioned him about it.

We went inside and I was shown my room. It was a bit clinical but nice enough, with a normal bed, chair, and desk. However, I noticed that the glass of the windows had been wire-meshed and that there was a lock on the sturdy door.

'We'll leave you to get settled in,' said Bennett. 'Nurse Besson will be along soon with some food.'

He left and I heard the lock click in the door. It all seemed rather melodramatic and needless.

However, Bennett was as good as his word and Madeleine soon arrived with a meal far superior to any I'd had at the other hospital. She seemed uncomfortable.

'I don't like this place, Bill,' she said. 'The rest of the rooms are full of German soldiers. There's about thirty of them as far as I can tell.' She shuddered. 'It feels more like a prison than a hospital. And I don't like that man, Pfumpf. Why have they brought us here?'

'They want to know why I survived that bullet wound,' I said, soothingly, although I felt some of her disquiet. 'I suppose it's only natural.'

Madeleine glanced at me then with a look I got to know very well. 'There is nothing natural about your recovery, Bill. We both know that.'

I was about to ask her what she meant, when the door opened and an MP came in.

'They're waiting for you, Sergeant.'

I stood and smiled at Madeleine, who was collecting up the meal I hadn't touched. 'They just want to know why I survived,' I told her. 'I'd like to know too.'

I followed the MP down the corridor until we got to a metal door without any markings. The MP knocked and then stood to one side so I could go in.

It looked like it had once been some sort of stock room, but now looked like a normal doctor's surgery: except for the metal gurney that stood in the middle of the room surrounded by ranks of all sorts of strange machinery. Sitting at a desk in the corner of the room was Pfumpf, now wearing a white lab coat. He stood as I entered and favoured me with one of his elastic smiles.

'I hope your accommodation is good?' he asked. I nodded.

He indicated for me to sit on the edge of the gurney and pulled a chair up to face me.

'Cigarette?' he asked, offering me one. We smoked in silence for a while.

'I've been going over your records, Sergeant Taylor.'

I nodded again, saying nothing.

He inhaled deeply on his cigarette, regarding me quietly before continuing.

'Of course, what they don't tell me is why you call yourself Taylor, when we both know your real name is Robert Deakin.' He smiled a little at my reaction, waving away my protestations.

'Don't worry about anyone else finding out about you. It seems unlikely they will. You've been quite good at keeping your little secret.'

I didn't know what to say. I was dumbstruck. 'Who are you,' I finally managed.

'You know my name, and you know my job. However, apart from my work at the university, I also do occasional, erm, favours for the American Government.'

'FBI?'

He laughed. 'I know the FBI is an organisation you tried to keep out of the way of during your brief stay in my country.' He laughed again when he saw my face. 'Oh, yes. I know you were in New York and I know what happened to Mickey Donovan. No. The people I sometimes work with are not the FBI. They are a little more *shadowy*, shall we say.'

He leaned forward, suddenly earnest. 'Don't worry. No one knows about you except me. I used my influence with the government to come here with this equipment, but no one knows why. I only tell you of my connections to make you understand that I only want the best for my country. And for yours of course. We're allies, after all.' He sat back. 'We have other allies, at the moment. Allies that may soon not be allies, if you know what I mean.'

'What allies?'

I was completely caught off-guard here. How did this man know so much about me?

Pfumpf grimaced, a look of distaste on his lips. 'The Soviets. They are the real enemy. Oh yes, we're all buddies at the moment. But, when Hitler's gone, do you think that friendship will last? We are talking about enemies of capitalism, Sergeant. The Soviets, they are our real adversaries. Once the Nazis are gone, they will show their true colours, believe me. We have to be one step in front of them.'

I shook my head, in a complete daze. This man knew about me. He knew about me!

He seemed to read my mind. 'When I heard about your case, I had Bennett send me photos of you. It didn't take much to check out your past.'

Much later, I discovered exactly how he had checked out my past and it was nothing to do with secret government organisations; but just then I had no clue.

He leaned forward again, his eyes glinting behind his glasses. 'How long have you walked this planet, Sergeant? How long have you been alive?'

There was something in his eyes now that I didn't like at all. Something strange. I remembered Ducos' words about a quiet madness. I saw that madness in Pfumpf's eyes. I tried to stall him longer. 'Why do you want to know?'

If he was disappointed in my answer, he didn't show it. 'Think of the edge we would have,' he enthused, continuing on his previous train of conversation. 'Think! American soldiers who were immune to injury. Immune to death! The Communists would never dare to do anything against us!'

I frowned at him. 'So that's why you want to know why I survived? You think I'm immune to death? And what's the problem with the Russians, anyway? They seem like they've played their part in this war as much as anyone. More than anyone actually.'

He sat back in his chair, looking at me shrewdly. 'You're not the only one, you know. There have been others. Others with the same gift you have. Francois Valin, for example.'

My heart leapt into my mouth. Pfumpf grinned when he saw the reaction. He nodded.

'If you help me, we can rid the world of our enemies,' he whispered. 'You and me. We can make the world a better, brighter place.' He paused for a long time. 'If you help me, I have the power to set you up somewhere safe. And I'll help you find Valin. We will find out together about the magic that runs through your veins.'

'He's still alive?'

Pfumpf smiled his elastic smile one more but said nothing.

I found out quite soon that he didn't have a clue about Valin. He had just heard the name when he was delving through my past and had put the pieces together in a lucky guess.

But the thought of finally getting some answers was too much for me. If the Medic was indeed like me, I needed to meet him. To ask him why we were different.

Whatever Pfumpf wanted, if it was in my power, I would give it to him. Because if helping him meant I would find the Medic, I was willing to go through hell.

And before Pfumpf had finished with me, I did.

XVI

At first, the work Pfumpf did was fairly non-invasive. He took blood samples, x-rays, that sort of thing. But these examinations didn't seem to give him any answers and it wasn't long before he moved onto more direct procedures.

As he worked on me, the war ended. April and May came and went with the news of Hitler's suicide and the signing of the German surrender. Only Japan fought on but, on my forty-ninth birthday, Hiroshima was blown apart in an explosion that changed the world. After Nagasaki was sent to hell three days later, the planet finally heaved itself out of warfare and millions around the globe began to look forward to a future brighter than the blasted past of the previous twenty years.

It didn't quite work out like that for them. And it certainly wasn't like that for me.

Day after day the experiments got worse. I was now being strapped down to the gurney to keep me still as Pfumpf cut into various parts of my body and timed how long it took for me to heal. He broke my bones to see what would happen. He used scalpels and probes to delve beneath my flesh. I began to beg him for an anaesthetic as he did these things, but he said it might jeopardise his findings and so the pain relief was denied. Night after night I would be dragged to my room and flung onto my bed, only to be dragged out of it the next day for the torture to start again.

Nobody else knew anything about it. Madeleine fussed over me, knowing that whatever was going on inside that steel room was causing me agony. But I kept silent, simply telling her that the work was tiring. She begged me to end it, to tell Pfumpf I'd had enough of his experiments, but the professor had promised that he would help me find the Medic, so I continued with his work in the vain hope this would happen. I needed to find out what was so different about me.

But, as the months wore on and he discovered nothing unique about me except my amazing ability to heal, he began to become more and more unhinged.

Whenever I complained or threatened to stop the work, he made it clear that, if I did, Madeleine may have been at risk. He never said it explicitly, but I was under no illusion that he would hurt her if I resisted. He said secrecy was vital in the new war against the Soviets and he used the threats towards Madeleine against me, knowing that my feelings for her were beginning to run deep.

I was as surprised by this as he was.

I realised I had never really loved a woman. I had been fond of Molly, yes, and I had craved Grace like a drug, but love had been alien to me until I saw the serious, blonde-haired, rather ordinary face of Madeleine Besson.

She was no beauty like those other women. She had dark blue eyes and her hair was thick and golden, but those eyes were set rather too far apart in her face and her nose was a tad too long. She was plain, truth be told.

But Madeleine had such a smile. When she smiled at me, I felt something I had never felt in almost fifty years of existence. She brought me a peace I had never known, even with what I was being subjected to every day. I was besotted with her, and that was because goodness ebbed out from her like a warm wave. Whatever the darkness was that flowed through my veins, it had no chance against that goodness. It was swamped and silenced by her. Even after all she had been through, Madeleine did what was right, whatever the consequences. Her goodness found the guttering flame of humanity within my frozen heart and blew the sparks back into life.

As Pfumpf hurt me, Madeleine healed me and I realised, as she came to me each night and stroked my face after my days in the medical room, that I loved her. I loved her totally and absolutely, and her presence became my reward for the pain I endured.

Another reason I allowed Pfumpf to continue with his work was that, as the months went on, it seemed that he had been right about the USSR.

After the initial handshakes between Soviet and American troops in Berlin, relations between the two countries quickly soured, and that was the main reason why I let the experiments go on so long.

As well as being a way to find the Medic and answer the questions about me, I thought I was helping to do something good for the world Madeleine lived in. The Soviets seemed to be craving a power they had not had before the war, and the countries of Eastern Europe they had "liberated" from the Nazi jackboot soon found themselves with new masters to answer to. The Soviets did not go home.

However, I couldn't keep going on forever with the experiments and I certainly couldn't hide the truth from Madeleine. She was an incredibly clever woman. Although I lied to her, and told her everything was fine, she knew Pfumpf was engaging in things that could by then only really be described as torture.

And, being Madeleine, it was her who came up with a plan to get me out of there.

*

It was, I think, early October 1945 when Pfumpf finally cracked.

He had been getting more and more agitated as his blood tests and his photographs and his skin samples and his filming of my body healing itself continued to show him nothing. There was nothing about me out of the ordinary. I was, to all intents and purposes, a normal man in his early twenties.

Except we both knew I wasn't that age.

When he found out I was only forty-nine he actually seemed a little disappointed. I think he wanted me to tell him about Tudor England or the Wars of Independence or something. He wanted to think I had lived a lot longer than I had.

I tried to explain to him that I didn't believe anyone could live that long and still function as a human. God knows, I had started to look upon humanity as a sort of sub-species and at that point I'd only been in my thirties. To live two, three, four hundred years? That would be impossible. It would surely drive anyone mad. Nobody could live that long.

Pfumpf ignored my protestations. He just cut into me again and again.

Finally, as his work became more and more frantic and the pain he caused me became too much to endure any longer, I told him I was finished. I knew by then he had no more interest in finding the Medic for me than he had in creating a serum for making American soldiers indestructible.

What Herbert Pfumpf really craved was the power inside of me. He craved immortality. Not for the good of humanity; only for himself. He really thought he wanted to live forever, and he was simply using the money which his links with the government gave him to try and fulfil that wish. He was a madman, was Pfumpf. As mad as Hitler and Stalin. As mad as Valin.

On that October day in 1945 he calmly told me he needed samples from my brain. He was all set up for it. There was an electric saw lying beside the usual instruments on the gurney, and he waited patiently for me to lie down.

'You'll recover,' he said, matter-of-factly. 'Half your brain was shot away only a year ago. There's no danger to yourself.' He picked the small electric saw up and waited expectantly for me to lie down on the gurney.

I eyed the saw apprehensively. 'It's over, Pfumpf,' I told him. 'It isn't going to work. Whatever is in me can't be transferred.'

I was wrong about that, but it couldn't be transferred in the way he thought.

'You will do as I say,' he said. 'Lie down so we can get this over with quickly.'

'No. It's over. I won't do it any longer.'

At first he cajoled, then he shouted, and finally, as I knew he would, he threatened.

'I will have that nurse you like so much brought into this room and I will do things to her you can barely imagine!' he shouted, holding his scalpel like a butcher's knife. In his eyes I saw the same dark madness I'd seen in those of Mickey Donovan when he'd stabbed me in Molly's apartment. This man was crazy.

I think at one time, not so long before, I would have simply grabbed his scrawny throat and throttled the life out of the miserable bastard. But it was the thought of Madeleine that stopped me doing it. I knew she would have been horrified in me for letting the anger out, as I had done so many times in the past. She would hate it if I allowed myself to become anything like that excuse of a man standing in front of me.

So, instead of doing what I wanted to do, I consoled myself with belting him on the jaw as hard as I could. He went down like a felled tree. I made to leave but turned back. I couldn't help myself, and I gave his unconscious body a kick or two as he was lying there.

I made my way quickly to my room.

Since I had been so willing to be cut about, there had been no need for me to have an escort anymore. But guards still lined the corridors and I didn't know the way out; I needed help for that.

Madeleine turned up a few minutes later and, as soon as she was in the room, I hushed her and whispered in her ear, 'We're getting out of here. What's the quickest way?'

She gave me a look that said, *'Well it's about time'* and then thought rapidly.

'I go out through the main door, but there's always two guards there. Plus we'd have to get through the gate, which has another two men.'

I swore to myself. Pfumpf would be coming round any moment and the alarm would be raised. I suddenly wished I'd ignored what Madeleine would have thought and cut the bastard's throat.

'But I've been looking for escape routes for a while,' continued Madeleine. 'There's one window at the side of this building. It's on the first floor, but I've checked and it's big enough for someone to squeeze though and drop down. It's the one window I know of that's outside the complex. I'll show you where it is.'

That was the first time I kissed her, and it was only a triumphant peck on the cheek, but she smiled at me, happily.

'This way.'

We went out into the corridor and walked quickly back the way I'd come, the guards frowning but not saying anything. I suddenly had my first inclination that they perhaps did not work for Pfumpf. I'd always assumed his words about secretive government departments meant that he had the whole complex to himself, but the attitude of the men in the corridors told me they were just army personnel. They were only there to guard the building and the German prisoners. To them, Pfumpf was just another doctor engaged in work for the army.

As we hurried along the corridor, I cursed myself for my stupidity. I had been conned by a trickster who was only working for himself. I was an idiot.

At least I hoped I was.

Near the metal door to the lab was a staircase and we went up quickly. At the top was a wooden door which Madeleine opened to reveal a broom cupboard.

'It's in there. I'll go out and get the car. I'll pick you up.'

With that she was gone. I slipped into the cupboard and stared at the window in dismay.

It was tiny! I'm sure she could have slipped through it, as slim as she was, but I was going to struggle. I opened the small top sash, trying to gauge if I could get myself through it.

The sudden ringing of alarm bells made up my mind for me.

I clambered up, shoving my head and torso through the

small rectangle. The latch of the sash ground painfully against my stomach and crotch but I ignored it. The pain of it was little compared to what Pfumpf had put me through.

Screeching tyres and headlights below showed me that Madeleine had arrived. But I was stuck, half in half out of the window and, to top it all, there was a drop of about fifteen feet to the concrete below. I heaved and pushed, feeling the latch tear into my skin. I redoubled my efforts when I heard footsteps running up the stairs outside the broom cupboard.

With a final heave, I tore myself free and I popped from the window like a cork from a bottle. My hands scrabbled at the outside glass for a second but found no purchase. I tipped upside down and my hospital trousers, still attached to that bloody latch, were dragged to my ankles, showing my arse to anyone who happened to be looking. I hung there for a moment, half-naked and sweating. Then my trousers tore and I was falling.

I hit the ground with a clatter, my left knee taking the brunt of it. I heard it crack, and a white-hot lance of pain shot through my leg. I hissed at its intensity.

Before I knew what was happening, Madeleine was there, heaving me to my feet and dumping me into the back seat of her old Citroen. The door banged, the engine was gunned, and then we were off down the street.

'We need to hide,' I shouted at her, but she already had it planned. As I said, Madeleine was an incredibly clever woman. She had been working on our escape from the day I went in there.

*

In the end, no one came looking for us. I got the feeling I could have just walked out of that building without any fuss. I don't think I was ever a prisoner. I cursed Pfumpf constantly, not just for what he had done to me, but for taking me in as much as I had let him.

Madeleine had driven to an abandoned farm she had prepared

over the weeks of my incarceration, fifteen miles or so outside the town. It was empty and had a barn in which to hide the car under tarpaulin and hay, and a cellar which she had already stocked with enough supplies to last a couple of weeks. It was all a bit of a waste really.

We stayed there until my fractured knee healed itself fully, which only took a couple of days. I had half-expected the following days and nights to be full of armed soldiers on the hunt, but we saw nobody. It was during those days at the barn that I fully realised the truth.

Pfumpf *had* been working alone, and the MP's at the hospital were not under his command at all. He must have conned the money and equipment out of Washington for his mad experiments. I had no idea how much money he had cost them, but I hoped they would lock the bastard up forever when they found out.

But still, he had known about me. He had known about me and he'd known about Valin, which showed my movements had not gone unnoticed. And if he knew, then so could others. We had to be careful. I didn't really know why I wanted to keep myself secret from the outside world; something inside me just told me I should.

Once my leg was fully functional again we moved on, hiding by day, travelling by night, eventually arriving in Le Mans in mid-October. We had seen nothing to make us think anyone was remotely interested in us, and I began to relax.

Over that journey I started to grow a beard again as a disguise and Madeleine somehow managed, in a France that had just been liberated from five years of Nazi occupation, to get something to dye her hair dark. She also cut it short.

We had no money and so, with some trepidation, I got in touch with my bank and told them who I was, sending verification through various postal boxes. Because I'd already set up the account in the name of Taylor, the money arrived on Halloween. Still we waited, living like tramps until we were sure the transfer hadn't been noticed.

We took out all the money and moved swiftly south, eventually stopping just south of Bordeaux. I felt we were far enough away from Cherbourg to now be invisible. We scouted around the area and found a small house on the edge of an insignificant village.

No one seemed to be on our tail. Our first night there we sat outside the house on broken stools in front of a brazier, sipping cheap wine. The place was falling down, but Madeleine, ever the optimist even with all she'd been through, said we could together build a place where we would be happy for the rest of our lives.

I smiled at her, loving every part of her, but knowing by then that we would be together only for the rest of *her* life, not mine.

We made love for the very first time that night, by the light of candles on a sagging couch in a broken-down cottage. And it was better, sweeter, and more satisfying than I had ever experienced before. I realised what the difference was, of course, and it was simple: we loved each other.

We made the cottage our own. We spent most of my money on fixing it up into a house which we both adored.

I told Madeleine everything: when I was born, my encounter with the Medic, my life since. She had seen me heal from a lethal head wound in only a few months and she had watched in awe as my broken knee had knitted itself back together in just a couple of days in the barn. She could have left me then, and I wouldn't have blamed her for a moment. I even offered her as much money as I could spare if she wanted to go and start a new life somewhere else, with someone else. Someone not like me.

But, of course, she didn't. She wanted to be with me. She loved me as much I loved her. She had healed me, and I like to think I helped heal her too from her terrible, tragic past.

She got a job at the hospital in Bordeaux and I stayed at home out of the way as much as possible.

The years rolled by. The 1940s turned into the 1950s and we enjoyed every minute of them together. I began to believe that my curse had been, if not lifted, then at least halted for a while. Madeleine had found the humanity in me and had released it once more, and if sometimes I listened to the radio and cursed humanity for their stupid, brief, useless activities, Madeleine's presence would always make me smile.

She kept me human and I began to think I was finished with people like Professor Herbert Pfumpf. I began to look forward to our future.

But fate, that hateful bitch in which I have never believed, had other plans.

XVII

Over the next thirteen years I became more and more comfortable with our situation and on a sudden whim, in 1958, I decided to shave off my beard.

Madeleine, whose hair had been back to its normal colour for years, stared at me. I knew what she was thinking. She was forty-seven and I was sixty-two, but I looked more than twenty years younger than her. I was still cursed.

Our lives had settled into domesticity. She earned enough money to get us through each month, and the little that remained from my own money helped. We even managed to save and, in the summer of that year, I told her we should have a holiday.

She didn't want to at first. She still had nightmares. Terrors that would throw her from her sleep, screaming. Some of them were of black-uniformed, jack-booted monsters, but some were of a tall man with black-rimmed glasses laughing as he sliced open my writhing, bloodied body. She didn't want us to be found again.

But I persuaded her we should have a break from the norm. Pfumpf was surely no longer a problem. We hadn't heard a thing about him in thirteen years. Whatever shadowy department he'd said he worked for would surely be bothered more about events in Russia rather than the ravings of a Professor who claimed he had once met an immortal.

The ending of the Korean War five years previously had not helped relationships between East and West, and there were still repercussions between the USA and the USSR over the recent uprisings in Hungary. It seemed the Soviet utopia was not one the people inside the Iron Curtain either believed in or wanted and the American government, using the suppression of the uprising to its political advantage, must have had bigger fish to fry than us.

I suggested Britain as a destination for a break. For some strange reason I wanted to show Madeleine where I was born; I wanted to show her Northumberland. That place breeds a pride in anyone who is lucky enough to be born there, and I wanted her to experience its wild beauty.

She eventually relented and, strangely, I think the reason she did so was because it had become obvious we could not have children and she didn't have the excuse to not travel. God knows we tried often enough, but it never happened. I was to find out why much later in my life, but at the time I believe she thought those SS bastards had done something to her which had made it impossible for her to conceive. Maybe they had, but I don't think so now.

Anyway, I filled her head with images of rolling hills and mountain streams and, finally, she relented.

I wish we hadn't gone. I wish to God she had talked me out of it and we had just continued with our life. But these things happen. We grasped that line of non-existent fate and we pulled at it.

We flew to Britain, my first ever time on an aeroplane, and landed at the newly extended London Airport.

We took a taxi to the hotel. As we passed through the streets, some of them still showing the scars of the war, I remembered my last time in the city when I was on leave just before D-Day, blind drunk and totally alone. I smiled at Madeleine and squeezed her hand, loving the fact I was no longer on my own.

It was at the hotel when things went very badly wrong.

We booked in and went up to our room, which had a very nice view of Tower Bridge. Madeleine went to look out the window and I stood behind her, wrapping my arms around her waist. She turned to me and smiled.

I remember her being so happy that night. She had never been out of France and to see the famous landmarks of London was a great thrill for her. We made love as night fell on the city and the view outside was scuppered by one of the infamous, but thankfully now rare, *"pea soupers"* that rolled up the Thames.

We finally decided we should get something to eat and got out of bed, washed and dressed, and then went down to dinner.

It was a nice hotel. The restaurant produced some fabulous food and the waiters moved smoothly and silently amongst the well-dressed clientele. It was almost as if the war had never happened. Outside the hotel, Britain had only recently come out of the last of the war rationing, but inside everything was plush carpets and quiet, civilised conversation.

We had finished eating and I had ordered a couple of brandies when I glanced up and caught sight of an attractive woman staring at me with wide eyes from another table.

She wore a blue evening gown, with pearls at her throat, and her dark hair shone in the candlelight. She looked to be somewhere in her forties, and she was sitting next to an older man in a dinner suit and rather austere demeanour. I recognised her straight away; she really hadn't changed that much.

It was Grace Yeo.

I quickly turned away and stood, dragging Madeleine to her feet.

'We need to go,' I whispered, and she followed me as I hurried out, keeping my face from Grace's view.

Back in the room, I hurriedly explained who she was.

'Are you sure she recognised you?'

'Of course she did. I look exactly the same as when I knew her back in Aylesford. She recognised me, all right.'

'This is the woman you asked to marry?'

I had told Madeleine about Grace as well as everything else in my life before we met. I nodded. 'Yes. She was a ruthless bitch back then and I don't suppose she's changed now. I think we need to leave.'

'Why? What can she do?'

'I don't know, Maddy. But I don't trust her, and I don't like the look of that man she's with. I think it would be better if we moved on now.'

'We can't do that. The trains are all finished for the night.' She put a hand on my arm, trying to get me to see sense. 'We're leaving for the north in the morning. There's nothing we can do about her tonight.'

She smiled at me. 'It will be fine. Even if she recognised you, what difference does it make? Who would believe you were her fiancé twenty years ago? Everyone would think she was mad. She can't do anything to hurt us, can she? Don't worry.'

She was right. I still looked like a man of no more than twenty-three or so. Even dining with Madeleine, who still looked quite young for a woman in her forties, had earned us a few curious glances. There was nowhere to go that night.

She eventually persuaded me she was right and I nodded reluctantly. We got ready for bed, deciding to have an early night so we could leave first thing in the morning.

With any other person from my past than Grace Yeo, things probably would have been fine. But what neither Madeleine nor I knew at the time was that the man with her was her husband, the prominent Conservative backbencher Sir Charles Wheland.

We were also unaware that Wheland was an attaché with the American Consulate in London, working on joint scientific and medical developments between the two countries. Or, indeed, that one of his associates at the consulate was a tall, thin Professor of neurosurgery with a bald head and black-rimmed glasses and an insane need to find the man he thought was immortal.

Once again luck had turned against me. It was only a matter of time before Pfumpf would catch up with us.

I wish we'd heeded my advice and returned to France, but Madeleine persuaded me that it didn't matter if Grace recognised me. She couldn't do anything about it that would harm us.

So the next day, instead of going to the airport like we should have done, we got on a train to Newcastle. I tried to relax on the journey but, every time I closed my eyes, I saw Grace's shocked face staring at me.

And turning to whisper something in her husband's ear.

*

I took Madeleine to Rothbury, showing her where I was born and brought up. It hadn't really changed all that much. My sister's and my parents' small cottages were gone, replaced by a new estate of nice-looking houses. But the River Coquet, by which I'd sat on that day in the rain in 1918, still flowed by, and the bench was still there. We sat on it for a while as I talked about my early years when myself and other boys from the village would fish or lark about in the water during the summer. We dined in a little café where I stared at the old photographs on the walls, showing childhood friends who were now in their sixties. Later we visited the graves of Mu and her family, decorating their headstones with flowers for the first time in forty years.

We hired a car from a local garage and toured along the military road beside Hadrian's Wall, taking picnics to eat along the way. We went up to Bamburgh and wandered along the beach below the imposing castle, perched on its eyrie of rock. Madeleine walked barefoot, smiling happily at the feel of the sand beneath her toes. I smiled back at her and pretended to enjoy it as my mind dredged up dark memories of Dunkirk and Normandy.

By the end of the week I had started to relax. The visits to the old haunts had done what I hoped they would. They had brought back a bittersweet happiness but, with Madeleine there with me, I began to unwind. We even visited Eyemouth, the small Scottish fishing village I had told Mickey was my home town. We ate fish and chips there and watched the seals glide up and down in the oily water, looking for any loose fish the trawlers may have missed.

We returned to Northumberland and walked the quiet streets of Wooler, climbed the Cheviot Hills and took tea in Corbridge.

Madeleine told me she had never seen me so contented and I smiled at her and kissed her. But I noticed the odd strand of grey in her golden hair and how the lines around her eyes were getting deeper, and an inner despair tore at my heart as I thought of what my future may be like without her.

Madeleine was an anchor for me. She was what kept me from despairing at the ephemeral workings of man, that most arrogant of animals, and I sometimes believed that, without her, I would become something infinitely dark. Something perhaps very dangerous.

However, I tried to put these thoughts away. For a man such as myself to think about the future was stupid in the extreme. I had to enjoy every second, by the second. Nothing else mattered. We continued to tour around the vicinity and I delighted in the fact that she seemed to love the countryside of my youth as much as I did.

But, in the time between London and Northumberland, Grace must have said something to Wheland which sparked an interest.

Maybe, when he returned to work, he had made some innocent comment to Pfumpf about his wife seeing an old suitor who hadn't seemed to have changed in twenty years, and Pfumpf, who surely knew about my time with Grace as he'd known everything else about me, must have put a plan into action straight away.

He was nothing if not efficient.

*

He came in the night, accompanied by two hard-faced individuals, probably attached to the American Embassy in some nefarious business. God knows what tales he had spun for them; maybe they were little more than mercenaries whom he had promised money to. I'm sure the CIA, founded ten years or so before, had people with all sorts of backgrounds on their payroll. I don't suppose it would have been too hard for Pfumpf, a skilled conman if ever there was one, to think up a story and persuade them to come along. He was ever resourceful.

We had rented a cottage for the week, near Hexham. It was close enough to the town for meals, but far enough away for the privacy we both liked and required. The cottage was at least a mile away from any other dwelling.

We were due to leave the next morning so had already packed, and our bags lay beside the bed. The night was very dark, with shadows stretching everywhere.

It was Madeleine who woke me, shaking my arm.

'Bill. There's someone downstairs!' she hissed in my ear. It's strange, she always called me Bill, even though she knew my true name. I think she preferred it.

I frowned, listening, and heard the muted sound of a door closing softly downstairs.

'Get dressed,' I whispered, pulling on my own clothes quickly. I went to the bedroom door and listened, hearing the creak of a stair board.

I searched the dark room frantically, looking for a weapon of some sort, but I couldn't see a thing. I fumbled my way across to the gas lamp that stood on the bedside drawers, turning it up slightly to see better, and my eyes alighted on the poker from the fireplace. I picked it up, indicating for Madeleine to get behind me. She was just in time.

I briefly felt her racing heart fluttering against my back as the doorknob turned slowly. In the light from the quietly hissing lamp, I waited for the door to open wide enough and then brought the poker down on the wrist that appeared as hard as I could.

There was a crack, a yelp, then I grabbed the arm and dragged the man it belonged to into the bedroom. He was a burly-looking figure and, although I'd broken his wrist, his free hand was already scrabbling in his jacket for something. I didn't hesitate. The poker cracked down again, this time into the man's skull. He went down between the bed and the wall without another sound, and I bent down to remove the pistol he had been reaching for. But I was too late.

Another man appeared in the small bedroom and he grabbed Madeleine immediately, yanking her in front of him as a shield. He twisted her arm up her back and I heard her gasp in pain. He pointed the gun he held to her head and smiled, wickedly. I went still.

'Down,' was all he said. I threw the poker and the pistol to the floor.

'Turn up the light,' he ordered, which I did.

He was another big man, with fleshy lips and a face that looked like it had seen its fair share of fights. He reminded me a little of Mickey Donovan. They were clearly of the same ilk. He called down the stairs to someone.

We waited, his pig-like eyes never leaving mine.

Pfumpf stepped into the room.

He hadn't aged well.

Although only somewhere in his late fifties, his face was slack, and in the glow of the gas lamp it looked yellow. He'd lost a hell of a lot of weight too, and his remaining hair had turned white. His suit hung from the frame of a skeleton. He grinned his awful, elastic grin at me as he recognised my shock at his appearance.

'I know, I look terrible. The years are taking their toll, Taylor, as well as other things.'

I just stared at him.

'But you,' he continued, shaking his head. 'You look exactly the same. You haven't aged a day. It's incredible.'

'What do you want, Pfumpf?'

He stepped further into the room, his man dragging Madeleine out of the way. Pfumpf spread his arms.

'What I've always wanted. For you and I to work together. For the good of democracy.'

I shook my head in disbelief.

'Pfumpf, whatever the reason for the way I am, it isn't something that can be transferred. You know that. Your God-awful experiments proved it. You don't care about democracy. You don't care about the Soviet Union. You just want to live forever; that's what it was always about with you.'

Pfumpf's eyes narrowed. I heard the man I'd belted starting to wake up behind me, and then Pfumpf glanced at his watch.

'I don't really care what you think, Taylor, or Deakin, or whatever the hell your name is. I want your secret. I *need* it. Before it's too late.'

I suddenly understood.

Pfumpf's haggard appearance made more sense now. He had something, some disease. When Wheland had told him of my presence he must have thought he'd struck pay dirt. I was his last chance to live. Indeed, to live forever.

'So, what are we going to do?' I asked him, and he flexed his mouth again.

'You will come with me. Miss Besson here will go with these two gentlemen to a secure location. As long as you help me in my work, she will be safe. If not…' Once more he spread his arms in a form of explanation.

My mind was whirling.

I didn't trust Pfumpf for one second. He could not kill me, but he could kill Madeleine, and I had no doubt he would do just that to keep his little secret safe. I had to get her away from the man holding her, before they took her away from me forever. That thought caused another shot of ice to course through my adrenalin-soaked body. I could not lose Madeleine. I could not envisage any sort of life without her. I took a little step forward.

'You promise you won't hurt her?'

If Pfumpf was surprised by my demeanour, he didn't show it.

'On my honour,' he said, which of course meant nothing as he didn't have any.

I managed another imperceptible step towards them as the man behind me slowly climbed to his feet.

I was only a couple of feet away from them now. I sighed and dropped my shoulders, seemingly defeated.

'All right,' I whispered. Pfumpf grinned. The man with the gun relaxed and lowered his weapon slightly and Madeleine, God how I loved that woman, did exactly what I had shown her to do if we ever found ourselves in a situation like that.

She lifted her booted foot and scraped it rapidly and forcefully down the gunman's shin, stamping on his foot. He naturally yanked the leg back in pain, becoming instantly unbalanced, and she spun, brought up her other leg, and kneed him in the groin with all her might.

He buckled, but still managed to bring the gun up to fire. But I was already on him.

I grabbed his gun in one hand, his lapel in the other, and head-butted him on the bridge of the nose as hard as I could. He went staggering backwards but I kept hold of his collar and hauled him back, punching him in the throat. He made a strangled, keening sort of sound and brought his hands up to his wounded neck and face, then there was a bang behind me and I felt something slam into my back.

I staggered forwards into Madeleine's assailant but managed to rip the gun out of his limp hand. I turned and the first man fired again, hitting me in the stomach. I fired twice and he went down, knocking over the gas lamp, blood spreading swiftly.

Pfumpf stared in horror as his world was suddenly turned upside down. A second ago he had me where he wanted me, now one of his men was dead and the other was injured and weaponless. He stared at the barrel of the gun in my hand.

I stepped towards him and smacked the pistol into his awful, smug face. He banged into the wall and slowly slid down to the floor, whimpering.

However, things were not going great for me. I'd been shot twice. We all knew I wouldn't die, but there was a good chance I'd pass out soon.

Madeleine ran over to me, ripping my shirt and tying it around me to try and stem the flow of blood, but I pressed the pistol into her hand and told her to cover the man whose nose I'd broken.

I stumbled over to the dead man and took his weapon. I was becoming light-headed, my vision beginning to swim.

And it was then that the gas from the lamp ignited.

God only knows what had happened. The wick must still have been hot enough probably and the leaking fuel had found it. Whatever it was, there was a *'whumpf'* sound and suddenly the bedroom was full of dancing, orange flames.

'We have to get out of here,' I hissed.

'What about these two?' she asked.

'Leave them.'

Madeleine turned her shocked face towards me. 'Bill, no. We can't.'

I was going to ignore her. I was quite happy for those two bastards to burn to death. But of course Madeleine would never have condoned that. On top of this, Pfumpf had woken up and was crawling as fast as he could away from the first gunman's body, which was now engulfed in flames. He pleaded with me to get him out.

I shook my head and relented. But it had to be done quickly; I was fading fast. There seemed to be a darkness around my vision and everything was viewed like it was in a tunnel. A wall of crackling fire grew quickly as the bed itself began to burn. The flames soared higher.

'Fine,' I muttered to Madeleine.

Between us, we hauled Pfumpf to his feet, pushing him to the bedroom door. I looked around.

'Where's the other man?'

He was gone. He had legged it as Madeleine was helping me. No time to think about that now. We had to get out.

I pushed Pfumpf down the stairs, not bothered if he fell and broke his neck.

The pain from the bullet wounds was beginning to fade, and I knew what that meant. I would soon lose consciousness. My body demanded blackness to begin its strange healing process.

We made it to the ground floor and saw the kitchen door was

open. We got outside just in time to see the taillights of a car roar off into the night. The gunman had made his escape.

Madeleine opened the doors of our hire car and I stuffed Pfumpf into the boot, ignoring his muted protestations as I slammed down the lid.

Madeleine and I turned back to the burning cottage. Flames were now emerging from the windows and licking at the eaves of the roof. The place was finished.

I tried to say something to Madeleine, but my vision was becoming even more blurred. I forced myself to stay awake.

'You better drive,' I whispered.

We got in and left the cottage's crackling ruin. Behind me, in the boot of the car, I could hear Pfumpf shouting.

'I have cancer, Taylor,' he shouted. 'I'm dying. Why? Why is it fair that I die and you continue to live? Why can't I have what you have?'

He then broke off into self-absorbed sobbing.

I ignored his whines. I was concentrating only on staying awake. I had no idea what we were going to do with Pfumpf. He had tried to kidnap us, but we could hardly go to the police. Any sort of background check on me would show up some very strange results.

But, as it turned out, I needn't have worried. The gunman who had escaped the fire did our job for us.

Madeleine had stopped at a crossroads, unsure of which way to go. I was panting now, feeling blood slide sickeningly from my body. I was no help; I could barely talk.

Madeleine made a decision and was just turning the wheel when headlights appeared from nowhere and a car slammed into us.

Our small Morris Minor was no match for the gunman's heavily built Jaguar. It crashed into us doing about fifty miles an hour and we smashed sideways. The wheels hit the kerb and the Morris banged over onto its side and then its roof. Madeleine and I were thrown wildly around the interior in a welter of screeching metal and ended up lying on the roof of the car in a tangle of arms and legs. It suddenly became very quiet. We were upside down.

The only sound was the purring of the Jaguar engine, still running. Then the opening of a door and the crunching of footsteps on gravel, coming towards us.

I could barely keep awake. The car crash hadn't even raised my heart rate, as my body was already going into shock from being shot. I knew the feeling by now. I was dying.

I glanced at Madeleine and, to my horror, saw that her eyes were closed and a trickle of blood ran down a cheek from a cut high up on her head somewhere. I couldn't even begin to think what my life would be like if she was gone, so I ignored the clawing panic that swept through me and turned my attention to the immediate situation.

I glimpsed, as if far away, two feet stop by the window of the Morris. My hand went to my pocket where the revolver lay, and I managed to pull it out just as the man bent down.

I was pleased to see his nose was split and swollen: I'd definitely broken it. He had another gun in his hand. Those sorts of people always have two, and he smiled cruelly at my predicament as he began to point the gun at me. He was still smiling when I shot him in the face.

He didn't make a sound; I think the bullet killed him instantly. He just collapsed to the road, his body illuminated by the one headlight that was still working on the Jag.

Everything was going wrong. I couldn't grip the pistol in my hand, and it clattered to the roof of the car. I tried to get to Madeleine; I needed to know she was still alive. I needed to know she would be alright.

But the black tunnel in my vision finally caved in and I was falling, falling down a deep black well. Madeleine's face seemed to waver and fade. She disappeared.

*

The next thing I knew was waking up in the back seat of a strange car. It was daytime. I tried to move but my stomach and back howled in protest. I felt my body and found that bandages seemingly made out of silk were wrapped around me.

A sudden panic swept through me as I remembered the crash. Pfumpf. Madeleine!

Ignoring the pain, I struggled up and looked out of the window. And sighed, thankfully.

Madeleine was there, crouching by a small stream, washing something in it. She stood and came back to the car, her face breaking into that wonderful smile as she saw me watching. She ran across and opened the door of the car, which I recognised now as the gunman's Jaguar.

She kissed me and kissed me, and I held her tight. She began weeping and I just held her. My Madeleine. My life. My love.

Eventually, I asked her what had happened.

'I woke up and you were unconscious,' she said. 'That other man was there. He was dead. Shot.' She looked at me, but there was no accusation in her voice. She must have known it had been necessary.

'Pfumpf?'

She shook her head. 'He's dead. Must have been the crash.'

'What did you do with him?'

She swallowed and tears of shame glittered in her eyes. 'I dragged him into the bushes, along with the other one... I didn't know what else to do. I...'

I took her in my arms. 'It's okay, sweetheart,' I murmured. Even though I knew it wasn't. *She* wasn't.

I had wanted to ask Pfumpf how he had known about Valin, how he had found out about my past. But now I couldn't.

Nearly twenty years later I did find out, but right then I had to assume he'd used his connections to find me. Things like that happen in life.

'How did we get here?' I asked her, trying to forget about that crazy Professor.

'Our hire car was wrecked, so I put you into this one and drove north. We're in Scotland. I didn't know where else to go.'

I wondered what would happen about the house and the crash and the dead bodies, then I forgot about it. Whatever would happen would happen. Our real names were not in any registers either in France or Britain so we should be safe enough.

Madeleine made me comfortable with more of her cleaned silk-stocking bandages, then we began to drive south.

We both just wanted to go home.

XVIII

That was the last I ever heard about Herbert Pfumpf, apart from a rather poignant episode in 1977 which explained a lot.

I assumed that, whoever the gunmen had worked for, they were adept enough to cover their, and thankfully our, traces: for there was never any news about burned-out cottages or bullet-riddled bodies being found in the Northumberland countryside. But even though he was gone, Pfumpf still haunted my dreams at times. He still occasionally does now.

I did hear the news that Grace and her husband parted ways, though. They went through a messy public divorce, full of incriminations and acrimony. Grace Wheland, nee Yeo, then thankfully disappeared from my life. There were the rumours she ended up with nothing, but a woman like Grace would always get on. I'm sure there were plenty of other fools willing to believe her golden lies.

Madeleine and I eventually returned to our cottage near Bordeaux. On that first night of my recovery, she drove us to a hotel in York where I spent half a week getting better. The bullets pushed themselves from my body within a couple of days and my skin knitted itself back together. Then we went home.

The following years were the best I have ever lived. And they were the best because of Madeleine. As she grew older, she only got more beautiful to me. She went back to work at the hospital, eventually becoming a Matron there. Even before we had left for Britain I had already taken on another identity, as William Taylor was getting old now. My French was so good I could easily pass as a native, so I changed my name to Guy Besson. Although Madeleine and I never formally married, I took her name and bought her a ring. I had to keep out of the way of her friends at the hospital of course, and she lived a lonely life because of me.

As time went by, she could no longer introduce me as her rather young husband and so, if anyone asked, she said I was her son. She was the love of my life and she gave up everything for me. No children, no friends, no family. It was a lonely existence in that French cottage, and yet we very rarely argued, very rarely fell out. I never tired of her company and I like to think she never tired of mine.

I had been teaching myself carpentry for some years now, something I used to enjoy as a child, and eventually I became good enough to be able to sell some of my pieces in the shops around the area. Madeleine got older, her hair got greyer, and I stayed exactly the same.

I hated my curse, but in those years it was nullified by Madeleine's love. If it had been the other way around, I don't know if I could have stood it as she did. To watch yourself growing inevitably older, whilst your partner stays exactly the same? That is a very real horror, and I saw the fear in her eyes at times, although she never said anything about it. We lived a good life together, Madeleine and I, as short as it was.

Because of course, one day it would have to end. And that day came around far too soon.

*

October 1962. We were in the kitchen. I was cooking dinner— Madeleine had taught me to become a passable enough chef—and we were listening to the radio.

Over in Cuba, there was a tense stand-off between America and the USSR. Kennedy had set up his blockade and it looked like the Soviet ships were going to ignore it. If that happened, God only knew what might become of the world.

Trying not to think too much about the situation abroad, I was bent over the stove, and I asked Madeleine to pass me something. I forget what it was now.

'Maddy?' I asked, still with my back to her.

I turned to find her staring at me, totally immobile. The pupil of one of her eyes was hugely dilated. It looked black.

I grabbed her arms in alarm.

'Maddy? What's wrong? Maddy?'

Slowly, slowly, her eyes seemed to re-focus and she looked at me in alarm. She frowned, touching a hand to her head.

'Do you mind if I lie down for a minute?' she asked. 'I've got a terrible headache.'

I led her to the bedroom where she slept for the next fourteen hours. I stood over her the whole time, worried out of my mind.

When she woke, she seemed fine. Nothing else happened for a while. We both tried to forget about the strange occurrence and went back to our lives as normal. But over the next year or two, there were the odd things that only made me worry about her more.

Her memory wasn't as sharp as it had been. In November 1963, we were listening to the news about the assassination of Kennedy and, out of the blue, Madeleine asked who he was.

I frowned.

'The President of the USA?' I said, and she thought for a second or two before nodding. 'Oh yes,' she said, distractedly.

It went on. She grew clumsy; I would find jars of food smashed on the kitchen floor where she had just left them. I would clean the mess up and say nothing. She forgot to bathe until I reminded her. Over those few, short years her condition worsened.

Eventually, despite her protestations that she was fine, I drove her to the hospital. They did their tests and only a couple of weeks later we were back in the doctor's office. The expression on his face revealed to me a shadow of despair so deep I could barely comprehend it.

'Your mother has a tumour, Monsieur Besson,' he said. 'Deep inside her brain.' He turned to Madeleine. 'I'm sorry. It's completely inoperable.'

The silence that followed was awful. I had flashes of my past: people I had known, things I had seen. God only knows what went through Madeleine's disintegrating mind, but she turned and took my hand and squeezed it tightly. *She* smiled at *me* and comforted me as I broke down completely. Madeleine had always been the strongest of us.

We went home and lay face-to-face together on the settee, not talking. I stroked her greying hair and she held me and we just stared at each other. She was still not yet even sixty, yet she was being taken away from me, piece by beautiful piece.

I still see Madeleine when I close my eyes now. Hers is the first face I remember in the morning, and the last thing I think of at night. People say you often forget loved ones' features when they are gone, but I remember everything about her. The lines on her face, the colour of her eyes, her scent. I remember it all.

By the following year, Madeleine was no longer the woman I had known. She lay in the hospital bed, her hair now snow-white because of her disease, her ravaged face thin and wasted. Her memory had gone completely in the end. She forgot about me, forgot about us. She raved and raged. She became demented and, finally, she become catatonic. It was only then that I took her into the hospital.

And on a dark and rainy November evening, six years to the day that Kennedy had been assassinated, Madeleine left me.

As the nurses went about their business with her cold body, I sat outside the room in a numb world of disbelief. Nothing seemed to make sense. The day-to-day sounds of the hospital—a typewriter clacking, a trolley rattling past—blurred into a soundscape I couldn't understand. I sat there for hours, I think.

Eventually, they came and asked me whether I wanted to see her one last time. I went into the room and gazed down upon the woman I had loved eternally. We had been given only twenty-five years together. Twenty-five years of happiness and dedication. Twenty-five years of perfection. And now she was gone. She was gone.

It was only then that the tears came. I sat next to her, cradling her, weeping silently. She had given me everything and I had consigned her to a life alone. I hated myself. I wished with all my heart that I had never met her so she could have spent her days with someone worthy of her love and devotion in the short time she had been allocated on this planet. I told her I was sorry for what I was, but it made no difference.

She was gone.

Finally, as the night drew in outside, I kissed her sweet face and said goodbye to her. I was alone again.

I walked the corridors of that hospital endlessly. For some reason I didn't want to step outside, because that would mean I had accepted the fact that she was gone. I would have accepted she was dead, and I just couldn't. Maybe if I stayed within the confines of the hospital, I would return to her room to find her smiling at me. Asking me where I'd been. Holding me tight.

I went from ward to ward, wandering aimlessly, my eyes red-rimmed and unfocussed, my mind in a vacuum. I came to a large sitting area and took a seat. There was a TV playing and someone was reporting about the Apollo 12 mission that had recently returned to Earth. I stared at the smiling face of the NASA man who was talking, but I didn't take in anything of what he said.

I was numb. I was no longer capable of emotion. I had cried myself out at Madeleine's side. I just felt empty, used-up. Once again I felt like a husk of a man, with no reason and no purpose. I didn't want to go on without her, but I didn't have a choice. I tried to suppress the old anger for her sake, but I could feel it once more bubbling like molten lava inside me. It was already beginning to consume me again, now that she was no longer there to stop it.

I turned away from the TV and looked at a far wall. It was covered in photographs and I went and stared at them, simply for something to do.

It was the very first one I saw. It showed a middle-aged man with thinning, greying hair, wearing a white doctor's coat. He smiled out of the photo. He had a dark face, a bent nose where it had been broken at some time in the past and a scar on his right cheek. His eyes were as black as night.

And so it was that on the night the only true love of my long life died, I found the Medic.

*

Or so I thought.

After Madeleine's funeral, after I had drunk myself into a stupor, after I had lain on the floor of the cottage and wept helplessly, clinging to a picture of her, once her scent began to disappear from my life, I returned again to the hospital and stared again at the photo of the Medic.

The name underneath said, *'Doctor Franz Liebnicht: Consultant Surgeon, 1931-1936'.*

It was now late 1969. The Medic had been at this hospital thirty-three years ago. Would there be any records of his movements? I began to investigate.

I honestly think I became interested again because Madeleine was gone. I believe that if she had still been alive and I had seen his picture, I would have ignored it. It was because I was so inconsolable that I went after him again. I had nothing else to do.

I became a regular patron of the hospital's library. I spoke to older members of staff who may have been around at the time, and I found out everything there was to know about Dr Franz Liebnicht.

He was apparently born in Austria in 1888 and had fought in the last two years of World War One. After the war, he returned to medical training, getting his doctorate in 1920. He had worked in Austria and had then moved to France in 1930, taking up his position at the hospital. In 1936, however, he had returned to Austria.

One of the old Matrons, who had been a young trainee nurse at the time, told me she remembered he had said he had family problems. Someone had died and he was returning to help out. She was a bit vague on details. I couldn't find out anything more about the reasons, but I did find out that Franz Liebnicht was a Jew. There were no records of him after 1936. The Matron said she believed he must have perished in one of the Nazis' death camps. She believed he must have died during the war. But why would a Jew have returned to the anti-Semitic Austria of 1936?

I searched frantically for the best part of half a year. I sold the cottage—the memories were too hurtful, and it was nothing without Madeleine anyway—and I went to Austria, where I combed the records there. My German was almost as good as my French after my time in Berlin and, although a little rusty, it soon came back to me enough to get me through.

But I found nothing. Franz Liebnicht seemed to have disappeared off the face of the Earth in August 1936. I was once again left with nothing.

I eventually gave up on him again. I told myself it didn't matter; I told myself he was dead. The photograph at the hospital showed a man twenty years older than the face I remembered from my death bed in St Theresa's.

Whatever—or whoever—he was, he wasn't like me because he was getting older. Pfumpf's words came back to me: 'You're not the only one'. But he was wrong. I *was* the only one. If not, how could the photograph show a man who was obviously ageing?

I was alone again. I had no one: no family, no friends, no acquaintances, and my future roared ahead of me like a road that would never end.

I remember standing at a crossroads, just outside Vienna, in March 1970. I had been alive for almost seventy-four years and there was a terrible, horrible chance that I would go on living forever.

I stood at that crossroads and looked each way. Whichever road I took, I didn't think it would make one iota of difference. I closed my eyes and turned around three times. When I opened them, one of the roads stretched before me.

I tightened the straps of my backpack around me and started walking.

Part Two

XIX

Over the intervening years I learned to limit my experiences. There was always something new to learn, somewhere new to see, but I knew that if I let myself I would have eventually done it all and seen it all. I rationed myself.

The road in Austria eventually led to Switzerland. I could only really move around Western Europe. In 1961, Khrushchev had built his wall through Berlin and the Iron Curtain cut me off from a lot of places I wanted to see. That would have to come later.

So I stayed in Zurich for a while, setting myself up as—of all things—a toy maker. Using the carpentry skills I had taught myself, I made little wooden cars and tractors and puppets and sold them at markets around the area. I took my time with each trinket I made, making sure every angle, every joint, every dowel was perfect before assembling the finished product. I rented a small apartment on the outskirts of Zurich and, when I wasn't making toys, I wandered around the city, becoming familiar with all the streets and alleyways.

I kept away from making any connections with the people of Zurich. I was still grieving for Madeleine and would often wake in the night having dreamed of her. The echo of my greeting to her mocked me, and on those nights I would wipe my eyes, rise, and sit by the window, smoking endless cigarettes, watching blindly as the sun rose over the mountains in the distance.

At first, life without her was a nonsense. I survived rather than lived and, even though the horrible pain slowly began to recede, it never left me. I missed her. I missed her so much, and I still do. Without her, I saw no point in life. A blackness seemed to cling to my soul and other people sensed it. I couldn't have got close to anyone even if I had wanted to. I believe I frightened people.

I stayed in Zurich until 1971 and then, feeling unsettled again, I moved on.

I left in the high summer of that year and went south, into Italy, walking all the way. I had decided on this mode of transport as it was the cheapest and would take the longest. I eked out every minute of every day, trying to find something to interest my broken soul. I visited Bologna, Florence, and Rome. I went to the museums and stared at the Renaissance glories and the paintings and statues and they all meant nothing to me.

I found that my disinterest in everything grew. Everything bored me. I had moved from a world of steam to a world of nuclear weapons. When I was a boy a trip to the nearest market was an exciting prospect. Now man had walked on the moon, TVs were everywhere, cars clogged the streets, new technologies were being created every day, and it all passed me by with a monstrous indifference.

Everything seemed like a complete waste of time. Nothing interested me; nothing kept me in one place more than a few months. But again, I made sure I stayed at least a moderate amount of time in each town or city to fully understand it, to find its hidden secrets. I believe I walked every alleyway and every street, from Venice to Naples and back again.

I wondered again and again how I could be the way I was. Why was I like this? Why did I continue, exactly the same, when my love had withered and died? What was the point?

I decided that, if nothing else, I should use my unique existence to try and better myself. I would force myself to learn new things, even if everything left me cold. That was what Madeleine would have wanted me to do, I was sure. She would want me to use the immensity of time that belonged to me to absorb, to know, to understand. I started doing it for her, but I found that it took the memories of her off my mind for short periods of time, so I began to pursue new talents with a rising vigour. Anything to stop the hurt from the loss of her from tearing me apart.

I picked up conversational Italian. From some buskers in Milan I learned how to play the guitar, and when I left the city I walked with it on my back. Another busker showed me how to play a reed flute and I practised every day.

I divided my time into segments of two hours. Two hours of day carving wooden toys, two practising the guitar, two working on the flute, two learning a new language. I made myself concentrate only on those two hours before moving on to the next thing. I tried not to think about tomorrow, or the next week or month or year, or decade. Or the next century.

I let my beard grow again, and my hair got long as was the fashion of the day. I met a few women along my wandering, endless route and I stayed with them for a while before moving on once more. They were brief, carnal pleasures only. Some of those women I still remember, most of them I don't. I got close to none of them. I knew I couldn't, even if I had wanted to. None of them could ever live up to what Madeleine had meant to me. Whatever the purpose or the point of my existence was, I knew by then that relationships were not allowed.

I lived with, but apart from, the ordinary humans who surrounded me. In the blink of an eye they ripened, faded, and died: like rotten fruit. I grew older and stayed the same. Once more, the idea they were below me began to slink through my mind. I viewed them impassively and kept away from them as much as I could, because I could feel myself becoming more and more different. I grew aloof to their pain and hardship, their luck and their greed. I began to dislike them. My walking kept me fit and healthy; that, and the poisonous curse that ran through my blood.

I got to know Italy well, and it was in Italy in 1975 where I joined the circus. And, in a strange and roundabout way, the circus ultimately led me to the truth about Herbert Pfumpf. I've said it many times and I mean it: there is no fate.

But sometimes coincidence makes it seem like there is a destiny.

*

I came upon the circus one autumn afternoon outside Sienna, and I acted on a spur-of-the-minute intuition. What did I have to lose?

I'd been in Sienna for only a few weeks and had spent my afternoons busking with my guitar and flute and my evenings sitting outside cafes, whittling away at wooden figurines and dispassionately watching the people go by.

One afternoon, I saw some men pull up in a van which had a huge, grinning clown's face on the side. They began putting up signs for the circus and I wandered down to the area outside the town to find the Big Top erected and the cages with the animals already set up around it.

I'd never visited a circus before, so I bought a ticket for the evening show then sat on a low hill, drinking from a bottle of wine and eating bread and cheese as I watched the circus folk get ready for the show.

I saw men going into caravans and emerge dressed as clowns. I heard lions roaring and saw them being fed. A man and a woman dressed like a Red Indian and a saloon girl were doing their make-up outside in the warm evening air. Trapeze artists flounced about, warming up for the show.

At the allotted time I joined the small crowd and took my seat inside the tent. The smell was wonderful: warm and sweet, the tang of fresh sawdust in the ring. It reminded me a little of the stables back in Rothbury when I was a lad, and I smiled at the memories.

I watched the show and it was entertaining enough. The lion tamer was good, although I could see that the lions were not all that fierce; they kept going up to him for a hug and a lick of his face, even though he tried to coax them to roar from time to time. The elephant parade was okay, but only to watch in awe at the size of those wonderful beasts. The trapeze artists were excellent, the clowns were stupid and boring. But I liked the idea of it; I liked the circus.

After the show, I hung around outside. I saw the ringmaster and sauntered over to ask him if there were any jobs going.

'What can you do?' he asked, gruffly, in thickly accented Italian.

I shrugged. 'I can carry things around.'

He looked at me sideways. 'Come back tomorrow. Senior Gravaldi will be here then. He's the owner. We'll see what he says.'

I shook his hand and left, returning the next day. Gravaldi shrugged and said there was always room for one more set of shoulders. He warned me the job would be seasonal and on a bed-and-breakfast basis only. I agreed and he sent me off to see the boss hostler, who would be my immediate superior. He asked if I had any experience with horses and I told him I had been a stable boy when I was a kid, which was true. Of course that had been nearly seventy years ago, but I wasn't going to tell him that.

He checked me out as I worked and saw that I knew what I was doing. Over the years of touring with the circus I became responsible for all of the show horses and even mucked out for the elephants, remarkably intelligent animals which have remained a favourite of mine ever since.

Working in the circus was good for me. My boots lasted as I was no longer walking them into the ground, I had a bunk to kip in, and there was hard physical work to keep me fit. But the best thing about it was that, apart from one notable exception, I was never fully accepted by the circus folk.

It wasn't that they gave me the cold shoulder or anything, but it was very quickly made clear that I was not like them. I was an outsider. They spoke to me—said hello, that sort of thing—but I was never invited to their campfires at night and they never really asked too much about me. Which was perfect for me. I kept my distance, I did my job and before long I became a *"trouper"*, a veteran of the circus circuit.

My years with the circus allowed me plenty of time to think. I didn't want to think of Madeleine because that hurt too much. Instead, I sat at night and strummed my guitar, harking back to my past and how the Medic had changed me

*

October 1917. It was pouring with rain. It had been raining for months now and the trenches and shell holes were full of freezing, filthy water.

A lot of the men had gone down with trench foot, which wasn't surprising as we were all constantly soaked and frozen. There was no shelter, no hiding from the incessant rain. We couldn't even get into in our dug outs as they were all underwater. We huddled in the filthy pools and shivered and sneezed, waiting for the attack we knew was coming.

The German guns had been battering us for days, and reams of men had already been killed. Those of us left alive had been driven almost mad by the continuous barrage.

But the guns had stopped, so we knew an attack was imminent. We crouched, up to our waists in the freezing water, waiting.

A flare went up from the German lines and we heard them shouting and cheering as they scrambled over their trenches.

'Not long now, lads,' came Greene's calm and confident voice. 'Not long now. You know what to do.'

I glanced at his soaked, exhausted figure and he winked at me and smiled. The man was incredible. I turned back to the enemy trenches.

No Man's Land was a boggy mess, so it would take a while for them to get to us. But come they did. We jumped up and began shooting at the oncoming figures.

Men went down in twos and threes. At first it was easy for us because they were slipping and sliding over the deadly, sucking mud, some of them disappearing completely into its cold, dark embrace, but

then their guns opened up again in a creeping barrage that covered their advance.

The shells crashed into our trenches; the gunners' aim was perfect, and deadly.

Beside me, Tom Laidlow, a new recruit and only eighteen years old, was eviscerated as shrapnel tore into him. His body was flung to the four winds and his blood splattered into my face: a sudden warmth in the cold rain.

I ignored his death and kept firing, shouting at the lads around me to do the same. The shells kept coming.

Along our lines, the machine gunners finally got their act together and started firing into the murk, shooting at anything they could see.

Another shell exploded, high above us this time, the shrapnel throwing itself mercilessly into our trench.

There were screams as men were struck by the metal balls inside that shell. I heard the noise as they hit soft, wet bodies. It was a thud, thud, thud sound, muted in the rain.

Men were thrown down all around me, and I felt at least two pieces smack into my left arm and shoulder. My arm immediately went numb, but I continued to fire one-handed.

The Germans advanced inexorably.

We kept firing and we kept dying. The shells were doing some wicked work that day. Men were killed and wounded all around me. Me and another new recruit, Billy Fryer, pulled the corpses of friends from a Lewis gun and began battering away at the grey figures, seeing them fall like stalks of corn.

Billy and I were almost the only men left in that trench when the advance was finally pushed back two hours later. Incredibly, Billy had not been hit. His face, however, was white and his eyes were black holes of terror. Billy was killed a week later by a random sniper shot. We found out then that he had been only sixteen years old.

I had holes all over me, but I believed nothing vital had been hit. I had survived. Again.

When we were relieved and I got patched up, I watched as the torn bodies were carried away, the blood already washed from their carcasses. I followed them through the support trenches, towards the rear where we could hopefully find some rest and some shelter.

It was only later, sitting in the dubious shelter of a dank barn on an abandoned farm, that I discovered I had been hit in the chest as well as the arm.

The hole was small and round, and already forming a scab.

It seemed to be right over my heart.

I lit a cigarette and tried to forget about it. It had obviously not hit anything vital.

Luck. That's all it was. Just luck.

*

My disinterest in other people continued to grow at the circus. I tried to fight it, but it was impossible, and the crowds who turned up every night for the performances only seemed to reinforce my beliefs. They started to resemble cattle to me: stupid and unthinking.

I was so different to them that their lives seemed insignificant. It seemed they were born only to die, mostly after pointless existences. The odd news reports I read of disasters and loss of life left me cold. I watched the Cold War wax and wane across the globe, and new Presidents and Prime Ministers and Premiers grasped at their powers and ultimately fell from grace. And all I felt was disinterest. It didn't matter, for they would all die one day. I didn't care about them. I didn't really care about me; but then again, I didn't need to. Life clung to me like a leech. For them, it sucked them dry and left them dead in a heartbeat.

I really began to despise them for their pointlessness. I would see people grubbing and scrabbling to create wealth for themselves, wondering all the time what the use of it was. Each and every one of them seemed to think they would live forever and I, who had every reason to believe I would do just that, watched them sardonically. I remembered my feelings the day the Great War ended, thinking that I was a watcher now, not a doer. I seemed to have fulfilled that destiny. From my impervious throne, I watched humanity live and die. And it left me cold.

Yet that was the problem. If humans were so pointless, if their fleeting lives meant nothing, then what was the point of me? Logically, it would seem I was different for a reason, yet I had no idea what that reason was. Everything seemed to point to the fact that my special life was just a twist of nature, a mistake. I was an aberration, created for no good reason, and I didn't even have the luxury of knowing it would all end someday. I began to hate myself as much as I hated everyone else.

God knows, I tried not to. I knew Madeleine would have been disappointed in me, but I couldn't help it. It seemed to be inherent in me. I began to think that whatever it was that kept me alive, whatever kept me young, demanded payment. And that payment was a growing belief that humanity was an utter joke. A waste of time.

It was the Yin to the Yang, the up to the down. My body was eternally young, but my soul was slowly being strangled and embittered and darkened by my condition.

I think it was because of this growing arrogance and hatred of humanity that I decided to seduce another man's wife.

*

In my defence, I didn't make the first move.

Her name was Anya and she was a trapeze artist. She was twenty-nine and married to an ugly fellow called Bruno, who was built like a tank and who also swung high above the crowds in the circus shows. They were a double act: *"The Flying Gombos"*.

I had noticed her around the circus. As I've already said, although I had a growing disenchantment with other people, and despite the fact that the circus lot kept themselves to themselves, I still had the physical wants and needs of a man of twenty or so. So yes, I had noticed her.

Primarily because Anya Gombos was the most beautiful

woman I have ever met, even more beautiful than Grace. She was nothing compared to Madeleine of course, but I had loved her not because she was the most physically perfect woman in the world, but because she was perfect for me. I ached for Madeleine every day. But Anya Gombos was in a different league as far as looks go.

Being a trapeze artist, her body was amazing. She was lithe and graceful and slim, with breasts that seemed to strain against the thin material of the leotards she wore for the show, and legs that went on forever. She had long, straight dark hair and her eyes were electric blue. Her face was a perfect heart, with wide lips and teeth of pearly whiteness. She was absolutely stunning.

I often watched her and her husband practising high above the floor of the Big Top, and it always amazed me how they could make something so complicated and dangerous look so easy. They trained hard. Every day they were up there with Bruno shouting his gruff instructions to her, telling her when to let go, when to grab on, and so on. It was all very exciting.

I loved to watch them, but only because I loved to see Anya's amazing body contorting itself into unimaginable shapes. However, I would always tire of it soon enough. The old darkness would come along and swamp any fascination I had with their expertise and I would leave and get on with my tasks.

Neither of them really noticed me down there, but on a couple of occasions Anya had smiled at me as she passed me by when I was outside the caravans or mucking out the horses. I would nod back and then watch her walk away, her backside swaying deliciously in the tightest jeans I have ever seen anyone wear.

I had been with the circus almost two years before Anya and I became more than just acquaintances.

The last performance had ended and I had been finishing up some tasks, ready for the Top to be taken down early next morning. We were moving on again.

It was getting dark and I was walking through the ranks of trailers and caravans, looking forward to nothing more than sitting in front of the radio in my own trailer, maybe with a whiskey to top off the night before getting to bed.

I went past the Gombos' trailer, and from inside I heard Bruno's hoarse voice bellowing. Anya screeched back at him and I heard a crash; she must have chucked something at him. I never found out which East European country they had originally come from, but their voices sounded like wet barbed wire as they screamed and shouted at each other.

I shook my head and moved past the trailer, annoyed by their passionate altercation. There was always an argument going on somewhere around the circus, as the travelling folk were pretty zealous when they got going. I think they liked the arguments only so they could make up again later on. One would see a couple having a proper old ding-dong and then twenty minutes later they would be ensconced in a passionate embrace. It was just the way they were.

I had barely moved past the door when it banged open and Anya stormed out. She turned and bellowed something incomprehensible to Bruno inside and then slammed the door shut with such force that the trailer rocked. She stormed off and, before I could move, she had banged into me; she hadn't seen me in the dark.

She jumped back and stared at me, glowering in the night. I remember she looked stunning. Her high, Slavic cheekbones were pink with fury and she was panting hard. She wore a tight t-shirt and jeans, and her pert breasts heaved up and down in time to her breathing.

She hissed something at me that sounded like a rusty knife scraping on a wall and then stormed off again into the darkness.

I shook my head again. Bloody stupid people.

I had hired my own trailer, sick of having to share with three other men, and it was set a little away from the others, where I liked to be. When I got to the door I spotted a red glow wavering just beyond it.

I squinted into the darkness and made out a slim form, accompanied by the sound of a muted voice as Anya smoked a cigarette and muttered to herself. I ignored her and opened the door of the trailer, climbing in and turning on the gas lamp. When I returned to close the door she was standing there, looking in.

I nodded to her. 'Everything all right?'

She nodded too. 'You have vodka?'

I raised my eyebrows. 'No. But I have whiskey, which is much nicer.'

She thought for a second and then stepped up into the trailer.

'I have whiskey with you.' She paused, staring at me fiercely. 'Unless you do not want to share.'

I shook my head once more, a little dumbfounded by her. 'No. Please, have a whiskey with me.'

She sat down and I opened the bottle, pouring a couple of glasses. I gave her one and sat opposite her. She lit another cigarette then, as an afterthought, offered one to me. We smoked, Anya deep in thought and me wondering what the hell was going on.

'Bruno is bastard,' she finally said.

'Really?' I didn't know what else to say.

She nodded. 'He always tell me what to do, where to go, who to see, what to think. He's bastard.'

I scratched my bearded cheek. I had suddenly had enough of her. I didn't care what her husband was or what she thought of him.

'I suppose you shouldn't have married him then,' I muttered and drained my glass, hoping she'd get the message.

But she didn't. She just cocked her head to one side and studied me.

'You are strange man,' she eventually said. 'You work and sleep and never go anywhere. Why you with circus? Are you thief, or criminal?'

She wasn't frightened of the prospect, just curious.

In spite of myself, I poured another drink and topped her glass up when she held it out. 'No. I'm not a criminal. I just want to be left alone, that's all.'

'Ah!' she said, as if she had solved all the problems of the world.

'A woman. You join circus because of woman, eh?' She smirked at me and I felt the old dark anger begin to flow within me.

'Why I'm here is no business of yours,' I snarled. 'Please finish your drink and leave so I can get some sleep.'

She didn't look shocked by my outburst, she just nodded slowly. 'Okay,' she said, knocking back the whiskey and standing. When she was at the door, she turned back to me, and those pink spots were on her cheeks again. But I didn't think it was anger that caused them this time. She licked her lips quickly and it was one of the most erotic things I have ever seen.

'If you want me to go, I go,' she murmured. Then she shrugged slightly. 'I don't want to go.'

I frowned. 'What the hell do you want from me?'

She just stared at me, those wide blue eyes communicating everything I needed to know silently.

'A one-night stand?' I asked, still angry but with a growing excitement. 'Is that what you're after? To get back at your husband?'

She hesitated, and for the first time, I saw indecision on her face.

'Not with anyone,' she whispered. 'Only you. I have seen you. I like you look.'

The anger suddenly disappeared as I laughed at the turn of phrase. She smiled too.

'I'm pleased you like my looks,' I said. 'Because I'm bloody sick of them. Take off your clothes.'

So she did, and I discovered that, undressed, she was even better than I had previously imagined. I went to her and picked her up, dumping her on the bed. She lay there, naked and waiting as I quickly stripped off my own clothes.

She most definitely got her revenge on Bruno that night. She made love like an alley cat, scratching and clawing at my back as we both cried out in ecstasy at the end.

She left after an hour or so and I lay on the bed, drained, thinking about her and about some of the other women I had known in my travels around Europe. I tried not to think about Madeleine. It still seemed wrong to be sharing any sort of intimacy with anyone but her. She had been dead by then for almost eight years but, at times such as those, it seemed like only yesterday. I climbed out of the bed that now smelled of Anya and poured myself another drink. In spite of myself I stood, naked, staring at Madeleine's photo. I sighed deeply, feeling nothing but an incredible sadness. Eventually, in the deep blackness of early morning, I slept.

Anya would come to me from time to time over the next few months. I knew she was still having sex with Bruno because I'd heard them at it as I walked past their trailer on occasion.

I didn't care. Sex with Anya was just a distraction for both of us. I felt nothing towards her, and I doubt she felt anything for me. It really was just great sex. But you can't hide anything in a circus camp—they're too small and full of gossips—so of course it all got out.

And Bruno came to me looking for his revenge.

*

I was asleep in the trailer when he smashed open the door and heaved himself inside. He filled the doorway, his massive shoulders almost touching the frame.

He pointed at me and shouted something in a strangled, Slavic voice. I sat up, rubbing my eyes and staring at him resignedly. I had known this day would come soon.

It was Anya; she couldn't help herself. I think every time they'd had an argument since our first encounter, she had hinted at some affair, some indiscretion on her part. Probably to make him jealous. By the look on his face, it had worked.

'I don't know what you're saying, Bruno,' I muttered.

He continued to rant and rave, his face contorted and his arms waving about all over.

I sighed. 'I don't understand you,' I said, slowly, as if I were talking to a very stupid person. I climbed out of bed and pulled on my jeans and a t-shirt. 'What do you want?'

'I vant to know!' he shouted. 'I vant to know. About you. About Anya. About you and Anya!' He broke off again into some anguished gobbledegook.

I waited for him to finish. A shadow fell across the broken doorway, and there was Anya. She jumped lithely inside and started tugging at his massive bicep, shouting his name over and over. He turned to her and pushed her away, screaming incoherently. They both started shouting at each other. Loudly.

I coughed politely. They stopped and turned to me.

'Are you two finished?' I asked. 'Because, if you hadn't noticed, my door is broken. I want to get it fixed and get some sleep. Take your drama elsewhere, please.'

Bruno stepped threateningly towards me, Anya hanging ineffectually from his arm. A few of the circus folk had gathered outside the door by this point, alerted by the noise, and they stared in, loving the break to their tedious lives.

'You vant to sleep?' screamed Bruno. 'Sleep? I make you sleep, bastard. I make you sleep forever!'

With this, he delved into his belt and pulled out a vicious-looking knife, brandishing it at me. Anya howled and held a wrist to her forehead, but I saw she was enjoying all this testosterone on her behalf.

I suddenly became furious. The dark shadow within me, never far from the surface, exploded and I felt my eyes widen and my lips twist in rage. Who the hell did these people think they were? This bastard had come into my house, threatening me? This *insignificant flea* was threatening me?

I stepped right up to him, my face inches from his own. I was as tall as he was, but he was much broader.

'You want to stab me, Bruno? You think you have the balls to do it? You're a joke. Your wife couldn't wait to be with me because she knows it. Go on, then: stab me, you useless bastard. See what will happen. Let's see if you have the guts to do it you piece of shit!'

I stood back and opened my arms wide, begging him to stick the knife into me. Then he would see. Then they would all see what I was. How different I was. How superior I was to all of them. I wanted him to do it just to see the looks on their faces when I didn't die.

He looked shocked at my outburst and my furious face. He blinked and took a step back, but I was having none of it.

'Oh no you don't.' I grabbed the hand holding the knife. 'Come on!' I shouted. 'I'll help you. I'll help you do it!'

I tried to force the knife into me, my hand grasping his own.

He was terrified by now. He had come to threaten me, to make me grovel and beg forgiveness, and to show Anya who the real man was. But instead he was suddenly face-to-face with a screaming lunatic who was actually trying to drive the knife into his own stomach.

'Let go!' he shouted, yanking the knife hand out of my hand. The blade slid across my palm and cut it deeply. I just stared at him. At them both.

'You irrelevant insects,' I hissed at them, and there must have been something truly awful in my eyes, because they both backed further towards the door in fear, the crowd making room for them as they stumbled outside. I stood in the doorway, staring down at them all.

I pointed my finger at Bruno.

'Keep away from me, big man,' I said, quieter now, but with no less power. 'You have no idea what I'm capable of. No idea what I am. I know what it's like to kill. I know what it takes. You don't have that in you. And you,' the finger swung to Anya, who was white-faced at what had happened and who shrank away from the finger as if it could shoot her. 'I suggest you stop offering what you've got to any Tom, Dick or Harry who happens to wander along. You married this idiot, so you better start showing him why.'

The crowd was silent, standing in a semi-circle around the ruptured doorway, staring at me. Blood from my sliced palm plopped to the grass.

'The entertainment's over,' I told them. 'Time to go.'

They just stood there, open-mouthed.

'Go!' I roared at them.

They scarpered.

'Bruno,' I yelled, and he stopped and turned back, fearfully.

'You owe me a new door.'

He just stared for a moment and then nodded. He and Anya turned away, holding each other tightly.

I went back inside and wrapped my hand in a cloth, pouring myself a drink. I gulped it down.

The darkness inside me was huge and I had to forcefully stop myself from going to the Gombos' trailer and starting again.

Because if I did, I knew I would kill him.

XX

After that, I thought it would be for the best if I moved on. The incident with Bruno had happened whilst we were in Northern Spain, and I walked away from the circus and made my way to Barcelona where I caught a plane to Britain.

For some reason, I craved once again the land of my birth. I still thought of myself as English, even though most of my life had been spent in other countries. And so, in that year of 1977, when my time with the circus was obviously over, I said my goodbyes to the horses and the elephants. The clowns and the troupers and the animal trainers said nothing as I left. They were pleased I was gone, I suppose, and I didn't blame them. I never saw Bruno or his mad wife again after that night.

I sat on the plane to Heathrow. I knew where I was going; I'd been thinking about it for a while in my circus trailer.

Longwood was not that far away. I caught the train to the station near to where Hector and I had sheltered in a hedgerow all those years ago, booked into a hotel in the village, and then walked the old country lanes which were now infested much more with vehicles than the last time I'd been there.

Before long, I came upon the old Gatekeeper's cottage I had lived in with Hector. It was pretty dilapidated now, and obviously unused. Moss covered the old stone walls and, when I wiped a greasy window with the palm of my hand, I saw that the inside was dust-covered and empty. No one had lived there for a long time; I wondered if anyone had lived there since I had.

A sudden memory flared of me and Hector, sitting by the fire. He was looking up at me with a dedication I had never deserved as I stroked his head and sipped a whiskey, talking to him about my past. In that instant, I missed that long dead dog with an intensity that actually brought tears to my eyes. I turned away from the dirty window, feeling more alone than I think anyone ever has.

The gates were open, so I strolled past the big sign that stood there now, up the drive to a copse of trees. I had planted those trees as saplings in 1920, but they towered above me now, and provided a perfect hiding place.

I'd asked in the village about Longwood and had been told it was now a nursing home, and this was confirmed by the sight of the wheelchair-bound ancients who sat about on the lawn in front of the house, attended by white-coated nurses.

This was no NHS-run establishment. I could almost smell the money coming from those skeletons sitting under their tartan blankets in the watery sunlight. They reminded me of lizards, soaking up the meagre heat of the last of their days. Even as they slid inevitably towards their deaths they were spending the last of their wealth on making it as pleasant as possible. I sneered at their pointless existence.

A figure emerged onto the lawn and grabbed my attention. My heart began to beat faster as I stared at him. The girl at the shop in the village who had told me about Longwood's function now had also told me something else. She said the man who used to own it and the land it sat on still lived there as a resident. It seemed part of the contract for the sale of the building had stipulated that Sir Jonathon Greene could stay at Longwood for the rest of his life in return for the conversion of the house into a nursing home.

It was Greene I was looking at. I quickly worked out how old he would be now and shook my head in wonder. He was,

I think, a year younger than me, so he would be about eighty. Not an incredible age by any means, but he was certainly getting on. He was standing, talking to a man much older than him in a wheelchair. He was dressed in a Houndstooth suit and his once-black hair was thin and grey. He was bent and shrunken, and I once again thought about the frailty of human life and how quickly youth deserted them.

His appearance instantly made me melancholy and I cursed myself for going back. One should not look back, only forward, because the past, in my experience, is always immersed in nothing but heartache and regret. Greene said something and I saw the old man laugh. It seemed he still had a ready wit about him.

I smiled sadly to myself. The last few years had tainted my view of humanity somewhat; indeed, the episode with Bruno had almost let the wild darkness inside me out. It would have been so easy to snuff out his pointless life and I don't think it would have mattered to me at all. It was frightening how inhuman I was becoming.

But Greene was like an anchor to a previous existence. He had been there at the beginning, when I still believed I was normal. When I didn't yet know that I had been turned from an ordinary man into something strange, something different. I watched from afar until Greene turned away from the old man and walked slowly back towards the house.

'Can I help you?' a voice asked sharply from behind me.

I jumped and span around, confronted by a young man, aged about twenty. He wore the white tunic of the home's staff. I must have been staring intently at Greene, lost in my thoughts, for I hadn't heard his approach.

I shook my head. 'No. I… I used to work here. Before it was a residential home. I was just in the area and thought I'd come back to have a look at the old place.'

I could see he had his suspicions, and I could understand why. He was looking at a tall, suntanned man with long, unkempt, sandy hair and a dark blonde beard, wearing jeans and boots and t-shirt. He probably thought I was some burglar casing the joint.

'I see,' he said, although he obviously didn't. I remembered belatedly that the girl in the shop had said Longwood had been converted sometime in the early sixties. How could a man of my apparent age possibly have worked here then?

I made to move past him before he asked any more questions, but a rustle in the undergrowth behind me gave me pause. An instantly recognisable voice shouted, 'Hello! What's all the ballyhoo here, then?'

My heart stopped.

'This man says he used to work here, Sir Jonathon. But that's impossible.' The boy smirked at me triumphantly.

'Plenty of people have worked here over the years, Richard,' said Greene. 'Let's see you, then.'

I slowly turned around to face him.

God. Even now I remember the wave of sadness that engulfed me as I looked at the old man I had once followed into war. He had been like a lion in the trenches. He never gave up, he never stopped fighting. He had been young and vital and strong, and he had taught me what it meant to be a man. Much more so than my own father ever had. I suddenly realised, in that second of silence between us, how much I owed this man.

His soft, jowly face was smiling at me. His hair, as I've said, was very thin, and liver-spots tattooed his forehead. He was pink and shiny. He was old. But his eyes were the same behind the spectacles. Sharp, appraising. They seemed to look right through me, straight into my time-damaged soul.

The smile on his face wavered as he searched my own eyes. His lip trembled and he whispered incredulously: 'Rob?'

The young boy tried to say something, but Greene held up his hand and he shut up instantly. Whatever age had done to Jonathon Greene, it had not dimmed his presence. Some people are born with a natural charisma. These are the leaders, the people who make things happen, the people other people want to be around. Madeleine had this and so did Greene. It didn't fade with age.

'Thank you, Richard, that will be all,' he said and the boy, after another glance at my profile, left us.

Greene and I looked at each other.

'It is you, Rob, isn't it?' he asked in a tremulous voice. And I couldn't deny him.

'Yes, sir.'

'My God. You haven't changed one bit,' he murmured, shaking his head. 'Apart from that awful long hair and beard.' He looked at me sternly. 'You've let yourself go, Sergeant.'

I suddenly laughed at the look on his face, and Greene joined me. We laughed so hard we doubled up and clutched each other. I hadn't laughed like that in years. Not since Madeleine and I had shared our short time together.

'I've been keeping tabs on you, Rob,' Greene eventually said, wiping his eyes. 'No one believed me, but I kept tabs on you.' He wagged a finger at me. 'I always knew there was something special about you. That business at the Somme. You should have died. We all knew that. The men knew it. But you didn't die: you came back. You came back to me and the men and we won, didn't we, Rob. We won!'

'We did, sir. We won because of men like you, though. Not me.'

He smiled a soft, disbelieving smile, then he replaced his spectacles and indicated for me to follow him with a turn of his head. As we walked across the lawn I had spent so much time in the past keeping in order, he told me a little of his life.

'Jane left me, of course,' he said. 'We never married. She had her head turned by another man whose wealth was a little more, erm, portable than mine. He was some sort of investment banker, I believe. Owning land was all well and good, but it was never going to last. If there's one thing to be said about Jane, it's that she knew a good investment when she saw it.' He chuckled at the poor joke.

We paused at the kitchen door he had led me to.

'She died, you know. Just last year. I went to her funeral.'

'Was she happy, sir?'

He nodded, smiling sadly. 'I believe she was. I hope she was. It's all we can ask for in the end, isn't it?'

He stared at me with watery eyes, and I nodded, cursing the memory of Jane Godley to hell and back. I'd known she was a horror and I had been proved right.

We went inside and he showed me into the old library. The smell of the books brought memories flooding back to me. There was a photograph of Brewis, the old butler, hanging on the wall, looking even older than he had been in my time at Longwood. Greene saw my gaze and smiled.

'Brewis died in 1949,' he said. 'He was ever a good friend. I often wish I'd sold this bloody house earlier, so he could have spent his last years here, but he ended up in a decent enough place. I made sure of that.'

I smiled. It was a typical act for a man such as him.

The library now contained seven or eight tables, laid out for meals. He led me to a table by the window and we sat down.

'Did you ever marry?' I asked him and, as I feared, he shook his head.

'No. After Jane I sort of stopped bothering, really. I thought, well, what's the point? I was happy enough here so I just kept the old place going and, when they offered to buy it and let me stay on indefinitely, I jumped at the chance. It's not bad, you know. I still have my old bedroom and I get to wake up every morning to this.' He swept an arm across the view from the window.

A staff member brought us a pot of tea

'Shall I be mother?' asked Greene, and busied himself making two cups. He sipped from his and looked at me over the rim.

'Now then, Sergeant. I believe you have some explaining to do.'

He stared at me, keenly. I offered him a cigarette and we smoked in silence for a while. Where the hell would I start? He gave me an option.

'I followed your progress,' he said. 'In those days, I had a bit of influence, as you know. I received reports about you over the years. I heard about your exploits in New York, working for that awful

Irishman. That must have been exciting; I've seen lots of gangster films.'

He flashed his dentures in a smile at me and then continued. 'I know you were searching for something or someone after that when you went to France and Germany. I supposed it was that doctor, Valin, was his name?' I nodded, listening carefully.

'I heard about him as I kept my eye on you. I used my influence in the American Embassy to follow your progress. I had an uncle who worked for the Yanks and he told me about your exploits. He sent someone to come and see me once in, oh, what was it, forty-three, forty-four? During World War Two, anyway. I took an instant dislike to the fellow. Awful man. Smiled like he was supping sewage. Said he was a professor of such and such. Seemed very interested in your history.'

I closed my eyes, momentarily. So now I knew how Pfumpf had first found me.

'Anyway, as I've said, I'd been following your exploits. You see, I felt terrible about how I treated you, Rob. Simply terrible. I turned away a good friend for a woman who tossed me aside as soon as the better option turned up. She never loved me, and I think you knew that from the moment you met her. You were right and I was wrong.'

He suddenly looked like a very old man indeed and his liver-spotted hand scrabbled for mine.

'I'm so sorry, Rob,' he said, his eyes glistening. 'I'm sorry for how I treated you. It was her I should have got rid of. Not you. Not you. Can you forgive me?'

I swallowed hard and licked my lips. This man had saved my life on numerous occasions in our time together in those God-damned trenches.

'Sir, you have nothing to apologise for. Nothing at all.'

He nodded his thanks, taking a handkerchief and wiping his eyes.

'I've prayed every night since then that I would meet you again one day so I could tell you that,' he said. 'And God has answered those prayers at last. Thank you, Rob. Thank you.'

We both stared out of the window for a while, two old men from an era long gone, unwilling to show their emotions to the world. But I smiled to myself for all that. If he hadn't let me go I would never have started down the road that led me to Madeleine. How could I be angry about that?

'So you kept an eye on me?' I prompted him, eventually.

He nodded. 'I knew something strange was going on with you. I saw the odd photograph over the years, and I saw you were not changing at all. I remembered your tale about the medic in France.

'It's my belief he did something to you, Rob. God knows what, but he did something to make you like this. Look at you! You're exactly the same as you were all those years ago! How is that possible? Is he the same as you? Are there others?'

I shook my head.

'I don't know. I don't know why I'm the way I am. You're right, though: I think the Medic did do something to me. I don't know what it was, or how he did it. But he made me like this, I'm sure of it. That Professor, Pfumpf, the man who came to see you, he caught up with me a couple of times. He tried to find out why as well, but he never did. He said Valin was like me.'

I didn't tell Greene that his interest in my life had almost caused the death of the only woman I'd ever loved, or about the months of pain under Pfumpf's knife. He had simply been interested in an old friend. If he thought he had caused me any suffering, I think it would have killed him then and there.

'I saw a photograph of that man, the Medic,' I said. 'In France. It was taken in the thirties and said his name was Liebnicht and that he was an Austrian Jew. But he was older than he had been at the church where I first met him, so he isn't like me.' I sighed. 'I thought for a while he may have been, but he's not. Whatever the hell I am, I believe I'm the only one of my kind.'

Greene stared at me in wonder. He shook his head. 'How can it be?' he asked me. 'How can you be like this? What is it like?'

I decided not to tell him the truth about this.

He told me he'd followed Valin's movements as well as mine, but found, like me, that the trail went cold in 1936 when Valin had apparently returned to Austria.

So Pfumpf had lied about that too. He hadn't known anything about the Medic. His promises to help me find another like me were based on nothing but lies and hearsay, a name picked up from his conversations with Greene. He had never known where Valin was. It didn't really surprise me.

I didn't want to discuss the Medic anymore, so we spent the rest of the afternoon just talking about our time in the war and what we had done since. I didn't tell him everything, and I certainly didn't say anything about the encroaching cold darkness that I felt creeping through me like a shadow. A man as sunny and engaging as him would never have understood. I did tell him about Madeleine, however, and, strangely, saying her name didn't hurt when I was discussing her with a friend.

As the sun was lowering through the window, I finally stood to leave and, to my surprise, Greene hugged me as a father would hug his son.

'I'm sorry for you, Rob,' he said. 'I hope you find yourself some peace. I believe you are the saddest man I have ever known.'

I nodded slowly. I believed he was right. I smiled at him, shook his hand and left Longwood for the last time, walking back to the village.

I was still alone, still no further forward. My future was still an open road with no ending yet in sight, and my feelings towards humanity were still as depressing and disinterested as usual.

But Jonathon Greene, like Madeleine, had shown me that not all human life was a waste. Even though Jane had turned out as I knew she would, even though he'd spent his entire life in one place, he was still a good man. A good friend. Perhaps the only friend I had left in the world.

When I closed my eyes that night, I dreamed, as I usually did, of Madeleine.

And this time, the dreams comforted me.

XXI

I spent the rest of the seventies and all of the eighties alone again. I didn't think I had any choice.

Jonathon Greene, the last person to know my real identity, the last person to know *me,* died in May 1984 and I returned to Hampshire for his funeral, although I didn't go back to Longwood. I stood at the back of the church, knowing my secret had died with him. Nobody else knew about me. Pfumpf, for all his talk of secret government agencies, had been nothing but a liar, a man out only for himself, and had obviously not disclosed his secret quest for me to anyone else. The thought that I wasn't on any sort of "hit list" did nothing except make me feel even lonelier.

When everyone had gone, I went and stood by Greene's grave, remembering the short time we'd had together. Our friendship had been forged in battle and hardship, and we had relied on each other completely. I had fought another war after that, and I didn't believe either of them had made one bit of difference. New wars continued to come and go.

America had only pulled itself out of Vietnam nine years before, the UK had gone to the Falklands, and the Soviets were now in Afghanistan where more men were killing and dying with a depressing regularity. Conflict seemed to be the norm for the shallow creatures I shared the planet with.

But Greene had been someone to whom war had been abhorrent. He had fought because he believed it had to be done and, thankfully, he had survived the following conflicts. He had been blessed with the good death he deserved, tucked up in his bed in the house that had meant so much to him. Greene had been a true warrior. A true friend.

A single tear trickled down my cheek as I pulled myself to attention and saluted his grave.

I stayed in Britain but I kept moving around. I couldn't remain in one place longer than a few years as my continual youth would always start to bring about questions. I worked at all sorts of jobs.

I was a taxi driver in Coventry, I worked as a gardener in Manchester. I did anything that did not require too many background checks and I never stayed in each job long. I saved my money over the years and my old French bank account continued to add up the small amount of interest from the sale of the cottage back in the early seventies, as well as the money left over from Wall Street. It wasn't a lot, but it was enough to get by, which was all I could ask for. I just existed: a part of, but apart from, humanity.

I wandered eternally. I lived in cities and towns and villages. I watched the humans around me going about their ordinary, useless lives and my disdain of them grew by the day.

I watched with a cold indifference as the eighties ended and the Cold War spluttered out of existence. Gorbachev was voted out and Yeltsin was voted in. Previous to this, I had seen the crowds cheering as the Berlin Wall came down. It seemed to mean a lot to the people cheering, but as usual it all meant nothing to me.

But I should have taken more notice. Because the collapse of the USSR opened up an opportunity for me. Eventually, after decades of fruitless searching, it led me to the Medic.

*

I've said before that, when I was wandering around, I had to limit myself to Western Europe. This wasn't strictly true, of course. One could travel across the so-called Iron Curtain back then, but you needed permits and visas, that sort of thing. There was no way I was going to try that: the identities I had created for myself would never have withstood the scrutiny. So I had contented myself with the West.

However, now that the Curtain was no more, I felt the wanderlust fall upon me again. I had a passport, this time in the name of John Foster. His was the identity I had taken. He had never existed, but I had concocted a National Insurance number and, as well as a passport, I had acquired a driving licence and everything else I needed. It wasn't all that difficult, even in the early nineties. So I could travel. And travel I intended to do.

In the summer of 1992 I took a flight to Moscow, Russia. For half my life the Cold War had been a background noise heard on the radio, but I had never been to the capital of the now former USSR. I had never even met a Russian before, even during World War Two when we had been allies, and now that travel was easier I decided to visit the Russian capital and see what, if anything, it could offer my broken humanity.

It was not, in hindsight, the best time to go.

I took a taxi from the airport, passing the parliament buildings where, the year before, Yeltsin had stood on a tank and demanded the release of Gorbechev from a last-ditch coup attempt by the hardliners trying to preserve the former USSR. Outside my hotel, the homeless seemed legion, and the faces of the people on the streets were gaunt and blank. The populace seemed to be trying to come to terms with the collapse of the USSR, and Yeltsin's government didn't seem to know how to make it better for them.

In attempting to "free" the economic market in the January of 1992, Yeltsin had made a huge mistake. The state-run system that had existed for so long under the likes of Lenin, Stalin and Brezhnev was in no condition to be changed so quickly and so radically. Hyperinflation, matching even that of Germany in the 1920s, ravaged the country. Unemployment surged. The Russia I experienced seemed mortally wounded by things it didn't really understand, and a malaise of unease and fear seemed to hang across the city of Moscow.

Undaunted, I visited the cathedral of St Basil and gazed down at the brown and waxy visage of Lenin in Red Square. His embalmed corpse seemed to me to be a reflection of the city around him. He, like me, was a relic from the past, lost in a frightening and unknown future.

I found that Russia did nothing to change the rising darkness of my soul. I tried to interest myself in its culture and history, but it was useless. Everything still bored me. Everything was still a waste of time. Moscow's broken people seemed to reflect back at me my broken soul, and all my visit did was make me even colder towards the humanity around me. I was totally and utterly alone in this world, surrounded by a species I was truly beginning to hate. Going to Russia was a huge mistake and I left after less than a week.

I headed for the sun. I flew to Greece and got myself a summer job on the quays of Piraeus, offloading fish and octopus for the restaurants of Athens. After a year or two I went to Turkey and once more made a meagre living making and selling my little wooden toys. I wandered and wandered, never settling, never happy. Every single person I encountered looked upon me with revulsion and fear. The blackness of my condition seemed to be emanating from me more and more, and the ordinary humans who came across me recognised that there was something very wrong with me. Something alien and repellent. I think I frightened every single person that I met.

By the summer of 1996 I had exhausted any interest I had in anything. I was unmoved and uncaring. Nothing I saw elicited any kind of response within my blackened soul and the darkness swamped me. It was even worse than my time in Africa during the war. I was almost totally de-humanised, and even the realisation that this was so did nothing to make me want to change. I existed only in a world of simmering hatred towards humanity.

However, one August morning I awoke in the hostel I was living in and realised that I hadn't dreamed of Madeleine as I usually did. With a rising horror I realised I hadn't even thought of her in months, and this in turn brought a shocking revelation within me. Was I becoming so cold that even Madeleine's memory would be lost to me? Would the darkness just get bigger and bigger and drown her memory from my mind forever? I felt a huge wave of shame that her beauty and love and devotion, her very memory, was being thrown away by me. How could I do that to her?

It was then and there, in a dirty, cockroach-infested hostel in Istanbul, where I swore to myself I would not let that happen. I would make sure that some form of humanity remained in me, even if it was just enough to keep the memory of my beloved Madeleine close.

I looked at the date on my watch and an idea of how I might do this came to me. I nodded to myself. I had been thinking about it for a while and now the idea seemed apt. There was a big anniversary coming up in my life, and I now knew what I wanted to do with it. I would spend the day of my hundredth birthday at the sight of the worst atrocity mankind has ever seen. I would visit Auschwitz.

This may seem a rather macabre birthday wish, and in a lot of ways it is. But I had fought in both of the wars of that century. I had seen death and destruction on a massive scale. I had fought against the Nazis and everything they had stood for.

Like everyone after the war, Madeleine and I had watched in revulsion as the footage came back from places like Auschwitz and Bergen-Belsen. I had known what horrors man could inflict upon his fellow man; I'd seen it with my own eyes. But the images we saw then... There are some things that stay with you more than others and those bodies, those pathetic, stick-thin, mannequin-like bodies being bulldozed into their final resting places: that was one of them. It was unbelievable

It was life and death, you see. I had lived, they had died.

Because of a whim, a twist of some invisible string, I had been turned into something indestructible. Those poor people had lost everything. Their homes, their families, their hope and their lives. They had been exterminated on an industrial scale and I wondered at the mentality that would allow this to happen: indeed, to be part of. I wondered if the darkness within me could lead to horror such as that. And the idea terrified me.

So I would go to Poland and to Auschwitz, not only to see for myself what I had fought against and won. But also to see if I cared.

Although visits to the camp had been available for Westerners before the breakup of the USSR, I had never tried to go. It had, of course, been compulsory for the schoolchildren of Eastern Europe during the Cold War, where it had been used as propaganda against the West. But by 1996 it was open to everyone and tickets were available to buy from street vendors on the streets of Krakow. So on the sixth of August 1996, a one-hundred-year-old man looking like a boy named John Foster climbed aboard a rusting coach and travelled to the camp.

We pulled up outside Auschwitz I. The more infamous Auschwitz II, or Auschwitz-Birkenau, was a couple of miles down the road. Where we stopped had once been a Polish Army barracks which the Nazis had converted into a camp when they invaded. It was now the main museum of the Holocaust.

The tickets included a guide who would show us around. She was a middle-aged woman whose father had actually been interred at the camp. She knew what she was talking about and spoke in a matter-of-fact way that somehow perfectly encapsulated the horror of what had gone on there.

We wandered through the camp. It was strange to be there in high summer with the hot sun on my face, as most of the footage I had seen was from when the camp had been liberated by the Soviet army, back in the snowy January of 1945. There were trees lining the barracks and the warm air glowed gently on the brickwork. It was actually rather pleasant to start with.

The guide led my group with through the infamous gates with

its legend of '*Arbeit Macht Frei*' forged in wrought iron above it. We stopped at various different places, being shown where prisoners were tortured, where prisoners were hanged, where prisoners were shot. She showed us a room where human hair had been piled up to the roof and old, rusted spectacle frames sat tangled together, the last remains of people who had once lived and loved and smiled and wept but who were now long gone. I began to wish I hadn't gone.

In a strange way, I was pleased the place horrified me. Surely that meant I still had some form of human emotion inside me and the memories of Madeleine were perhaps safe. I had not yet descended into total callousness. As we went into the next building, I wondered how many more years that would take.

The door to the museum's barrack hut led straight into a long corridor lined with old photographs of men and women in the now-infamous striped uniforms. The men had shaved heads and the women wore scarves. They stared out at me from the past: victims of the monstrous acts that mankind can perform. Their lifeless eyes reminded me strangely of Pfumpf. They were dead eyes in faces still alive. I caught up with the group and followed them into the room at the end of the corridor.

And it was in that room where I first came upon a photograph that was to change my life. Where fate, which I didn't believe in, took me once again by the hand.

The photograph was huge, covering an entire wall and it showed the unloading area at Auschwitz II. The infamous arched gateway was in the distance, and in the foreground a train was disgorging onto the platform people who would soon be corpses. SS guards stood with Alsatian dogs that barked silently and eternally at the prisoners. One man, in the uniform of a high-ranking SS officer, stood with his hands behind his back. He seemed to be talking to the crowd, no doubt telling them the lies about having to go for a shower before being admitted into the camp.

But it was not this man who held my attention. It was another figure, standing near to him.

He wore the uniform of a sergeant, I believed. His Death's Head badge glittered and he seemed to be smiling at the officer. I could make out his features clearly as he was turned towards the camera. He looked to be somewhere in his late fifties and his nose was bent, as if broken in the past. On the right cheek of that dark face was a line that could have been a scar.

I had seen a photograph of that face before, in the hospital the night Madeleine died, and I had seen a younger version hovering above my ruptured body in a church in France in the summer of 1916.

From beneath the cap of a Nazi Death Camp guard, the Medic smiled out at me.

*

I must have stared at his face for quite a while, because the guide touched my arm and made me jump, telling me it was time to leave Auschwitz I and make our way to Birkenau. I asked her about the people in the picture, but all she knew was that the officer in the foreground was Josef Mengele, the so-called *"Angel of Death"*. In a daze, I followed her back through the camp, and we boarded the bus for the short drive to Auschwitz II.

I'm afraid to say I didn't take in much of the camp, apart from the loading bay where the Medic had stood fifty-odd years before.

In the end, I said I felt ill and waited impatiently beside the bus until the group came back and we set off for Krakow once again. The guide asked me if I was alright, probably thinking I'd been sickened by the atmosphere at Auschwitz.

I had, but it wasn't just because of what had happened at that cursed place. That evening, as I sat outside a café in the main square of Krakow, the face of the Medic burned through me.

What the hell had he been doing in the SS? Liebnicht was a Jew, for God's sake. The general feeling at the French hospital was that he'd perished in one of the camps, not worked at one! It made no sense at all until I thought about my own existence. How many different identities had I gone under over the years? What made me think it had been different for the Medic? How did I know what his real name was? He'd already had two identities I knew of and could very easily have had more.

Maybe he *had* been some sort of spy, with a myriad of different identities to use. I cursed myself for thinking that he was Liebnicht and not Valin. I didn't even know whether he was French or German or Austrian or any other nationality.

And he was definitely not the same as me. He was plainly just an ordinary man. Maybe he had nothing to do with what had happened to me. Maybe he had just been at St Theresa's that night only because he was a crazed German spy and was being hunted for murder. That made sense as he'd obviously been a member of the SS later as an older man.

But what about his work at the French hospital in the thirties? Why would an obviously nationalistic German pretend to be an Austrian doctor? Or maybe he really *was* Austrian? Hitler had been, after all.

My head spun with the thoughts tumbling through my mind. I had come to Krakow to search for the little that remained of my own human compassion, and instead I had stumbled upon a new mystery of that constant man in my life.

But then realisation hit me. It didn't matter anyway. Whoever the Medic was, he must be dead by now. The man I'd seen in St Theresa's had been in his late twenties or early thirties. The face in that photograph from Auschwitz had been that of a man somewhere in his late fifties, taken more than fifty years ago. Whoever the Medic had been, he would be long dead. He could not help me or explain anything about my condition.

Despite this immovable truth however, the next morning I started searching through the records. I might find out something about him. I might at least discover who he had been, where he had come from. It may have been enough to extirpate his damnable memory from my mind and, if nothing else, the quest to find out about him at least helped me to think and behave as a human being once more. If only for a while.

There were plenty of files on Auschwitz and I found a copy of the photograph easily enough, but the man in the records department could give me no more information. He indicated that it was in Germany where most of the records were now kept. At the German Historical Museum, Berlin.

I had no choice. If I could find out anything about the Medic, I would.

I caught the next flight.

XXII

'Hans Holmann,' said the young man.

'Are you sure?'

He nodded. 'Yes, definitely. Hans Holmann. Stabsscharführer Hans Holmann. You can see him here in another photograph. The one you have is from June forty-four. This one is from October 1947, when Holmann was taken to Spandau Prison.'

I had gone straight to the museum, and the young man I was talking to had been very co-operative. He seemed genuinely interested in my questions and had shown me to a room containing several microfiche machines. He'd sat me down at one of them and had then gone through some microforms, slowly honing in on the man I was after.

'He wasn't executed?'

The young man flicked through a few more frames. He shook his head.

'No. According to this, he was put on trial at Nuremberg, but it was never proven he had anything personally to do with the deaths at Auschwitz.' The young man's lip twisted momentarily in distaste.

'But he's there,' I insisted. 'In a photograph. At Auschwitz. In an SS uniform, standing beside Josef Mengele! He *must* have had something to do with it. Surely no one got away with it.'

The young man laughed, humourlessly. 'Oh, plenty people got away with it. Mengele himself got away with it. He managed to escape to South America. He didn't die until 1979. That was proved when his body was dug up for identification in eighty-five. He lived a very nice life.

'The top brass were sentenced to death, of course. Himmler and Goering were captured but killed themselves before they could be executed, and of course Hitler and Goebbels were already dead, but some of the minor figures were given prison sentences rather than execution. The commandant of Auschwitz, Rudolph Hoess, was executed—at the camp actually—but yes, some of the guards and what-have-you got away with it. Claimed they were "just following orders" and, unless it could be proved categorically that they had intended to kill those poor people, they were sent to prison instead of to hell where they belonged.'

I looked at him.

'Did you have family who were killed?'

He was quiet for a long time, but eventually he said, 'No. It was a member of my family that did the killing.'

I kept quiet. The generation that took part in the Holocaust had a lot to answer for, but it seemed the shame of their deeds still stung with the German population, even years later. The young man was about thirty years old. Probably a grandparent had been involved. I changed the subject.

'So were they all sent to Spandau?' I finally asked. 'Those who weren't executed?'

'Most of them,' he said, seeming to rouse himself. 'Let's see what happened to your Stabsscharführer Holmann.'

He wheeled the knob on the machine and whizzed around the microfiche with aplomb.

'Here we are,' he said. 'Yes, sent to Spandau in 1947 and released in 1965.'

'Released?' I was shocked.

He nodded. 'They had done their time,' he said, sarcastically and with a cold smile. 'Paid their debt. Your Holmann did eighteen years and was then released to live the rest of his life as he saw fit. That's the beauty of the law.'

I slumped. Released! So how the hell would I ever find out when he died? I needed to know. I wanted the Medic gone from my life for good, but it seemed I had failed again.

'Is there anywhere I can search records for deaths?' I asked.

He nodded. 'Spandau was demolished in 1987 after Hess killed himself; but yes, we can do that here. We have computers!'

I followed him to a little office where he typed Holmann's name into the national births, deaths and marriages register. I shook my head at the computer's boxy little screen. What would they come up with next?

'Can't find anything about his death, I'm afraid. Although that's not too unusual: not all the records have been put in yet.'

He saw the look of disappointment on my face.

'However, I do have an address. Maybe it's where his surviving relations live?'

He wrote the address down and I thanked him, exiting the museum onto the Unter Den Linden: not far from the address the Medic had written on the telegram Ducos had given me in Paris, and beside the little house I had rented in the 1920s and 1930s. Strange how things work out.

I was desperate to find out what had happened to the Medic, but I was curious as to how the area where I'd lived for six years had changed. I wandered the streets, in my mind's eye seeing the swastikas hanging from the balconies and hearing the cheering of the crowds. I walked past the grey stone apartment block. There was still a restaurant on the ground floor. It hadn't changed that much really, and I wondered idly what had happened to the old woman I had spoken so briefly with.

I went to where my house had been, but the street was completely different to how I remembered it and the house was no more, a modern block of flats in its place. Maybe the street had been rebuilt after being flattened in the war.

Eventually, though, I steeled myself and caught a tram to the address the young man had given me.

It was in Hohenschoenhausen, in what had been East Berlin: now an industrialised and pretty rundown area. Blocks of anonymous-looking, Soviet-era flats littered the skyline, and the shops on the main street sold mostly shoes or work clothes. I walked down the road, past the old Stasi prison that was also now a museum, until I came to the street I wanted.

I was confronted by a squat, concrete building with what looked like a large garden to the rear. I walked through the rusting gates and up some steps, finding myself in a foyer-like room. An unshaven and grubby looking man in his forties was behind the counter.

'Yes?' he asked me, in a bored voice.

I wasn't really sure where to start, so I just dived in.

'I was given this address from the German Historical Museum. I'm trying to find out about a man called Hans Holmann and this is the only address on record. I thought it may have been the address of his family, but I can see this is some sort of hospital?'

'It's an old people's home,' said the man. 'Not a hospital.'

I nodded, waiting politely for him to continue, but he just stared at me, breathing through his mouth.

I sighed, pointedly. 'Do you have anyone here by the name of Holmann?'

He begrudgingly bent to get something from under the desk and pulled out a ledger with an alphabet running down the front of it. He opened it at 'H' and ran a finger down the page and then nodded.

'Yes, we have a Hans Holmann here.'

My blood seemed to freeze in my veins, but I forced myself to calm down. It couldn't be him. It must be his son, that's all. Or a nephew?

'Can I see Herr Holmann?'

'What's it about?'

I considered telling this oaf the truth. That I was immortal, searching for the man who may have made me that way. It would have been funny to see the look on his face, but I was too eager to see this person by the name of Holmann and, anyway, I believed he was so stupid he wouldn't understand a word I said.

'I believe he might know someone I met once. I wanted to ask him about that person.'

The man continued to breathe at me stupidly. He stared at me like a cow; all he needed was some cud to chew on and the picture would have been complete.

'I don't see why not,' he eventually muttered. 'I'll get someone to take you to him.'

He indicated to a row of plastic seats by the wall and I sat down, purposefully not thinking about anything.

Presently, a young woman appeared. She conversed briefly with the man and then turned to me, again with an open mouth. She seemed to be as stupid as the man. The place was a long way from the comfortable retirement home of Longwood, back in the 1970s.

She buzzed me through a glass door and I followed her down a corridor, with rooms either side. The carpet was dirty, with bits of old food lying around on it, and the whole place had a vinegary smell about it, the stench of old people and air-fresheners. Under this was the sharp, electric smell of urine.

Some of the doors were open as we passed and I glanced into the cell-like rooms at the sagging, hollow faces of the inmates, their shoulders narrowed and hunched, their mouths bereft of teeth.

Even though it was late afternoon, a lot of them hadn't been dressed and, by the smells emanating from their rooms, it seemed they hadn't been washed either. They reminded me of the Death Camp victims. Their eyes were just as dead, that was for sure. Their bodies lived on but their souls had already perished, simply waiting for their used-up carcasses to follow them. They were the complete opposite of me. I quickly averted my gaze and hurried after the young girl.

She led me through a sort of communal room with a TV playing away to itself. More skeletons sat in there, staring at each other in a desultory way. The smell almost made me gag. Didn't anyone *do* anything for these people?

We went through some double doors and I found myself in the large garden I'd seen from the outside. I breathed in the clear air deeply, to wash away the awful smell of the home itself.

The girl led me halfway across the lawn and then stopped, as if she couldn't be bothered to walk the rest of the way. She pointed to a lone figure who sat in a wheelchair with his back to me. All I could see of him was a bald, wrinkled head.

'Herr Holmann,' the girl intoned and then walked back through the double door. I saw one of the old people inside ask her for something, but she shook her head and went out the far door. The old woman who had stopped her stared after her, forlornly. I turned back to the figure of Holmann.

There were others there in the garden and their wheelchairs were set in a circle, like a wagon train in one of the old Westerns I'd seen at the movies, but Holmann sat by himself as though the others wanted nothing to do with him.

I slowly made my way towards him, my heart banging with suppressed hope, but also fear at what I would soon find. If this was Holmann's son, he may not have known anything about his father or, perhaps, knowing that his father had belonged to the Nazi Party, he wouldn't want to talk about him. It may be another dead-end, but it was the closest I'd come so far in my long quest to find out who the Medic was and, at the very least, I might discover when he had died and be allowed to put his memory to rest.

I had to know. I needed this eighty-year search to have an end. I needed to know who Hans Holmann really had been and what, if anything, he had done to me to make me so different to other people.

I stood in front of the old man.

His head was totally bald, as I've said; not a hair remained. He was small and brown and wizened, innumerable wrinkles thrown hither and thither across his face. The creases were everywhere; there was not one centimetre of skin without lines criss-crossed over it.

His hands, folded in his lap, were the same: the skin covering the bones seemingly paper thin. He looked like he was made of crumpled wet card that could tear at any moment. His eyes were closed, as if sleeping and, as I took in his face, my world swayed. My hand scrabbled behind me for the small wall of a raised flowerbed and I sat heavily, my eyes never leaving that ancient face.

Although incredibly old, his skin was still swarthy. The nose was still bent to one side and, on his right cheek, a deeper wrinkle than the others was plain to see.

His eyes snapped open and I gasped at their depthless blackness, my hand unconsciously raising to my mouth. He stared at me for a long, long time until a hideous grin split across his face.

'You've found me at last, eh, Mr Deakin?'

I couldn't speak. I just stared at this man whom I had met only once, but who had been a part of my life for so, so long.

'Now that you have,' continued the Medic. 'What are you going to do about it?'

XXIII

It took a long time for my racing heart to slow. For me to stop just staring at this man and start listening to what he had to say. For me to be able to question him about his influence in my life.

'Hard, isn't it,' he said. 'When after years of trying, you finally get what you have been looking for.' His voice was papery-thin.

I only just managed to nod.

'I know what you're thinking,' he continued. Which was good, because at that point I didn't have a clue.

'You're thinking of when you saw me last. You're thinking about how I looked in the little clues I left lying around for you, how I've aged over the years. You're wondering how I'm still alive.'

'Clues?' I managed.

'The photographs. At the hospital in France. The one from Auschwitz. The one of me here in Berlin.'

'Berlin?'

'Oh, you never saw that one? It was good. I looked very dapper. It was taken in 1930. Just before I went to France.'

'You were in Berlin then?' I asked, shocked, and he giggled and nodded.

'I have been near you quite a few times, Mr Deakin. Keeping an eye on you. Seeing how my touch had developed on you.'

I frowned at him. 'Your touch? What do you mean?' I leaned towards him. 'What did you do to me? How did you make me like this?'

A thought struck me then, as he just smiled insipidly at me. I licked my dry lips. 'How old are you?'

'Chronologically?' he asked. 'Or from when I became mortal once more?'

My frown deepened. He wasn't making any sense at all. 'Once more?'

'How old would you say I was when we met so briefly in 1916?' he asked, ignoring my last question.

I shrugged, shaking my head at this mad conversation. 'Twenty-nine?' I guessed. 'Thirty?'

'So how old does that make me now?' He chuckled again. It was an unpleasant sound, like water gurgling down a drain. He answered his own question. 'That would make me one-hundred-and-ten years old.'

He suddenly looked pensive, glancing down at his bony hands.

'I think it's the remnants,' he said, musingly, almost to himself. 'The remnants of the immortality I once possessed. The wispy fragments of the God-like status I once held.'

His eyes came back into focus and he grinned at me again. His teeth were just brown stumps.

'Or perhaps not. Maybe it's just luck that I reached this grand old age, eh?' He rubbed the back of one of his hands, wincing. 'Of course,' he continued, 'if you're asking me about my real age, I'm afraid I'm much older than that. I was born in 1782.'

I fumbled in my jacket for a cigarette, offering him one, which he declined. I lit it and smoked hungrily, my mind whirling. There was so much I wanted to ask him that I didn't know where to start.

'How…?' I started. Then stopped, lost for words.

Holmann wasn't smiling now. He got himself comfortable in his wheelchair and his gaze went past mine, over the flower bed and across the distant city.

'There is much you don't know, Deakin. In fact, you know

nothing. You've blundered around on this planet for a hundred years and you are but an infant.'

He sighed, as if consumed by a great burden. 'Let me tell you my story,' he said.

*

'My name, my real name, is Louis Mandrin. I was born, as I have already told you, in the year 1782, in Paris. My father I never knew, and my mother was a seamstress, making a little money when she could.

'I think, when I was younger, she prostituted herself to keep a roof over our heads and some food on the table, but I don't know that for sure. I had two older brothers, but they both died in the wars after the coronation of Napoleon. I had a sister too, but she perished only a few weeks after I was born, so I never knew her. It happened a lot in those days. I think it was when she died that my father left us.

'Anyway, when I was old enough I began to help my mother out in the shop, as did my two brothers: fetching and carrying, that sort of thing. And then the Revolution came along and changed everything for us. I was only seven at the time, but as I grew I witnessed the old aristocracy losing their lands and losing their heads.'

He laughed at the memory.

'Snip, snip, snip, they went. I think it was then, even at such a young age, that I first began to understand the brutality of human beings. Their inherent wickedness. I began to know them and their ways.

'Day after day, week after week, the bodies and the heads piled up higher and higher and the crowds continued to howl for more; until, of course, the grand man himself, Robespierre, lost his own head in 1794. When Napoleon came to power ten years later, I and my brothers flocked to his side along with all the other young men of France. I was twenty-two and desperate to make things change.

I had seen how ideals could be twisted, and how people could move from wanting to change things for the better, to become nothing more than an unthinking, violent mob.

'The things I saw, Deakin. The horror I witnessed. Violence, murder, fear, suspicion. *This* is the nature of humanity. *This* is what they are, what they have always been. They crawl and preen and scrabble in the shit because they think, they actually *believe*, that they are worth something. The Revolution showed me their reality. They are worse than any other animal on this planet. They are the stupidest creatures to have ever walked the Earth, and they cause misery and death wherever they go. They do not deserve to breathe. They should all just go! Disappear. All of them!'

He paused, breathing hard, glancing in disgust at the others in their wheelchairs. He seemed furious and I despaired at what he was telling me.

He was like me! He was just like me. He was, or at least had been, immortal. And his anger and vitriol towards humanity was even greater than my own. I wondered, with a terrible, morbid curiosity, if I was looking upon my own future. I opened my mouth to speak but he held up a hand. He seemed to have got himself back under some sort of control.

'Please,' he said. 'Let me finish.'

I nodded, and he eventually continued.

'I wanted something better, and the Emperor seemed to offer that. I went to him, like I've said, and it wasn't long before I saw my first war. Not my last, by any means, but my first. I fought in most of the major campaigns for Napoleon, I was lucky to survive on more than a few occasions and, even after both my brothers had been killed in his never-ending quest for glory and power, I went to his side again in 1815 where I watched his defeat at the hands of Wellington. I thought he was different, you see. I thought he was better. But I was wrong. He was just the same as all the rest of them. Just as twisted. Just as wicked'

He glanced at my face, and smiled a sly, secret smile. His eyes, his black eyes, seemed to see straight inside my soul and his weak voice was hypnotic. I listened in silent awe to his tale.

'It was at Waterloo where I got my face bashed in by a British Rifleman. He left it in rather a mess I'm afraid. But I still managed to skewer him.'

He tittered as I frowned at him.

'Anyway, after the defeat I returned to a cowed Paris to find my mother living with another man, a local merchant. She didn't love him, but she needed his money to survive in the now once again Royalist city without her sons. He didn't like me coming back to her, though, and his dislike very quickly turned to hatred. He didn't want anyone else in his house, you see. He already had a son and a daughter of his own, and he didn't want a cuckoo living on his money too. So he set me up.

'A man came to the ale house I was living in and said I had slighted his fiancée, and that he demanded satisfaction. I hadn't done anything of the sort of course, I had been in Belgium, fighting for him and his whore of a fiancée while he cowered in the city. It was a charade. The merchant, by now married to my mother, had paid for the whole thing to be played out. However, I was a proud fool back then, and a veteran of war. I wasn't going to let anyone slur my good name.

'So we met, as was the norm of the day, in a clearing at the Bois de Boulogne forest. The seconds made sure the weapons we were using—pistols—were correct and in order. I fired first and my bullet took him in the head. My honour had been restored.'

His lips twisted as he said those words, and I once again glimpsed the pent-up fury in this ancient creature.

'But, of course, that was not what was supposed to have happened. It was I who should have ended up with a hole in my head. The man my stepfather had paid was a champion pistol shot, but I'd killed him. So the two men who had been with him, acting as seconds, shot my second and myself, leaving us for dead.'

He seemed to gaze at the view of the city, but I don't think he saw it. I think, instead, he saw a forest in France and a body lying drenched in blood.

'My second died instantly, I think. He was a decent enough lad, a comrade from the Peninsula campaign. I lay there, the grass turning red and the day turning to night. I remember staring up at the stars in the darkening sky and wondering whether I had been good enough to reach heaven. I didn't think I had been.'

His words reawakened a similar scene of myself lying, choking on my own blood in the church in 1916, staring up at the wooden figure of the saviour, thinking I would die that night.

'At the end,' he continued, 'as the blood from my wound slowed almost to a standstill and my heartbeat grew weaker in my chest, as I was dying, I heard footsteps on the grass and I looked up into the face of a woman.

'She was dressed in the finest clothes of the time. I remember them vividly. She wore a gold-coloured gown and she had pearls at her neck. She carried a fan and her blonde hair was piled on her head. I still remember her face: she was the most beautiful thing I had ever seen. She seemed like a golden angel, come to carry me off to my death, and I smiled at her, trying to beg her not to judge me too harshly.'

He broke off and turned away briefly. I saw his throat working as he seemingly choked off some emotion the memory had wrought.

Then he sighed and turned back to me.

'But the real memory I have of her was her smell. She smelled divine, some sort of soap. Lavender. Every time I have smelled lavender since, I am reminded of her. She smelled clean and fresh after hours of the stink from the blood and shit leaking from my stomach.

'Her face hovered above me in the dusk light. Above her head I saw bats hunting and, in her green eyes, I saw something else. Something that twisted and heaved. Something dark.'

His own eyes were haunted now as he remembered what had happened.

'There was a madness in those eyes,' he continued, his voice shaking slightly. 'They terrified me, but they also captivated me. It was like looking into the eyes of something immensely *alive*, something old, older than time itself, something primordial, but contained within the beautiful face of a woman no more than twenty-five years of age.

'She reached down and touched my chest and she leaned very close to me. She seemed a little unsure of what she was doing, but determined to carry it out. She lowered her mouth to my ear and at the time I didn't understand what the words were that she spoke. I recognised the language, it was Russian, yet I didn't understand what she had said. But the words stayed with me, and later, I found out what they meant. She said, *"Ya imel dostatochno. Ne bol'she, ne bol'she. Ya peredayu eto"*. "I have had enough. No more, no more. I pass it along."

'I felt a warmth from her hand, and that warmth seemed to move through me like a wave that filled my body with heat. It was rather like when you are in a bath and someone adds more hot water, except this was on the *inside*. Do you understand?'

He raised his eyebrows at me and I nodded, dumbly.

I sort of did understand him. His words were bringing back memories of my own, suppressed for eighty years. Of the touch of a hand, some murmured words and a spreading warmness, heralding a rebirth of immense proportions.

'I fell asleep then, or perhaps I died, I don't know. When I awoke, it was morning and the woman was gone. My second was still there, lying where he'd been shot, and our horses cropped happily at the grass nearby. I staggered to my feet, as I felt much stronger. I looked at my stomach and, as I opened my torn shirt, I found two bullets lying in its folds. My body had pushed them out in the night. The bullet wounds were almost completely healed.'

I remembered my own body doing the same thing back in my apartment in New York and I nodded again for him to continue. Nodding was about all I could do.

'I was obviously mystified as to what had happened, but I was sure it was something to do with that woman. Perhaps she *had* been an angel and had saved me for some reason as yet unknown. I took my second's body back into Paris for burial, then I left. I never saw my mother again and I didn't know at the time about my stepfather's betrayal. By the time I realised it had been him and went for my revenge, they were both dead.

'And I was different. My mother's death didn't seem to matter anymore. Nothing seemed to matter. I moved to Normandy and met a girl there, staying with her for a while. But she died after a few years, and soon I began to realise I was not ageing. The touch of that woman, and her words, had frozen my body in time. She had healed me, yes, but she had changed me.'

'What is it?' I asked, finding my voice at last and leaning even closer to him. 'What did she do to you? What did you do to me?'

He shook his head.

'I don't know. I have thought about it a lot, as you may have imagined, but I have never truly known. I have hunted for years, trying to find any other examples of life and death such as yours and mine, but found very little.

'There are a few medieval texts that mention a touch that brought forth a *"life bereft of death"*, but they don't necessarily mean the same thing. The earliest I ever found comes from around the time of the First Crusade and mentions a knight who was mortally wounded but who was healed with just a touch by a Muslim soldier. Supposedly he went on to live well into the thirteenth century.'

He shrugged. 'Wherever it first came from, my belief is that it is a different way for life to continue. An older, darker way, separate from the norm. An alternative form of procreation if you will. A touch, from one infected person to another which means the life energy goes on and on.'

'Infected?'

He laughed softly. 'I sometimes think of that energy, that life force as a living thing. Almost as if everyone it touches are simply hosts for it to survive in. And I believe it has been around for a very long time. Like bacteria, a disease, it infects whoever it enters. Its hosts are infected with life.'

'Did you find out who the woman was?' I asked, my voice shaking. The idea that the energy that had once poured through his veins and now poured through mine was a living thing, a sentient, parasitic thing, made me squirm. It was an uncomfortable thought. Infected with life!

He shook his head. 'No, and neither was I interested to do so. It was only years after we met that I realised just how different I was when I thought about her. But I never looked for her.

'I moved from place to place. I think it has probably always been so for whoever is touched. It's hard to stay in one place for long as the people around you grow older and die. I found it was best to keep myself to myself. Like you, I wandered the world, seeing new things, experiencing as much as I could.

'But all the time, in the back of my mind, the knowledge that I was different hovered. I couldn't settle; I couldn't fall in love. I realised I couldn't have children. I believe the touch does this. What is the point of producing squalling infants when life has already been passed on? I would have to experience the changing of the world instead of the love of any children. But I couldn't share my strange existence with anyone else, because everyone, *everyone,* was different to me.'

I thought of my own, lonely life, my own losses, the babies Madeleine had craved and had blamed herself for not being able to produce.

What was the point of it all? Why were we so different to others? I brought my attention back to him as he spoke again.

'Eventually, I found myself in a Europe once again desperate for war. I was in France when it broke out. I had trained as a doctor in Vienna before this. I became a surgeon. I was obsessed by this point. After so many years of not caring, I became obsessed with finding out about human physiology. I wanted to know how the body worked, why the body aged. By learning these secrets, I believed I might understand why I was different. Of course, I never did. When World War One broke out, I joined the French army as a medic, and I worked in many different hospitals and field hospitals. And that, of course, is where I met you.'

He smiled his brown-toothed smile at me again.

'I hated humanity by then,' he continued, his face twisting again with some old, unresolved rancour. 'They were like cattle to me, no more important or different than all the other animals nature produced. They all lived and died in a heartbeat. I was happy the war broke out, because then more of them would die and they would not pollute the world with their stupid, brainless continuance. I worked in the field hospitals and I watched them die and it fulfilled me in a way I suspect you are beginning to understand.'

He held up a withered arm at my protestations.

'Please, I know how you think, I know how you feel about them. Don't try to lie to me.'

I wanted to deny him. I wanted to tell him he was wrong, but I couldn't. It was as if he could see inside my soul. I waited for him to continue.

'On the first of July 1916, I was at the field hospital you were brought to. I believe Ducos filled you in on the details, back in the late twenties?'

I nodded again. Had my quarry been around me my entire life?

'The British army came after me because they had found out my identity was false. They thought I was a spy.' He laughed at this. 'As if I gave a damn about nationalities by then. But anyway, my previous identity had been German, and someone found out about it, I don't know how. Probably a slip-up on my behalf. Like you, I had discovered I had to keep reinventing myself so my real identity was kept secret. The Commandant at the field hospital called me into his office to show me the telegram and, well, you know the rest of the story. I killed him in the heat of the moment. I didn't mean to. I just lost my temper, and he was only a human.'

He said this as if he was talking about a chicken whose neck he had wrung for dinner.

He didn't seem to notice the look of disgust I gave him, but at the same time I remembered how much I had wanted to kill Bruno Gombos in my circus trailer. I sort of understood his callous, offhand opinions of the relative importance of human beings.

He began talking again.

'But as I cut his throat, so a startling revelation came to me. A sudden compulsion if you like.

'I wanted to pass it along. I wanted the infection to leave me. For some reason, as I stood staring down at his body, I just wanted it to stop. And the only way to make it stop was to pass it on to someone else.'

I leaned even further forward, gazing at his gaunt face in fascination.

'The idea had been hovering around me for a while,' he continued. 'I don't know why. I think that eventually, life becomes too much for those infected. Those words the lavender woman spoke to me—"no more, no more"—there was such desperation in her voice. Such melancholy. I think it had been the same for her. God only knows how old she was by the time she came across me. But I also think it can't be passed on until the infected person has come to this point in their life. And the only way to get to that point is to live. To live until you can't bear to live anymore.

'I also suspect that whoever it is passed onto must be near death for the infection to work. At the very point of death: within minutes of it in fact. I tried to pass it on to Forest, the man I killed, but he was already dead. I had been rather too energetic with my scalpel.'

He sniggered again here, and I began to realise that whatever madness the woman's touch had wrought in him, it was still there. Maybe he had been infected for too long.

'So I escaped into the night, searching for someone to pass it on to. I believe I felt something like stags must feel in in the rutting season. Only one thought raging through their minds: to mate. It was the same for me. Suddenly, nothing was more important for me other than to rid myself of the disease. I had to pass it on!

'I came across the church and the first person to fit the criteria was you, as most of the others in there with you had already died. I touched you and I passed it along.'

I rubbed a shaking hand over my jaw.

So this was it. The question that had haunted me for almost a hundred years was finally answered. And, in a way, it was just down to luck, as I'd always thought. No mystery. No reason for my difference, just pure luck that the first person Valin saw was me, and pure luck that he had come to his decision to rid himself of the infection of life at that time. No magic. Just luck. The roll of a dice.

No purpose. There was no purpose or reason for my immortality. Whatever this disease was, I had not caught it to fulfil some great, unknown destiny. I had simply been the only one available. All this revelation did was make me feel slightly sick. My thoughts turned to Madeleine, aged before her time as she lay in the hospital.

'I had a wife,' I said, dully. 'If you had come to me and told me, I could have passed it on to her.' I stared at him. 'She could have lived.'

Valin seemed to think for a second, then shook his head. 'No. Although she was near death obviously, you were not ready. It wouldn't have worked.'

'How do you know?' I insisted. 'You may have been wrong about that.'

He just shook his head again. 'Even if you had succeeded, what would it have done to her? You would have consigned her to the same fate you and I have endured. Would you really have wanted that for her? Seeing her begin to realise what her life would be like? Seeing her start to hate, as you and I hate? How would she have felt watching you grow old and die while she stayed the same? Do you think she would have forgiven you?'

I was silent, not willing to give this man an answer.

Because he was right. Madeleine did not deserve that fate and, as horrible as her death had been, as much as I still so desperately missed her, as much as I clung to her memory, she was at least now at rest.

Unlike me.

'Why did you write the address in Berlin down on the back of the telegram?' I asked, eventually. 'What was the point in that?'

Valin smiled his smug little smile again. 'I knew I was going to pass it along. I had to. I could feel it trying to burst from me. But I wanted to know what the person who received it would do with it. I was curious. I have spent my entire life trying to find out what was different about me. That's why I became a surgeon. I searched for an answer to a question that has no answer. But I wanted to keep an eye on you for as long as I could, to see if you came up with anything different. I wanted to see if your curiosity would match my own. So the address was a magnet, a fly trap if you like.'

He glanced at me with a quick, secretive motion. 'I watched you, you know, watching the apartment. I watched you as you drank in the bars and clubs of Berlin. I was around you all the time and you never even knew.' He sniggered again and I felt a burst of anger towards him.

He was so alien, this man. He was repellent, and I wondered if he had been like that before his duel all those years ago, or whether it was the touch of the mysterious woman that had changed him into the deranged monster he now seemed to be.

'So,' I said, taking in a breath to calm myself down. 'You followed me around Berlin?'

He nodded. 'Yes, although I lost contact with you when you returned to Britain. And after that, my old curiosity was satiated in different ways. I used the chaos of World War Two to further my investigations. I still wanted to know if there were others, like you and I, even though I was now obviously mortal once again, getting older every day. But I wanted to know if you were truly the only other person on the planet like that. I had to find out if there were others, and I used the Nazis to help me.'

'Auschwitz,' I said.

He nodded, eagerly.

'I got myself posted there, again using a false identity, the one I'm using still. Ostensibly, I worked for that madman Mengele on his experiments. In reality I used him to look for others like you, like I had once been.'

'You experimented on those people?' I asked. I stared at him in horror. 'How could you do that?'

He flapped a hand at me in a desultory manner. 'I care not what you think of me, Deakin. Even though I no longer had the infection running within me, I had seen too much by that point. Human life and death meant nothing to me. It still means nothing now. I simply wanted to know if there were anyone else like us.'

He slumped a little. 'I confess, I never found anyone like that.'

I stood and turned my back on that wizened monster, lighting another cigarette and smoking it slowly.

Was this my future? Was I cursed to become a cold and heartless murderer and torturer? How long would it be before I ended up looking upon the rest of humanity as a disease worse than the one that had stopped my body clock, yet kept me young and strong?

This was the payback. I suddenly understood. This was the Yin to the Yang of eternity I had previously envisioned. This was the down to the up of never-ending existence. This was what Pfumpf had never understood in his cravings for immortality.

No one should live this long. At that moment, I believed no one *could*. That was obviously why the craving to pass it along had caused the woman to touch this man I still thought of as Valin. Why he had felt the compulsion to touch me. Why, one day, I would presumably feel the same.

My body would live and live and remain young and healthy, but my soul would shrivel and blacken until there was no human emotion left in it at all. That was the reality of the touch. That was its curse. Valin had said it was a God-like existence. At that moment, I believed it to be the very opposite.

I turned back to Valin, who just grinned up at me. A silver line of drool dribbled down his stubbled chin, but he ignored it. His mad eyes jumped around me. I finished my cigarette and ground out the stub on the floor, then I shook my head at him.

'Thank you for telling me everything, even though you've made me sick to my stomach to listen to you. Sick to be even in your presence.

'But I promise you one thing. I will never be like you. I will never descend to whatever it is you have become. We may share the same disease, but I will not become a thing as lost as you are.'

He sniggered once again, the drool hanging from his lip. 'Maybe you just haven't lived long enough yet.' He nodded to himself, his eyes still on mine. 'Give yourself another hundred years and then tell yourself that.'

I crouched down in front of him and put my face very close to his. He had an unpleasant, sour smell about him. I was pleased to see that, even though he was completely insane, he drew back from me in sudden fear.

'You will die soon,' I whispered to him. 'And when you do, the world will be a better place. I may go on, but I will not be like you. I will not allow myself to become whatever it is you are. And I will never allow anyone else to suffer this disease.'

I stood and stared down at him. 'I will not pass it along.'

I turned and walked away, leaving him in his chair.

I heard him laughing at the uselessness of my words as I left that stinking, decrepit home, and I could still hear him laughing in my hotel room later that night.

Sometimes, I still hear him laughing today.

XXIV

I left Berlin the next day feeling numb and empty. Feeling so unutterably alone.

Everything I had experienced, all the hopes and dreams that every person feels, multiplied by a thousand, was all for nought. I had been given something, something that made me different from every other person on the planet, and if Valin—or whatever his name really was—had been correct, all it would do was just turn me into a monster. I would become even hollower than I was now, even more remote. I would descend to such depths that I would be bereft of anything approaching humanity. Cursed to walk the world forever until the compulsion to pass it along came upon me and another person would be changed. Another person would be cursed.

I ruminated constantly on the point of it all. Everything I had been through—the wars, the heartache, the people who had flitted oh-so-briefly through my long life—was all pointless. Nothing mattered. Nothing they did meant anything at all; and nothing I did, or would do in the future, would ever matter either. Everything was just a huge waste of time.

Time.

That word hung over me like a sword. How often have we heard people complaining they never have the time to do the things they want, or know they should do?

People make excuses for not doing things, for not living their life the way they want to. They say, *'If only I had the time'*. They complain about it and yet they do nothing about it. It seemed to me, as I sat on the plane back to the UK, that humans are essentially nothing but time-wasters. And life itself, that infection running within me, laughed at them like Valin had laughed at me. They both knew that they were right, I was wrong, and it was all just a sick joke.

I returned to Britain and tried to go back to the life I'd had before, working in odd jobs around the country, but the memory of the Medic, what he was, and what I might become would not leave me.

Madeleine was also constantly on my mind. Was Valin right? Could I have saved her? Should I have tried? But worse, much worse, was knowing that if I had—if I had given her this disease, this curse—she would have hated me for eternity. She would have turned out just like me.

She was everywhere I went, she was in everything I saw. Every time I passed young, laughing lovers on the street—or worse, watched old couples sitting side by side in companionable silence on park benches—her ghost burned in me, and the knowledge that I would never be allowed to share such an ordinary existence cut deeper and deeper into my already wounded soul. I would stare mournfully at these fortunate, normal people, who had spent their entire lives together and who would be with each other until they both died, and the memory of Madeleine stabbed at me mercilessly.

She haunted me. Why could I not have what these people took so much for granted? Why should they have happiness when I had lost my love and was doomed to this non-life that would last forever? Why did the humans around me have so much freedom, when I had none? Despite the compassion I had been moved to at Auschwitz, the mortals surrounding me continued to irritate and anger me to such an extent that, within three months, I'd had enough of them. I hated them for their contentment.

Tiring of the charade of pretending I wanted to be anywhere near them, I decided to give up on them. If I was so different to them, if I was such an outsider, then I would be an outsider on my own terms. I would disown them and their hateful lives.

With the memory of Madeleine boiling within me, I made my decision and travelled as far away from humanity as I could. My stinging loss would be suffered by me and me alone. Humans did not deserve my presence. I made my way up to the far north of Scotland, to the Western Highlands. I bought a small stone croft there. It was miles from anywhere and anyone. There weren't even any farms in the surrounding area, just mountains and glens. Here I would give up on my useless, never-ending life. Here I would suffer my pain alone.

The croft had an old-fashioned boiler which was fed from a peat fire, a stream nearby for fresh water and the odd fish, and it was tucked away from prying eyes. I lived off the land, hunting rabbits and wild grouse for meat and growing root vegetables in the back garden. As infrequently as I could I visited the nearest village, which was twenty miles away, for cigarettes and alcohol and tinned goods.

It was a raw, wild existence, but it was the only sort of existence I believed I could have. I occasionally listened to the radio to keep in touch with what was going on in the world of the humans I no longer belonged to.

On my first night there, I lit the fire and poured a whiskey. I sat and stared into the flames. My thoughts were as black as the night outside. Trying hard not to think of Madeleine, Valin instead consumed my mind.

Because he was right. I now knew he was right.

I despised humanity. Yes, the trip to Auschwitz had caused some emotions to surface, but I remembered all the times I had viewed life with dispassion. All the times I had witnessed the violent acts of man and had ignored it because it simply did not interest me.

His touch had changed my body, but it had also changed *me*, and I now knew why. Its function was simply to make me survive until I could bear to survive no longer. That was all. No grand plan. No reason for it. It was simply my lot in life. I was just a temporary host for the immensity within me.

All life, whether human or animal or plant or germ, is designed to one day end. No one could stand to live forever, for it was not natural. Not normal. Valin's touch had made me abnormal, and the touch of the lavender woman had done the same thing to him. But it shouldn't have been so!

What was the point of life, if it never ended? What was the point of love if, one day, that love would wither and disappear to leave one utterly alone? What was the point of existence if that existence was never-ending?

I stared into the fire, imagining that the flames were like the disease within me. The peat and coals fed that fire and it burned brightly at first but, eventually, the flames consumed the source of their power. They needed new combustion or they would eventually die out themselves. The fire was the power within the touch. The peat and the coal were the poor souls the touch kept alive, but ultimately destroyed. It would always need to be one day passed along.

This was probably why the compulsion to pass it on eventually came upon those people infected with life. Because, finally, life would become so horrifying and cold for them that they would crave death. They would yearn for it. They would *need* their life to just *end*.

How long would that take for me? How long would I stumble onwards, watching the world change, watching new wars and new diseases sweep the globe? How long would I be the watcher of an existence I could never be a part of?

I stared at that fire as the flames grew weaker.

What if it never got the new coals and peat? What if it was not fed?

I sat and watched the flames slowly expire, drinking more

whiskey. When the fire was gone, I nodded to myself in the darkness, renewing the vow I had made to Valin.

I would not be like those who had gone before me. I would not allow this awfulness to continue.

I would not pass it along.

*

I stayed alone in my croft, up there in the Highlands, for years. I contained myself in a little world. The mornings consisted of making breakfast and coffee. I allowed myself only to concentrate on that, then I would leave the croft and walk.

God, I must have walked thousands of miles over those years. I would take a direction based on nothing and just walked until I could walk no more.

I trained myself to think of nothing. Not Madeleine, not Valin. I kept my mind blank. When I returned to the croft I would make my evening meal and then drink whiskey until I woke the next morning and did the same thing again. I did not allow myself to think.

Like some form of mad hypnosis, I stopped myself from contemplating anything further ahead than the next minute, the next second. Time was too immense for me to consider, so I ignored it the best I could. The years roared quickly by.

On New Year's Eve, 1999, I listened on the radio to the booming of Big Ben and the cheering of the crowds and the crackling of the fireworks. I drank whiskey.

I was drinking a lot by then. Why not? It couldn't do me any harm. It got me through each lonely day and dark night. It stopped me thinking coherently. Sometimes it stopped me thinking at all. Three years since my meeting with the Medic had changed me completely once again. I was becoming incapable of any cogent thought process, even if I wanted to.

The seasons came and went with boring regularity. I ate, I drank, I walked. I existed. And, every day, my thoughts grew darker and darker. Every second, my hatred of those I shared the planet with grew and grew. I wanted no part of them or their miserable existence, and I was too miserable myself to even wonder why.

I stopped shaving. What was the point? My beard grew very long, as did my hair. On that early morning of the new millennium I had to tie it behind my head to keep it out of my eyes. I looked like a savage.

I turned off the radio; the sounds of the crowds had made my lip curl in anger at their stupid, pointless lives. How could they enjoy themselves when they would soon all be dead, along with their children and grandchildren? I hated them. I contemplated my existence for the millionth time, not even realising I was becoming just what Valin had said I would.

Slowly, I turned around and stared at the rope I had prepared over the main beam in the kitchen. The noose regarded me curiously. *Will you?* it seemed to ask. *Dare you?*

It had been hanging there for over a month. I licked my lips and stared at it.

I sniffed and took another long draft of whiskey, grimacing as it burned its way through me.

What the hell was I doing? What was I trying to achieve by hiding myself away like a recluse? What was the point of me? What was the point of *anything*?

I looked at that rope and felt the weight of my past pressing against me. All the things I had done, all the things I had seen. And they were as nothing to what stretched before me. What might my endless future bring? The cheering of the New Year crowds on the radio mocked me. I was apart. I was alien.

I was a man completely out of time. A strange Victorian cast-off, still continuing to exist in a shimmering, silvery world of technology and digitisation, still moving relentlessly forward long after I should have just lain down and given up. I was out of place and out of time. A misfit, lost in a frightening, futuristic nightmare.

Why me? Why had it happened to me? I should have died. I should have been just another name carved on a pristine white gravestone in Northern France. I should have been forgotten by now, like the rest of my generation. That had been my fate. That was what I should have become. But it had all changed when Valin stole into my life and touched me, unleashing this hell upon my soul.

Suddenly decisive, I grabbed the nearby stool and placed it under the noose. I stood on it, reached up and tightened the rope around my neck.

Won't pass it along, won't pass it along, won't pass it along.

The thought tumbled through my whiskey-sodden brain.

And yet still I hesitated. Even then, after everything Valin had told me, after everything I had experienced, I felt the cold fingers of fear stroke my spine. To end it all, to just cease to be. What would it be like?

Could I even have it? I had been shot, stabbed. I'd had half my head blown off for God's sake, and still I had lived. What would it take for me to die?

This was the reason for the rope. Maybe only this was the answer. Maybe I had to do it myself. Perhaps only suicide would kill the eternal, infernal energy inside me. This had been the thought going through my head when I had made the noose and tied it around the beam. I realised I had to know. If only as an experiment to make me know I really would last forever.

I waited a long time, standing on the stool, the rope hanging limply around my neck. The awful, endless thought repeated itself again and again. Could I die? Would I? I needed to know.

I kicked the stool away.

The pain was instant and immense. My hands scrabbled at my neck to try and stop the agony; I couldn't help myself. I choked and spluttered. I felt cartilage crunch in my throat, and my lungs burned for air.

My tongue begin to emerge from my mouth, my eyes bulging, my vision fading. My legs kicked the empty air uselessly. My head felt as if it were about to burst. It went dark.

I awoke to the same sensations. My throat still burned, my

legs still kicked, my lungs still scrabbled for air. I registered it was daytime, though. I faded again.

I don't know how many times this happened, but I lived and died many, many times, each one as agonising and terrifying as the last. And as I did, I remembered at last what the Medic had done to me.

*

His hand descended from the gloom in the church. He was smiling: a strange, disturbing smile.

In his eyes I saw something flicker and twist. It was a dancing, turning blackness, a trailing snake of nebulous dark smoke that writhed endlessly.

I couldn't tear my eyes away from that blackness. It hypnotised me. I tried to reach out to touch it, but I could not move at all now, my body was on the very edge of eternity. He placed his hand on my chest and the black snake in his eyes seemed to expand until they became completely opaque. They were twin holes in time itself, and the blackness seemed to flow from those eyes. Into me.

'I pass it along,' he whispered.

I felt the blackness enter me, and it was a warm flow that calmed my ruptured chest and spread rapidly throughout my entire body. I felt it setting dying nerves on edge, I felt it beginning to heal, closing ruined flesh and bone, rejuvenating veins, creating new blood, infected blood to run through those veins. I felt my heart begin to beat, stronger and stronger.

I gazed up at those eyes, until the blackness faded from them, emptied from them. Into me.

My pain decreased, my breathing eased. I could still only stare up at the Medic, who was no longer smiling. Instead, his face was thoughtful, unsure what to do now. He removed his hand and stared at it, and the blackness spun within me now that it had left him. Healing my broken body. Cursing my broken soul.

He stood up and looked around the church as if in a daze. Then he turned back to me once more.

'Good luck, mon ami. I will try to keep an eye on you.'

He turned and disappeared into the darkness.

The infection swirled within me like electricity. I sighed. I was so tired. So tired.

I closed my eyes.

*

I awoke again to the awful, choking pain, then once more gurgled myself out of existence. And again. And again.

But slowly, over those brief, awful periods of agonising consciousness, a plan began to formulate in my mind. One thought at a time, interspersed with agony and terror and blackness, they formed themselves into an idea of rescue and, eventually, I was able to act upon them. I woke once more and instantly threw up an arm, managing to grab the rope and scrambled up it high enough to hang, one-handed, from the beam, taking the strain from my neck. I scrabbled and pulled at the noose and finally yanked it from my throat and fell to the floor, gasping, the pain of returning blood making my head feel like it would break. I passed out once more.

When I awoke again, my swollen throat had returned to normal, and the banging in my chest had ceased. I swallowed, feeling only slight discomfort. I scrambled to my knees, and slowly made it to my feet, only then noticing I had vomited everywhere and had fouled my jeans. Probably more than once.

Grimacing at the mess, I stripped and bathed in cold water, cleaning myself and dressing in fresh clothes. I inspected my neck in the mirror and saw only a faint, lightly-bruised line where the rope had strangled me to death so many times. The old thought raged through me.

It was useless. The power inside of me would not allow it.

I could not die.

I went into the front room and turned on the radio. It was the third of January. I had been choking and kicking and dying for three whole days. The new century stretched before me and I saw it only as a roaring red river and myself as nothing but flotsam, consigned forever to mindlessly follow its flow.

I opened another bottle of whiskey.

Maybe it had to be catastrophic.

I sat and drank and muttered madly to myself and thought my macabre thoughts again. Maybe some sort of explosion would do it. Or perhaps I could throw myself into the molten metal of a steel factory? That would do it, surely.

Even in the crazed state I was in, I shied away from the horror of that. What if it didn't? What if it just left me a melted, pain-filled mess, with the evil life force within me still keeping me captive? No, there was only one conclusion I could come to about that sort of suicide. The power, the force, the *life* that infected me, would not allow me to do it.

With this awful revelation ringing in my head, I slowly slumped to the stone floor once more, and for the first time in years, I wept.

*

I gave up on everything. I could not even begin to envisage my endless future, so I ignored it. I existed without living. I continued with my solitary existence and it slowly drove me mad.

The years went by in a blur of meaninglessness from the radio. The twin towers in Manhattan came down and the war in Afghanistan began. Brazil won the World Cup. Saddam Hussain was toppled. The Beslan school hostage crisis ended in dreadfulness and slaughter. On one Boxing Day, over two hundred thousand people were killed by a tsunami in the Indian Ocean. David Cameron became Prime Minister. An earthquake in Japan led to the Fukushima nuclear power plant going into meltdown. Somebody set off a bomb at the Boston Marathon. World population reached seven billion.

I listened to it all on the radio, my only connection with the outside world. All the horror, all the bloodshed, all the vice told me everything I needed to know, and my hatred for humanity grew and grew. I could barely bring myself to look at the villagers as they stared at the filthy mad hermit who occasionally came into their midst to buy his whiskey and cigarettes.

I collected the supplies I needed and slunk quickly back to my croft, away from the world. I didn't trust myself to be around the villagers, for I believed I no longer cared about hurting them. Indeed, I hated them so much now I was fearful I might stab one of them, just to see the light fading from their odious eyes.

One night, I awoke from another drunken stupor to the sounds of breaking glass. I jumped up and stalked, naked, into the main room of the croft, to find two dark figures inside.

They turned at the sound of my bare feet on the stone floor and I roared at them and ran towards them.

They both screamed at my appearance. I must have looked terrifying. My hair was long and matted and my beard hung almost to my waist. My toenails were like talons. I was filthy and stinking and grimed and I must have seemed like some sort of wild animal to them.

They turned to run, but I caught one of them by the scruff of the neck and slammed the figure to the floor as the other made his escape.

I grabbed the throat of the intruder with both hands and squeezed with all my might, screaming incoherently at the top of my voice.

I wanted to kill. There was a mad, burning anger inside me. How dare this pathetic, useless creature come into my house! I was a God! I would wreak my revenge on this impertinent insect.

But, as I stared down, I began to realise that the figure I was choking had the face of a youngster. A boy, no more than sixteen or seventeen stared back at me in terror, his eyes bulging, his face beginning to turn blue. He was just a child. He had short dark hair and the downy face of a teenager. He reminded me of the photo I'd seen of Molly O'Brian's long dead son and I gasped in shock, letting him go.

I stood up, watching as he clutched at his throat, retching and gasping for air. He stared at me in utter terror. I saw he had pissed himself in his fear and I felt a shame that almost overcame me.

He started to climb to his feet, still watching me warily. I went and pulled open the door, standing to one side. He just stood there, dread still plain on his face.

'Come on,' I snapped. 'Get out.'

Slowly, he came towards me and the door to freedom.

When he was beside me, I placed a long-nailed hand on his arm and he froze in panic.

'Do not come back here,' I said quietly. 'It's dangerous for you. Don't come back.'

He said nothing, but suddenly fled. I listened to his footsteps disappearing into the darkness. After a few minutes I heard a car start up and saw taillights vanishing quickly. I never saw the boy or his mate again.

I closed the door and stared at my hands.

I was right to stay away from them. I had wanted to kill that boy. Not for breaking into my shit-hole of a house, but for daring to go against a being such as I. It seemed the darkness within me was almost absolute.

I thought it would not be long until I was totally merciless.

And God help humanity then.

*

I did not think that anything would change my life. I thought I would stay in my croft in Scotland forever, hiding away from humanity, both to save myself and to save them. But the attempted burglary must have altered something within me. Because, on a fine September morning in 2015, the day after the two boys had broken into my home, something changed completely.

It was as if I had suddenly woken up from a nightmare. It was quite bizarre. For some reason I suddenly felt more alive than I had done in almost twenty years. I rose from my stinking bed and looked at myself in the bathroom mirror. I saw a wild, bearded, long-haired monstrosity; I saw a beast.

I looked like an animal and I frowned at my reflection, suddenly ashamed of how I had let myself go. It was an odd feeling to be suddenly aware once more of my *self*. My appearance was suddenly so foreign to me now. A compulsion came over me then, stronger than anything I had ever experienced. I had to heed it.

I ran to the kitchen, grabbed a pair of scissors, and returned to the bathroom to start hacking away at my beard, and then I shaved it off completely. I started on my hair.

When I was finished, the sink was overflowing and my head looked like a rat had gnawed my hair off, but for the first time in decades I saw my own face staring back at me, not a stranger's. It was the same face of course, albeit grimed with dirt, but it was the face of a man, not the animal I had been.

I made a fire and turned on the boiler, having my first hot bath in as long as I could remember. I had to fill the bath twice, the water turning black from the filth caked into my skin. I cut my hideously grown toenails and fingernails. Then I dressed in clean clothes.

I looked around the croft. It had been the one place in which I had lived the longest apart from the cottage with Madeleine, and I hated it. It stank. I couldn't bear it and no longer wanted to be there. It had suddenly been consigned to my past.

Something was calling to me. Something was telling me I had to return to humanity, even though they were a species I looked upon with no more respect or curiosity than I would look upon insects. It was an urge I could not resist. I needed to be near them once more.

I picked up the keys for my Land Rover and, without a backwards glance, I closed the door of the croft behind me for the last time.

I drove south.

Part Three

XXV

The shop never made me rich, but it did make me feel something I had not felt for most of my long life. It made me happy.

It was tucked away down a side street in Kentish Town, London; and, as soon as I saw it, I knew it was the place I needed to be.

I spent almost every last penny of my money on it. Years of untouched interest accrued in various banks around Europe meant I had a sizeable amount. I bought the equipment I needed, which was very little actually, and I decorated it plainly but with a panache I never knew I possessed. I sat at a worktable by the window, carving and painting the traditional wooden toys I made and sometimes sold. I called the shop *'Madeleine's'*.

For the rest of 2015 and, indeed, for the next two-and-a-half years, I concentrated only on making my toys and learning how to run a business. By August 2018 I was earning enough to live a sparse but comfortable enough life in the one-bedroomed apartment above the shop. Slowly, after years of self-loathing, I started to live again.

I still didn't mix, of course. I couldn't. I couldn't make friends and I avoided going to the same pubs or restaurants as much as possible. I still kept myself to myself.

But, strangely, I found being alone was quite easy in a crowded metropolis such as London. The people who hurried by me on the streets were all so wrapped up in their own little worlds that they ignored anyone they came into contact with, and so I just lived my life and worked from day to day, no longer staring into an abyss of never-ending existence and never-ending darkness. The inevitability of my life remained, of course; it was just that I didn't dwell on it as much now.

It was strange how much I had changed in such a short time, and I wondered what the reason for this may have been.

I was, by then, one hundred and twenty-two years old, although I didn't think about it a lot. My face and body remained as they had always been, and I knew that, one day, I would have to close the door of *Madeleine's* for good and try my luck elsewhere. But perversely, the thought did not haunt me so much anymore. The compulsion that had made me come to London had soothed me. I felt better. I had an income, I worked at something I enjoyed, and I had a small but comfortable place to live in.

I liked London, I always had, and its noisy bustle seemed to help me begin to live again. I started to go to the theatre and the cinema once more. I even went to see a restored version of Charlie Chaplin's *The Gold Rush*, and I enjoyed it just as much as I had when I had seen it back in the 1920s. I was as settled as a man like me could be.

I believed the urge I had felt to return to humanity was the beginning of the end.

I was almost as old now as Valin had been when he passed it along to me, and I thought that maybe this was how it started. I began to believe that my vow to never pass the disease on was as useless as my desire to still be with Madeleine, whose memory was now once again, thankfully, strong within me; and as useless as trying to die before my time.

I supposed I may have had no choice in the matter. But of course, to pass it along I needed to be near other people, and that was why I had woken on that morning of 2015 and driven hundreds of miles to London. The swirling vortex of power within me was readying itself for a change of host. My end, perhaps, was in sight.

As I became reinterested in life once again, I began to wonder what had happened to the man who had made me the way I was. I looked up Valin's records, a lot easier now because of the internet. He had died in 2003, seven years after our meeting, and had been buried in a pauper's grave in Berlin.

The news of his death did not make me sad, but I felt some emotion tug at me. He had been a monster, a man who had tortured innocents in the hideous death camp of Auschwitz, but maybe he had not been the creature he became because of his own making. Perhaps it had been the touch of the lavender woman that had made him the way he was.

But I also realised that he and I were vastly different. He had never really emerged from the state of hatred for people unlike himself, even when he had once more become one of them. I had suffered that too, but I thought I may have come through the other side, or at least was beginning to.

I remembered Bruno Gombos, and the face of the young intruder in the croft, and my desire to kill them for what I saw as their effrontery to my God-like status. But I had not succumbed. I had retained some glowing ember of humanity that had stopped me from murdering them. I believe Valin would have choked them both to death without a moment's hesitation.

As well as that, though, Valin was the last of the links to my previous lives. His passing left me as the last individual from a long-gone past. I was only now truly alone.

I still viewed the humans around me as inconsequential, but the hatred—the unfounded, frightening hatred—had diminished. I didn't want anything to do with them, but I tolerated them now, which for a man such as myself was perhaps all I could hope for.

As I sat in my apartment on a balmy August evening in 2018, I raised a glass, as I always did on my birthday, to Madeleine.

I stared at her photograph, the only possession I had taken with me from the French cottage, and the hurt stabbed horrendously. I still missed her so much, even after almost fifty years. I missed our cottage. I missed dancing with her to records in front of the fire. I missed her voice, her touch, her smile. I ached for her every single day. But I thought she would have been happy at how I had dug myself from the hole of remorse and hatred I had found myself in during those years in the croft. I hoped she would be proud.

Next morning, I went downstairs to open the shop as usual. And it was on that day, the seventh of August 2018, when I met the girl who would change my life completely and permanently.

That was the day I met Pearl.

*

I spotted her as I was sitting at my place in the window. She was hanging around on the opposite side of the street, trying not to show too much obvious interest in the shop.

She looked to be about fifteen or sixteen years old. She wore pink Doc Martin boots, dungarees, and a denim jacket covered in badges. Her young face was very pretty, and her Afro was huge. Her big brown eyes skittered away from mine every time I looked up from the toy tractor I was carving. After an initial appraisal of her, I ignored her.

The next time I looked up she was standing outside the shop window, staring intently at my hands as I scraped and shaped the tractor. I smiled at her through the glass.

The bell above the door tinkled as she eventually came in. I put the tractor down onto the workbench and stood.

'Good afternoon,' I said. 'Can I help you?'

She glanced around the shelves of brightly painted toys quickly. 'Just looking,' she answered curtly, with an East End accent.

I nodded and sat back down again to work on the tractor.

She wandered around the shop, picking up toys and putting them back down again. I continued to work on the tractor, amused at this young girl pretending to be interested in my work.

I was not in the least surprised when, from the corner of my eye, I saw her place a small, carved figure into the large bag hanging from her shoulder.

She was very good though. She didn't leg it straight away. She simply continued to browse, picking up toys and putting them back. Eventually, she turned to leave. The bell tinkled again as she opened the door.

'You do know you have a carved representation of *The Little Mermaid* in your bag, don't you?' I asked, quietly, still whittling away.

She went very still. I could almost hear her heartbeat banging across the shop floor. Fight or flight? I wondered. Would she run or try to brazen it out? I was curious rather than angry.

'I ain't got nothing,' she finally said.

'Dear me. Double negatives as well.' I sighed and put down my chisel, looking her in the eyes for the first time. I raised my eyebrows and waited for her next move.

I half-expected her to make a run for it and, to be honest, I would have just let her go. I was in no mood to start chasing her down the street for a wooden toy that retailed at £17.99, but I smiled to myself at her next words.

'Just supposing I had, accidently, knocked one of your toys into the bag,' she asked. 'What if I put it back?'

I folded my hands in front of me. 'Then I suppose I would say something like, "That's all right, accidents happen". And you would put it back and leave.'

Her hand delved into the bag.

'And never come back,' I added, forcefully.

She must have seen something in my eyes then, for she nodded hesitantly. She pulled out the figure and set it back on the shelf where it belonged. She gazed at it longingly for a moment before turning to me with a questioning gaze.

I frowned. 'What's your name?' I asked.

She immediately became more suspicious. 'Why do you want to know? You going to call the coppers?'

I shook my head. 'No. I'm just curious. I'd simply like to know

237

who to look out for when I hear of a desperate thief in the vicinity,' I answered. But I smiled when I did so, and eventually she smiled back.

'Pearl,' she said. 'Pearl Tulip.'

'Pearl Tulip?' I asked. My smile broadened.

She shrugged.

We regarded each other for a while.

'Why were you attempting to steal my property, Pearl Tulip?'

The half-smile that had been there on her lips faded. 'What's it to you?'

I shrugged. 'Just curious, as I've said. And it is *my* shop you decided to pilfer from. I think I have a right to know.'

She stared at me for a second longer before seeming to slump. 'It was for my sister. It was her birthday yesterday and I can't afford to get her a present. All right?' She was defiant now.

'Yesterday?' I asked. 'August sixth?'

'Duh,' she said, scornfully. 'That's the date that usually comes before August seventh. Which is today.'

I smiled again and walked over to her, noticing the slight look of apprehension cross her face. I forget sometimes that ordinary humans see something dark in me at times. It must be a natural thing. They can sense I'm different. I picked the *Little Mermaid* up and studied it.

'What's her name?' I looked up at her. 'Your sister.'

'Precious.'

I nodded. 'Of course she is. And how old is she?'

'Why d'you want to know all this? You some sort of paedo or something?'

'Don't be disgusting,' I said. 'Answer the question.'

'She's six,' she said eventually. 'She loves *The Little Mermaid*. Ariel and all that.'

I sighed. What difference did it make? I handed her the figure. 'Give that to Precious. And tell her happy birthday from the paedo in the toyshop.'

Pearl stared at me for a long time. 'I don't owe you nothing.' It was almost said as a challenge.

'We must speak about your terrible language skills at some point,' I said, then shook my head. 'No, you don't owe me anything. Take the toy and leave.'

I thrust it into her hand, suddenly sick of the whole conversation. By the time I had sat down again, she had gone.

I thought that would be the last time I saw Pearl Tulip.

But I was wrong.

She came back the next week and tried to give me some money for *The Little Mermaid*. I refused.

'You probably nicked it,' I explained. 'I don't want to become your money launderer.'

At first it seemed she was going to take offence, something her generation seem very good at, but she saw the curl of a smile on my lips and put the money away.

I had been boiling the kettle and I asked her if she wanted a cuppa. We took the drinks to the table by the window and sat opposite each other. She indicated to the almost finished tractor on the bench.

'How long does it take?' she asked. 'From start to finish?'

I shrugged.

'As long as it has to, I suppose. This one has taken me about a week, but I don't hurry. I work on them until I think they're done. I have plenty of time.'

She nodded and sipped her tea.

'Did Precious like her present?' I asked after a while.

Pearl grinned and I felt something I had never felt before. Something strange. It seemed to steal through my frozen heart. It seemed to warm it.

I frowned, trying to work out what the feeling was, but it was elusive. I didn't know then of course, what Pearl would come to mean to me.

'She loved it,' she enthused. 'Said it was the best present she'd ever had. 'Course, it probably was, seeing as she's never really had that many.'

I didn't ask why at that point. I was still trying to work out the feelings this young girl had seemingly awoken in me.

We sat in a companionable enough silence for a while, before she finished her tea and stood to leave.

She hoisted her bag onto her shoulder. 'What's your name?' she asked.

'Rob,' I answered without thinking.

'See you then, Rob,' she said, waving goodbye with a flick of her hand. The bell above the door tinkled, and she was gone.

I sat for a long time as my tea got cold, searching myself for what her presence had brought up within me. Then I shrugged and got on with completing the tractor.

She came back the next day for another cup of tea. And the next.

Before long, I had handed her a work apron and I was showing her how to carve some basic pieces; just simple figurines at the beginning, but quickly moving onto more complicated work.

I watched her, smiling, over the next few months. She was good. She had an eye for the natural grain of the wood and before long she was creating completely new figures. We painted and varnished them, and I placed them on the shelves next to my own.

'The first one sold is mine,' I told her. 'It'll cover the money you owe me, but anything after that, the profit will go to you. After tax, of course.'

She was delighted. Her figures became quite popular and I ended up handing over a decent amount of money. Nothing to me, but for Pearl it was a fortune.

It was still the school holidays when she had first come in and her visits had become a daily occurrence. She continued to call in on evenings and weekends when school started again. Over her time in my shop I began to find out about her and her life. It wasn't that pleasant.

Her father had come from Ghana and had met her mother at a local nightclub. She quickly fell pregnant with Pearl. They had very little money, so they moved into a bit of a desperate tower block where assorted criminals and drug dealers haunted the desolate walkways day and night.

When Precious was born, her father, a complete bastard by the sound of him, had upped and left. He reappeared every now and again, but those visits were usually not pleasant. He was a violent man and Pearl's mother had suffered from his fists on numerous occasions.

The last time he had entered their lives he had broken her mother's nose and Pearl had tried to defend her, earning herself a beating too. He had disappeared after that and Pearl had no idea where he was now, and certainly didn't care. She hadn't heard anything from him for three years and hoped she would never meet him again.

Her mother had struggled on, working in a laundromat during the day and a pub at night. Pearl had grown up quickly, looking after her little sister when she got in from school, making her meals, putting her to bed. She had turned into a surrogate mother for Precious and their bond was very close.

I said nothing as she told me this. I didn't know how to respond. I'd lived a life of such extreme loneliness that I had no words of comfort for someone who had seen so much of the bad side of the world from such an early age. I just nodded, but that strange feeling in my heart seemed to twist with anger and despair at her story.

One day after school, she brought Precious into the shop.

She was a tiny double of her big sister and she stood with wide eyes, holding Pearl's hand as I showed her a figure I had just finished. It was of a princess and she was captivated with it. When they left I gave it to her, and she took it and hugged my leg.

I stiffened at this contact at first. But then I put my hand on her head and ruffled her hair.

'Thank you,' she said, politely.

I gritted my teeth and swallowed hard as that strange feeling rushed through me again. It was weird. They both had the same effect on me.

'You're welcome,' I managed.

After they had gone I sat back at the worktable, staring into nothing and frowning. I shook my head.

What the hell was happening to me?

XXVI

One day, almost a year after our first encounter, Pearl came, as usual, into the shop. I frowned at the sight of her. I had noticed changes in her appearance for a while, and they were worrying me for some reason. I wondered why that was. What was she to me? But I worried all the same.

She seemed to be losing weight. Not much, but noticeable. She had strange bruises on her arms and once, while we were having one of our cups of tea together, her nose suddenly started bleeding and it took ages to stop the flow. Her visits had become less frequent of late, and when I asked her why she said she 'had a cold'.

Yes. I worried about her, and I wondered at that worry.

Why was I bothered? They were all pointless. They all just buzzed around me like droning flies, so why should I care about a few bruises and a bit of weight loss?

I didn't know why. I just did.

On that day, she came in and smiled a wan smile at me.

'Want a cuppa?' I asked and she nodded but, when I went into the back room, I heard a thump and a gasp of pain. I ran back into the shop to find her slumped on the floor, her nose bleeding again. This time, it wouldn't seem to stop. I was beginning to panic slightly at the force of the flow. The floor was awash, and I started to think I would have to call for an ambulance but, slowly, it began to ease and eventually stopped.

I sat her down at the table and got her a glass of water which she lifted to her mouth with trembling fingers.

'What the hell's wrong with you, Pearl?' I asked her. 'Look at you. You're not well. Have you seen a doctor recently?'

She shook her head. 'I'm fine, I've just had a bit of a bug recently. Can't seem to shake it. I'll be fine.'

'You need to see a doctor,' I repeated.

She frowned at me, seemingly annoyed at my insistence. 'What's it to you?' she asked, defiantly.

I kept quiet, and she seemed to soften

'Sorry,' she muttered. 'I'm not myself right now. Didn't mean to take it out on you.'

I nodded, but I wondered at her words. What *was* it to me?

'Come on,' I said, eventually. 'I'll give you a lift home.'

Pearl usually came into town on the bus, but I was worried her nose might start bleeding again so I drove her, the first time I had seen where she lived. We stopped outside the block of flats. Pearl saw me looking around the desolate landscape.

'Not like your place, is it.'

I just smiled.

It wasn't. It was pretty bleak. We were parked beside what had once been a playground but was now deserted and dusty. Broken glass littered the ground, accompanied by the odd used condom.

Pearl made to get out of the car but froze when she spotted a figure approaching.

'Shit,' she whispered.

'What?'

She turned to me, fear in her eyes.

'It's my dad.'

She got out to face the man coming towards us. He was a well-built guy of about forty, with a shaved head and what seemed like a permanent frown on his face. He was dressed in baggy jeans and a white t-shirt. A huge, chunky, gold necklace decorated his bull-like neck. I got out too and stood beside Pearl as he stopped in front of us. His eyes were a yellowish colour and his breath stank of booze.

'Where's your mother?' he growled at Pearl. Four years. He hadn't seen his daughter in almost four years, and this was his opening gambit.

Pearl stood her ground, although I could see she was frightened. 'She ain't here. She's at work. She don't want to see you.'

'I don't care if she don't want to see me,' he said. He had a strong African accent that seemed to drip with sarcasm. 'I want to see my wife.'

Pearl said nothing and he took a threatening step towards her. I stood forward and he halted, staring at me.

'Who the fuck are you?' he snarled. 'You her boyfriend or something?'

The idea was preposterous to me but I could see why he might think that. I only looked about four or five years older than Pearl.

'No, I'm just a friend. But I don't think Pearl wants to talk to you, and she's already told you her mother isn't here. Maybe you should just leave.'

He looked at me with an exaggerated demonstration of disdain.

'This got nothing to do with you, motherfucker. Move out the way. I want to talk to my girl here.' He grinned at Pearl. His teeth were as yellow as his eyes. He seemed like he was high on something.

'No.' I said. 'Just leave, eh? Do us all a favour.'

I could sense the old anger bubbling up inside me. It had been a while since I last felt its touch, but I had to clench my fists to keep my hands from his throat as it coursed through me now.

Who the hell did he think he was? Threatening, bullying. Frightening his own daughter with his menacing presence. I tried to keep myself calm.

But he had already started down the path he mistakenly thought was for the best.

He shook his head and made his move; he had obviously run out of words. As Pearl had indicated, he was a violent man and he was accustomed to using brute force to get what he wanted in life.

He swung a sledgehammer of a punch that would have laid me out had it landed. But it didn't get anywhere near. I had a hundred years of experience on him, and that old anger suddenly burst from me.

I ducked the initial blow and, while I was down there, I gave him a quick, hard punch to the balls. He hissed and bent forward, clutching at the sudden pain as I knew he would, and I instantly straightened, the top of my head smacking into his face.

He staggered backwards and I stepped towards him, belting my left fist into his already-bleeding nose. I distinctly heard it crack as I did so.

He howled at this second wounding and brought his hands up to his injured face, again as I knew he would, and my next punch went straight into his unprotected solar plexus.

The wind went out of him with a great whoosh of air and he staggered back again. My final blow crunched into his throat and he gurgled and sank to the ground amongst the broken glass and broken bricks. He lay on his side, concentrating on simply trying to breathe.

His downfall had taken only seconds, but I was livid now, the anger and hatred pouring from me in a cold, dark stream.

This piece of shit deserved everything I was going to give him. He would remember this encounter for the rest of his days. I drew a foot back, ready to smash it into his split and bleeding face.

But a hand grabbed my arm and I whirled round, seeing Pearl shrink away from the expression on my face.

I don't know what I looked like, but I saw the terror in her eyes, the sudden realisation that the man she thought she knew was perhaps very different to what she had previously believed.

The look in her eyes stopped me. The red mist of battle cleared.

'Don't hit him anymore, Rob,' she whispered in a frightened voice. 'He's had enough.'

I took in a deep breath, closing my eyes for a second, willing the darkness away. By the time I had opened them, Pearl had bent down beside her father.

'You need to leave,' she said to him. 'You need to leave and not come back. You're not welcome here.'

He looked like he was going to hiss some sort of retort at her, but I took a menacing step towards him and he flinched, dragging himself to his feet.

He looked at me, his nose swollen and bleeding, his face battered. Then he turned to Pearl.

'You ain't worth the fucking bother,' he muttered, then turned and stumbled away, wiping his broken nose roughly on his t-shirt.

I leaned against the car and took out a cigarette. My hands were rock steady as I lit it.

Pearl turned to me. There was a strange look in her eye now, as if something had happened that she had never expected. As if a trusted family dog had suddenly turned and savaged someone.

We stared at each other for a long time then, without another word, she turned and walked towards the flats. She disappeared inside.

I finished the cigarette and climbed into the car. I waited for hours, watching, making sure her deadbeat father didn't reappear. I watched as Precious came home, holding hands with a stocky woman in her forties whom I presumed was her mother. They went inside. I waited another hour before driving back to the shop, where I poured myself a proper drink.

It hadn't gone. Whatever the anger was, it was still there. My hatred of them was still there, I knew it. Because when I'd beaten Pearl's wayward father into the ground, it hadn't just been because of necessity.

I had enjoyed it.

*

Pearl kept away for a few weeks, but eventually she came back. She seemed even thinner than when I'd seen her last. She thanked me for my help with her father and confirmed he hadn't been back.

She seemed listless, however. Quieter. She looked like she had a lot to think about.

We sat at the table and picked up our respective pieces of work, but she just stared out of the window at the passers-by. Her eyes seemed sunken, her face a greyish hue. She looked unwell.

And so, on that July day in 2019, I asked her again what was wrong with her, because by then, I knew something was. And I knew it was serious. I just stared at her, at a loss for words, as she told me.

'Leukaemia,' she said, staring down at her cup of tea. 'It's like a blood cancer.'

I nodded. I knew what it was. I just didn't understand why a person as dynamic, as wonderful, as Pearl should get it. She, amongst all the people on the planet, did not deserve it.

'Apparently, it's pretty bad,' she continued. 'It's called chronic lymphocytic leukaemia.' She stumbled over the words. 'They don't think it'll go away.'

I couldn't speak; I was utterly shocked. The news was even worse than I had imagined, and I had imagined quite a few different scenarios. She had obviously known about it for a while. It was eating her up.

'Can I do anything?' I asked uselessly, and she laughed without humour.

'No. I don't want to talk about it, Rob.' She took a sip of her tea. 'Let's not talk about it,' she repeated.

When she was gone and I had locked up, I went up to the apartment and stood in front of my reflection in the bathroom.

That damnable face stared back out at me.

*

Over the next couple of months, Pearl began her chemotherapy. She lost her wonderful hair. She became stick-like.

Her visits to the shop became less and less frequent. The final time she came, she fell asleep over the figurine she now found so difficult to work on. I picked her up and lay her on the sofa in the corner of the room, covering her with a blanket. I stood over her, watching her as she slept, just as I had stood over Madeleine when her illness had first become apparent.

My mind was in turmoil. I could see this young girl literally dying in front of me and the feelings I had for her seemed to twist at my heart. Why the worry? Why the anguish? Humans were designed to live and die and disappear. Why did this one girl make any difference to me? Millions of people had died during my long life, either through war or famine or disease, and my darkening soul had dismissed them all without a second thought. Why was she so special?

I tried to put it down to the changes that had occurred within me since I'd left the croft four years before. Maybe that was the way it went. Maybe the beginning of the end was foretold somehow in a change of attitude within those who had caught the infection of life. Perhaps a rising humanity meant that the idea to live on became more and more abhorrent. Perhaps my feelings towards Pearl were simply a symptom of the power inside me getting ready to leave.

Perhaps.

But I remembered Valin and his eternal hatred of humanity, still smothering him in darkness long after the infection had left him, the abhorrence he felt towards them still so strong, and I knew that this was different. This was personal.

Pearl's eyes opened and she stared at me. I smiled and knelt beside her, pulling the blanket tighter around her shoulders.

'Hey,' I whispered, softly. 'You can't be sleeping on the job, you know. I'll have to dock your wages.'

She didn't smile back, but instead, she reached out a thin arm and touched my face. I felt tears pricking in my eyes at the look on her face and forced myself to swallow them down. Her features were serene, but they were also resigned. Resigned to the inevitable. She seemed to understand the raging emotions twisting inside me.

'It's okay, Rob,' she whispered. 'It's all okay. You've been a good friend, and I know you're sad, but it's all okay. It's just the way it is.'

My lip was trembling slightly as I grasped her hand on my cheek and rubbed it gently with my thumb. I had not felt anything like this since Madeleine had left me, all those years ago.

'I'll be going soon, I think,' she continued, and I shook my head in denial, but she just smiled softly at me for the first time.

'It's okay,' she repeated. 'I think I'm ready now. Had enough.'

Her hand fell away, and she just stared at me.

'I'm pleased I met you, Rob Deakin,' she murmured as sleep once again overtook her. I tucked her in again and went and stared out of the window, my head in turmoil, my emotions whirling.

I cursed life. Why had I found this wonderful girl now, when she was going to die? What was the point in making me feel like this towards her when she was being snatched away?

I roughly wiped a hand across my eyes, my reflection in the window showing a steely hardness spread across my features. I shook my head.

I would not succumb to this. Whatever it was, I would not succumb to it.

I woke Pearl roughly and drove her home.

*

She didn't return to the shop and I tried to get on with my life. I told myself to forget about Pearl Tulip. The weeks dragged on. I couldn't forget her.

I hated myself again. I wanted to go and see her, to sit with her and talk of things that had nothing to do with her illness. I wanted her to open the door of the shop with a tinkle of the bell and smile at me and sit opposite me and for us to drink our tea and quietly carve our toys and figurines together. I wanted things to be the way they had been. I missed her immensely, but I couldn't bring myself to visit her, because then I would be giving in to the sensation which the thought of her brought about. Giving in to the one thing that could destroy me.

And then, one day, Precious came into the shop.

I frowned and went over to her, looking around for whoever should have been with her.

'How did you get here?' I asked her.

'On the bus,' she replied, matter-of-factly. 'Pearl wants to see you.'

I stared down at her, shaking my head.

'No. I don't want to.'

Precious's eyes were full of unshed tears as she stared at me, and that feeling I had for her sister, whatever the hell it was, attacked me again.

'She says you've got to. She says she wants to see you. She says you have to go to the hospital. Before it's too late.'

'Don't say things like that,' I snapped at her, making her jump and causing a tear to finally break free and trickle down her cheek.

I hunched down in front of her and gently wiped the tear from her face. 'I'm sorry, Precious. But I can't. I'm not built for that.'

I could see she didn't understand.

'I just can't,' I repeated. 'Come on, I'll take you home.'

She looked at me despondently but said nothing. I closed the shop and drove her to her flat. I watched as she walked into the tower block entrance.

I once again sat in the car as the evening drew on and darkness fell. I saw Precious and her mother come out and stand at the bus stop. I watched the bus collect them and take them to the hospital. To Pearl.

I went home.

*

I tried once again to forget about them all. But that feeling—I was finally beginning to recognise it as some sort of new emotion— wouldn't leave me alone. I sat for hours in the shop window, staring into nothing, blind to the people walking past outside.

The window was like an analogy of my life. I was separated

from every other person in the world by an invisible screen, and had been for over a hundred years. I once again thought about how different I was to them.

I shook my head. What difference did it make to me that another of their kind died? I shouldn't go to the hospital. It was a stupid idea. It was nothing to do with me.

But then another feeling came upon me, a feeling of the utmost urgency. It was the same as when I'd woken that day in the croft in Scotland and cut off my hair, beginning my journey back to life again. That same feeling washed through me now. I could do nothing about it even though I cursed myself for what it told me to do.

I went to the hospital.

It was the first of September 2019. It had been a hot summer and the day was sweltering. I drove into the car park and switched off the engine, staring through the windscreen at the trees around the hospital and the clear blue sky.

I shouldn't go in. I should turn the engine back on and drive home, forget about Pearl and Precious and their mother. They were nothing to me.

But as I sat in the car, telling myself lies, I suddenly realised what the emotion was that Pearl had dredged up in me. I suddenly knew what I felt about her, and the revelation was shocking.

The feeling was love. Not the fierce, passionate love I'd had for Madeleine, but rather a different, warmer feeling. The feeling I believed a father, a good father, would have for his daughter. I wanted to protect Pearl. I wanted to stop the disease in her body. I wanted her to get better and live a life of joy and happiness.

That was it. My feelings had been jaded for so long that I didn't even recognise them anymore for what they were.

I just wanted Pearl to be happy.

I climbed out of the car and went inside the building.

I was directed to the ward she was on. I wandered down the corridor, glancing in on awful tableaus of children lying in beds, dying. Some had their relatives surrounding them, some were alone.

This is what it always comes down to, I thought. This is how life always finishes. At the end, no matter who you are, or what you've had in life, in the last moments you are truly alone.

Death. The only true meaning of life.

I found the room where Pearl lay. Precious and her mother were by her bedside. They turned when I came in and Precious whispered something to her mother, probably explaining who I was. I ignored them and looked down at Pearl.

Once again, the sight of her caused a pricking behind my eyes as I stared down at the figure on the bed.

She was thin and grey and bald. She was sleeping, or had been induced into sleep by drugs, I didn't know which. She had a tube up her nose and another stuck in her arm, attached to a plastic bag filled with some sort of clear solution. She looked awful.

Something caught in my throat as I looked at her, and I wondered why this young girl, whom I had known for only a few short months in my long, long life, had stirred up such feelings within me. Of all the people I had known, all the lives I had lived, it all came down to this urchin-like girl, dying in a hospital bed because of some damnable disease.

I asked, with a glance at her mother, if I could sit, and she nodded. Her face was as drawn and grey as her daughter's.

We all sat in silence, just gazing at Pearl's sleeping face. Her mother said nothing to me, and I said nothing to her. After an hour or so, Precious fell asleep in her mother's arms.

I had stood to leave before the girls' mother spoke. She didn't look up from her daughter, and her voice was desultory. 'Thank you for coming.'

That feeling, that God-damned feeling, choked in my throat.

There was such a helplessness in the woman's voice, such a maudlin hopelessness. Her daughter was slipping away from her and there was not a thing she could do about it. She didn't even want to glance up at the face of the man her daughter had known. She didn't want to waste even a second of not looking at Pearl, the girl she had brought forth into the world and who was now slipping out of it alone.

As I stood there, not knowing how to handle the newly discovered emotions within me, I saw a tear well in one eye and trickle down her face. She didn't even blink. She just continued to stare at Pearl.

'I'll come back tomorrow,' I said, finally.

She nodded, her eyes still on her daughter.

I left them: the woman with one safe, sleeping daughter in her arms and another on the verge of being taken away from her forever.

I drove back to the apartment, sitting staring out of the window at the night outside. I smoked cigarettes endlessly.

I felt the same about Pearl's situation as I had all those years ago when comrades had not returned to the trenches, their bodies decorating No Man's Land like grotesque Christmas baubles. Then, as now, I wondered what the point was in it all. Why should a girl like Pearl, dragged up in the harshest of conditions she had no say in, suffer what she was suffering? No chance of getting better? No chance of recovery? Why should a mother have to watch her child die?

For the first time in years I opened a bottle of whiskey, but the first swallow reminded me of my dark time in the croft and swamped me with countless faces, countless memories. I poured it down the sink.

The unfairness for Pearl and her family weighed upon me. I couldn't understand why it had to happen to her. Why it had to happen to anyone, but especially not that spirited, wilful, wonderful young woman with barely sixteen years completed on the planet.

She wasn't even yet an adult, she was just a child. Not even eighteen: the age I had been when I so casually joined up for what I'd thought would be an adventure. And what had turned out to be a nightmare.

My long life screamed in my mind. Faces I had almost forgotten, things I had done, places I had seen.

It wasn't fair. How could life be so immense for one person and so brief for another? Especially when that other had seen only its dark side and deserved so much more.

And a thought came to me then.

I shook my head. No. I had vowed not.

But it came again. And, once born, it stayed.

I stood up and stared into the mirror above the fireplace. My face—my same damned face—stared back at me, white with the insidious idea crawling inside my head.

'No,' I said aloud. But the thought persisted.

I could save her. I had something no one else had. I had eternity flowing through my veins.

I was infected with life.

I could pass the infection on. I could make Pearl whole again.

I frowned at my reflection.

'No,' I said again. 'I promised. No.'

But the life within me would not be quiet. It had told me what it wanted. The thought had been born and it grew inside me. I wanted to. I wanted to pass it along so much!

I remembered what Valin had said to me. That one day, I would be unable to stop it. It was the way things were. Maybe I had come to that time. God knows I had lived long enough, and why not use the power within me to help someone I knew was worth it?

But the results. Oh God, the results if I did.

Life. Endless life. Could I subject Pearl to something like that, knowing what I had been through? Everything I'd seen, both good and bad? The deaths of everyone and everything I had ever loved?

No.

I could not.

I would not.

I would not turn Pearl into a monster. Into a freak. She was better off dying.

But as I lay in bed that night, staring at the ceiling, the thought that had been born spread through my body like an unassailable itch. I believed I needed to soon pass it along. I began to think I didn't have any choice and never had.

Someone was soon going to have it passed along to them.

As my eyes finally closed, as my exhausted body slipped into sleep, one thought seemed to stay with me.

Why not Pearl?

XXVII

Over the next few days I became more and more fixated with the idea of passing it along. My previous determination to not do so was scattering with every minute of every day. I felt what I believe drug addicts must feel when they are going through withdrawal. Everything was centred on passing along my disease.

I fought against it constantly. Even though I'd promised I would visit Pearl again, I kept away. I didn't trust myself, and I hated myself for not seeing her. She could die at any minute. She may have already died, as I brushed my teeth or made a cup of tea or ate my evening meal. As I lived my selfish life. She could be gasping out her last breath while I lay in bed, breathing just one more of billions I had breathed before.

Yes, I hated myself. For staying away, for my indecision, for my want to touch her chest and to pour that power, that infection, that *gift* into her. To see her eyes open and her mouth smile… Wouldn't that be worth the downside? Wouldn't it be worth the knowledge that one day she would curse my memory for what I had done to her?

I was in a constant flux, forever on the verge of going to the hospital and yet holding myself hostage at the shop. I couldn't sleep and was lethargic, yet I couldn't stay still for more than an hour at a time. The thought twisted and heaved within me; it wouldn't let me go.

I was sitting by the window at the table on a muggy Tuesday afternoon, exhausted by yet another sleepless night, when Pearl's mother came into the shop.

My throat seemed to close. A cold, cold flash of something flushed through my system.

She was dead! She was dead and I had failed her. I, her supposed friend, the only person who could have done something about it. The only person who could have stopped it.

She glanced around the toys on the shelves and a sad smile flickered across her mouth as she looked at the figures Pearl had made. She turned to me as I stood.

'She's still there,' she said in response to my ashen face.

I sighed, relieved, and went across to her and took her hand, leading her to the chair where Pearl had sat so many times.

'You said you would come back to see her,' she said. It was an accusation.

I sat down opposite her. 'I know, but...' I didn't know what to say. 'It's hard,' I managed.

She nodded. She seemed more composed than the last time I had seen her. But I realised that was wrong. She was not composed. She was just resigned to the inevitable.

'Yes, it is. It's very hard. But that does not make it right that you don't spend her last day with her. She said you were her best friend. How can you desert her now?'

Best friend? I felt that emotion claw at my heart again.

'Last day?' I asked, fearfully.

She was making an effort not to cry, I could see that.

'She wanted you there. At the end. She told me weeks ago. When she could still speak. They're turning off the machine today. We've made the decision. Precious and I don't want her to suffer anymore. You need to be there. I've come away from her side to collect you. She might have died while I was gone, but I know my Pearl. She would have wanted me to try.'

She spoke these words in a flat monotone that conversely held all the emotion of an already grieving mother. I couldn't speak. Something was wrong with my eyes. I couldn't see properly.

'Where's Precious?' I managed to croak.

'Still at the hospital. The nurses there are very good. They said they would look after her for me until I came back with you. But we have to go. Now. Please.'

Her voice remained flat and metallic as she spoke, but I could sense the urgency in her. I knew that if Pearl went before she got back to her she would never have forgiven herself.

I stared at her, the life inside me pounding at me to stand. To go with her. To pass it along to Pearl. But still I resisted.

'I don't even know your name,' I said to her. I was stalling. I knew it.

She smiled, sadly. 'That's the reason Pearl came here in the first place. She said she'd found a shop that sold the best toys Precious would ever have, and she knew this as soon as she saw it. She said it was fate. My name is Madeleine. Now please. Come with me.'

I think my heart actually stopped for a second. I managed to swallow.

Fate, Pearl had called it. I have never believed in fate. I have said this so many times.

She put out her hand for me to go with her.

I took it.

*

She had come on the bus. Her daughter may have died at any minute, and she had taken a bus to go and collect the only other person her daughter wanted to be there at her side. Her friend. We took my car back to the hospital.

Heavy clouds were building as we parked up, and a flash of lightning momentarily lit the sky. Rain began to patter on the vehicle's roof as a growl of thunder rolled across the city. For some reason the noise reminded me of the last roars of those artillery guns back in November 1918. I felt the same sensation I'd had then of some form of new beginning. Or, perhaps, a sense of something ending. We went inside and rode up the elevator in a heavy silence. The lift was taking us to a place where everything would end. Life, love, hope.

We were walking faster as we went along the corridor to the room where Pearl lay. Was she still alive?

We went in.

Precious was sitting with a young nurse at the table in the corner. They were playing snap. Pearl lay with the tubes sticking out of her all over.

As soon as we stepped inside the door, it was as if Pearl had been waiting for us to get there; as if she was making her own choice of when she would die. The machine monitoring her clicked loudly and squealed a monotone note. We all looked at it. The line went flat.

*

It was only the nurse who moved at first.

She calmly went to the machine, checking the numbers as they fell, fell, fell away.

She turned to Madeleine and Precious. Her eyes were very kind, but also devoid of hope. Madeleine jerked a breath into her lungs, the noise loud in the sudden shocked silence. Precious stared at her sister with huge eyes, the reality of what was happening just beginning to register on her face.

For myself, I remember gazing at Pearl with a hunger I could not contain. I felt like a vampire. I could not take my eyes from her body as it began to die in front of me.

I felt something flood through my body; I cannot describe it. It was a desperate, animalistic need. I could not have controlled it even if I wanted to. I had to touch her. I had to touch Pearl.

It was as if she were a light and I was a moth. I swear I was not in control of my own body as I stepped towards her, my arm already rising in front of me.

Far away, as if the sound was coming from a distant galaxy, I heard Madeleine make that jerky noise again and part of me suddenly realised it was the beginning of weeping, but I ignored it. The nurse was watching me, but she didn't seem to be moving. Didn't seem to be breathing. Another flicker of lightning lit up the window and more thunder boomed. Everything around me slowed.

And stopped.

The thunder outside continued to growl; sounding like a never-ending barrel rolling across a wooden floor, and the lightning flickered endlessly, creating stark black-and-white compositions in the room.

And suddenly, like a white-hot explosion of knowledge and understanding, I realised everything. I suddenly realised the truth of my disease. It spoke to me. I swear to God, in that millisecond of endlessness, the disease spoke to me. It showed me everything. It showed me what it was.

The infection that ran through me was, indeed, life, just as Valin had said. But not life as he and I had believed. This life was an alien, timeless life. It was a life *eternal.*

I was infected with its eternity, and, in that golden, electrifying moment, it slowed time down to such a degree that I seemed to be the only living thing in the room. Madeleine and Precious and the nurse were just window-dressing in a scene that showed me standing by Pearl's bed, knowledge from the entire universe soaring through my mind.

It showed me the beginning of everything. Standing in that hospital room in London, I saw oceans swell and trees grow. I smelt the warm, damp odour of life manifesting itself on the planet. I saw tiny, mindless amoebae turning and twisting into the first version of life. I watched fish swim, saw them struggle onto land, saw them change and adapt. I saw life begin. The infection showed me what it was. What it had always been.

It had been there from the very beginning of the universe.

It was the first lifeform that had ever existed and was itself the instigator for all life on this planet. Its huge age battered at my sanity. It showed me its endless existence. Every second of its life fell upon me like a billion knives and I screamed at their touch. The infection burned with pain and horror, and that pain swept through me now. I felt its hideous, unwanted life.

And it told me something then that I had never once, not *once* in all my years of existence, had ever even begun to realise.

It told me it wanted to die.

Like me, and like everyone it had infected eventually felt, it craved its own death. It had lived too long. It had done what it was designed to do. It had created life. But it had been somehow trapped, moving from infected person to infected person. Never ending, never knowing why.

Pointless.

Those feelings of hatred and animosity. All the darkness that had flowed through my veins. They had not been *my* feelings. They had been the twisted, ancient emotions of the force within me. The force that had kept me alive but had soured my soul.

I was not the instigator of them. They were the bitter remnants of something that had wished for its death a million times over. As it craved it now. The disease wanted to pass it along.

The revelation almost killed me there and then. The life force, the infection. Whatever being or creature it was, it was older than time itself and it screamed at me to release it from its eternal prison. It begged me. And then it showed me something else. It showed me something wonderful.

It showed me that I could free it. It told me what it would do for Pearl if I did. But it also showed me the cost of that act.

And it was a cost I was so happy to pay.

All the others like me: Valin, the woman who had touched him, whoever had touched her, going back and back and back through time. They had all been given this desperate choice at the end, I knew that now. But none of them had even recognised what the choice was, that there even *was* a choice, and therefore each time it had been denied.

I remembered Valin saying he thought he had lived on long after the infection left him because of the remnants of its power. What he had so wrongly called his God-like status.

And he had been right. The infection had somehow rebooted him, renewed him, left him with the remains of its immense power for years to come. But he, like everyone else who had ever passed it along, had passed it along to a stranger. Simply the first person they had met who fitted the profile they needed. Someone close to death, found at the right time. When the souls of the infected were finally swamped by the horror the infection itself felt every single second and had felt for a billion years and more.

The people they had found had meant nothing to them; they were simply strangers to whom the disease could be passed on to. How the transfer would impact on the infection itself had never been considered, had never even been fully realised, because what happened to the people who received the infection was not the overriding reason for the transference in the first place. And neither was what happened to the infection. So the disease had been passed from person to person; a prisoner of its own existence, lost and alone in its own never-ending, horrifying existence.

I felt that horror now, the infection had shown me. I knew what it meant.

I suddenly knew how to save Pearl. I couldn't have saved Madeleine, but I could save Pearl. I knew how to make her better. And I knew why it was her who would finally bring peace for the power broiling inside me. Unlike all those who had gone before me, I had listened to its plea.

Because I loved Pearl. She was not a stranger; she was not just an empty vessel to be filled with the curse of never-ending life. I loved her like a father loved his daughter. And any father, if he had this choice within him, would have given it in a heartbeat. What happened to me did not matter.

I could save Pearl. I could save Pearl and I could free the infection. And I could free *me*. For a while at least.

I stared at her face, knowing that nothing could stop the transference from taking place. It was nature, even if it was nature of a twisted and secret kind. It had been part of the world since its inception. And I could give it what it had wanted for so long. I could make it end.

I stared at Pearl. I could not take my eyes from her.

I touched her chest.

*

I felt it move away from me.

I swear I felt it leave me and enter Pearl. It seemed to drive headlong, joyously, from my body into hers, released at last from its endless jail. It *pushed* itself into her, the warm, spreading flux seeping, *pouring* from my palm.

I saw the life force blasting from me to Pearl like a boisterous dog bursting into a new home. I envisioned it as old Hector, excitedly rushing from room to room, sniffing happily and trying to take in everything at once, full of glee and investigation and freedom. Soon he would hunt down what was wrong in Pearl. Soon he would re-energise every single cell in her body. Soon she would be healed. He would do what he had always done.

But this time, unlike every other time before, and like the faithful hound he had always been, Hector would retrieve her illness. He would fetch that disease back to his old master. He would take it away from Pearl and bring it to me before finally, after a millennia of existence, he would curl up in front of the fire. He would close his old eyes, thankfully, and sleep forever.

For this was what the infection had wanted for so long. This was the deal that had been made. The option that only a father would take.

I smiled as I passed it along.

And the transference occurred.

*

Everything seemed to come back to me with a bang and I swayed. The lightning flashed and then disappeared and the thunder tailed off into the distance. The nurse grabbed my arm and led me to the seat she had been sitting on. She checked me over briefly. I suddenly broke down and wept uncontrollably and I think she thought it was grief, but it wasn't. I wept with joy.

Joy and fear.

She then turned to Madeleine, who was somehow hunched over Pearl now. I hadn't seen her move, I don't know how she got from the door to the bed without me seeing. Whatever I had witnessed there by Pearl's bed, it was gone now. Gone forever. Madeleine was weeping, whispering Pearl's name over and over, and stroking her head gently. She was letting her daughter go.

I felt a hand on my arm and turned to see Precious staring at me, her young eyes aghast at the emotion and fear in the room. But I wiped my eyes and smiled at her, lifting her onto my knee, cuddling her into me.

'It's going to be all right,' I said, over and over. 'It's going to be fine. You'll see.'

The nurse left us to our grief, closing the door to the room behind her softly. I sat and hugged Precious whilst Madeleine hugged her other daughter who lay, still and silent on the bed. I think we stayed there a long time as the storm built and died outside, but I don't know how long.

Time didn't matter to me anymore.

Eventually I said we had to leave. Madeleine and Precious said their goodbyes to Pearl. I didn't.

I took them home and dropped them off. Very soon they would be getting a phone call. Very soon they would be getting a miracle, and I didn't want to be there when it happened.

I drove around for hours in the now light drizzle, not seeing where I went, not knowing what to think.

I was different. I could feel it. Whatever that power was, whatever it had done to me, it was now gone. It was a frightening, but somehow liberating feeling. I felt that, at last, I could now be who I wanted to be, what I wanted to be. For however long I had left.

I was free.

And so was Pearl. I had saved her. The infection, the power, the force, whatever it had been, it would heal her disease and then disappear. It would die, thankfully and comfortably. To begin whatever voyage is on the other side for all of us.

I got back to the apartment and saw there was already a message on the answerphone. I knew what it was. I didn't need to listen.

I also knew what would happen to me. When, I had no idea, but I believed it would be soon. Very soon.

Ever since that warm, bright, sunny August day in 1914, when everything had seemed possible, I had done my duty to the best of my ability. I had paid a heavy price for it.

But my duty was now over.

XXVIII

The years once more moved swiftly by.

2019 ended and 2020 burst upon the planet like a vengeful god. Once again, just as I had witnessed in 1919, a tiny, invisible germ showed humanity just how insignificant it was. That year was bad, very bad, and many a family lost loved ones but, as everything does, it eventually ended.

By sixth of August 2022, things were moving quickly for me. I was a sick man. The chemotherapy had extended my prognosis but it was never going to save me. I didn't think I had long left and in fact, just a few months before, I had told them I no longer wanted to continue with it. It was too awful. I was sick of the vomit and the pain. Best just to leave it now.

I ruminated constantly on my life. I'd had so much longer than most people get. One hundred and twenty-six years old was, I believed, a world record for longevity and, now that it was coming to an end, I was stupidly beginning to fear its completion.

Not that anyone knew about it of course. Apart from Pearl.

She would live a normal life because of the bargain between me and the strange power that had once lived within me. She would have the same chance as everyone else does to love and laugh and cry. She would have the same chance to live and die. I secretly believed it would be quite a while before she did die, but she would at least grow old normally. She would have children and they would pass on her wonderful genes to the next generation. The infection was now gone. It no longer existed in anyone.

It certainly did not exist in me. The diagnosis of the same leukaemia that Pearl had was given to me a year after she awoke and terrified the nurse in the room with her. They said that, with the right treatment, I could expect to live a good five to ten years but, as I'd now stopped the chemotherapy, I didn't know how long was left for me. At least my hair was starting to grow back, which was something. This had been the secret bargain between that power and me. It was a one-off transference, and it had happened because I had wanted Pearl to live. Not to just rid myself of eternal life, but because she needed to survive.

And because I loved her. Totally and unconditionally. The infection had known this and it had been easy for us both. We had both wanted the same thing.

I was stretching my legs in the local park when my phone rang. I dug it out of my jeans pocket.

'Hi, Pearl, how you doing?'

'Hiya,' came the answer. 'Where are you? I'm at the shop but you're not here.'

'That's because I'm here.'

'Lol,' she said, dryly. 'I've got a birthday present for you.'

'What is it?'

'Well if you were here, you'd know,' she answered. 'So you coming back, or what?'

'Nope. It's far too nice a day to be cooped up, cooking in a shop window. I'm taking the day off.'

'Nice,' she muttered. 'Is it still on for tonight, then?'

'Yes. Bring your mum and Presh over for seven. I'm cooking vegetarian.'

'Why, for God's sake?'

'Some of us have to look after ourselves now, you know. No more of that smoking malarkey or drinking too much. It's the gym twice a week for me.'

There was a pause as Pearl silently contemplated this useless jollity.

'You've been saying that since you joined and you still haven't been.' There was a sadness in her voice, and I cursed myself for putting it there.

I forced myself to laugh.

'Seven. Be there or be square.'

'You are such a dork,' she said, and closed the call. I continued my walk through the park. The grass was littered with people out enjoying the sun, and children ran and played. I sat on a park bench and watched a dog sniffing around the nearby fountain.

Although I was now free, I wondered if I would miss the world when it was finished with me. Valin had lived for over eighty years after he had passed it along, and doubtless it had been the same for the others before him. I probably wouldn't see another summer. Now that it had been taken away from me, I believed I wanted to see more of the world and what it held. I would miss it.

I regretted immensely what I had done with my life. I had lived for over a hundred years and had allowed myself to see nothing but the worst of it. I ruminated on how it may have been if I had seen more, done more. *Been* more.

Perhaps I could have helped humanity. Perhaps I could have used my special condition to aid them. Maybe I could have learned to be a doctor, a scientist. I might have worked towards them, *us*, having a better future. I perhaps could have led them to something brighter than their broken past.

There was so much more I could have done, could have experienced. In reality, life is a never-ending wonder but, instead of grasping it, I had turned my face away from it and had started to hate it.

I wished I'd had more time.

But then I cursed myself for my greediness. I had been given so many more years than most people could dream of, and all of them in the bloom of health. I had selfishly tried to kill myself once rather than continue with my existence. And now, when the end I had craved for so long was upon me, I wanted more. But in reality I wanted it not for me, but to see what would happen. How Pearl's life would turn out, how Precious would develop.

My phone rang again. I took it out and my heart sank when I saw the number.

'Doctor Fenwick,' I said. 'How are you?'

'Afternoon, Mr Deakin. I'm fine. I'm wondering if you have time to come into the surgery within the next few days? I have something to discuss with you.'

'I suppose I can,' I answered, evasively. I didn't like the doctors. 'What's it about?'

They must have found out something else. Maybe today was the day I discovered when I would die. The cold fingers of dread brushed me and I shivered. I still clung to life. It was very strange.

'Well, I don't want to go into it too much over the phone,' said Fenwick, 'but we've had word of a new treatment for cases like yours. Carville University, over in America, have been conducting tests on a new treatment for leukaemia and we're wanting to start the same testing over here. They've had some quite amazing results over there. As I've said, I'd rather talk to you face-to-face, and I don't want to get any hopes up, but I think it would be really good if we could talk soon.'

I frowned.

'The Carville University? In Washington?'

'Oh, you've heard of it? Yes. The doctors there are at the forefront of treatments against all sorts of cancer. The Herbert Pfumpf Memorial Research Centre has been working on things like this for years. Ever since the fifties I think. Have you already looked at their data? It's really interesting.'

I stared at my phone for a second, then laughed, shaking my head.

Fate. No such thing as fate. Never had been, never would be.

'No, but I will do,' I said. 'I can come in whenever it's best for you.'

We made an appointment for the next day. I tried not to get my hopes up too much, it was getting rather late in the day for that. But it was hard.

I left the park and walked the busy streets of London slowly, going back to the shop.

I sat with a cup of tea in the shop window and opened the birthday present Pearl had left for me. It was a new watch. I grinned, ruefully, fastening it around my wrist.

Tonight Precious and I were celebrating our birthdays, with my surrogate family, and tomorrow I would visit Doctor Fenwick and listen to what he had to say. Perhaps it would come to something, perhaps it wouldn't. Afterwards, I would sit at the table in my little shop and make wooden toys.

From its place on the shelf, the old black-and-white photograph of Madeleine smiled at me.

I smiled back.

*

Late September, 1959. The night was getting dark outside our cottage.

I lit the fire and put a record on. It was Glenn Miller, Moonlight Serenade. I turned as Madeleine came in with two glasses and a bottle of red. She wore a simple skirt and blouse, and her golden hair with its streaks of grey was loose over her shoulders. She glowed in the light from the fire. She smiled at me and I took the glasses and bottle from her, then took her hand. We danced slowly to that mournful, beautiful tune.

I breathed in the scent of her and closed my eyes. My happiness was complete, as it always was when she was near me. When she was with me.

We sat when the music ended and I poured us both a glass of wine. For a long time we just stared at the fire, my arm around her shoulders and her head on my chest.

Eventually, Madeleine turned towards me.
'Bill?'

'Yes?'

'We'll always be like this, won't we?'

I put down my glass.

'Of course. Why wouldn't we be?'

She didn't say anything for a long time, but I knew what she was thinking. She was getting older and I was staying the same. We both knew what the future held and it was something neither of us wanted.

She eventually sighed.

'Your life will be so different from mine, my sweet,' she started. I shook my head and put my fingers to her lips. I didn't want to talk about this, but she gently removed them and kissed them. She kept my hand in her own.

'Please. I need to say this to you, just once, and then never talk of it again. Your life will be different, and I want you to think about that. I want to give you some advice and I want you to listen to me. I want you to think about what you have, not what you may lose. You'll never be able to really live properly unless you come to terms with what life is. You think you are cursed but, in reality, you have been given a gift. Don't hate life. Don't miss out on happiness in the future because you think that happiness will be snatched away at any minute. That would be a monumental sin.'

'Maddy, please, I don't want to think about any of that.'

I leaned forward and picked up my glass, frowning. I didn't want this conversation. But Madeleine was not to be denied. She gently pulled me back towards her.

'Most lives are short for a reason, Bill. We all have to give way for others, to give them a turn on the wheel, if only for a while. Life is too precious to believe it will always be there.' She smiled at my frowning face. 'I know you deny this, but it's true. You know it's true. I won't always be here for you, my love, and I worry for your future. I worry about you. Life has been different for you. Life has been more constant for you than should have been allowed, and will continue to be long after I'm gone. Life will hold you longer than it should. Longer than anyone should endure.'

Madeleine smiled at the look on my face. She leaned over and kissed *my cheek, which had become damp. She wiped my silent tears away.*

'What you have to remember, Bill, is that life is a currency. A currency of time that has no worth, and yet is priceless. Without it we do not learn, we do not grow. Without time, how does the new born baby learn how to hold, how to grasp, how to stand, how to walk? Without time how does the tree grow, the seasons change, the years pass?

'You will see much on your travels, Bill. You will experience the highest and the lowest that life can bring. You will see terror and obsession and vice and bloodshed. And you will see love and laughter and warmth. It's the Yin and the Yang. The up and the down.'

Madeleine sighed and wiped her own eyes, sipping her wine.

'I believe you are the way you are for a reason, Bill. And I believe one day you will understand why you have been made like this. One day, perhaps a long time from now, you will realise that there is a purpose to your strange life. That you're not cursed. Instead, you are blessed.'

She took my face in her hands and she continued to smile at me, and her smile warmed my soul.

'One day, this will all make sense,' she said. 'And you will do what you know is right. And it will be wonderful. It's your fate.'

Madeleine looked deep into my eyes, and something inside me, something that had so many times in the past heaved with anger and hatred seemed to relax and settle, as if it agreed with her words. As if some sort of deal had been struck. She continued to stare at me until she suddenly nodded. She seemed satisfied that her words had been heeded. Then she sighed, contentedly and once more laid her head on my chest.

I held her tight, thinking about what she had said, and I knew she was right. Madeleine was always right. But the knowledge of this caused more tears to trickle slowly down my cheeks and into her hair.

I kissed the tears away and stared into the fire once more, that power inside me feeling warm and replete. After a while, Madeleine stood and selected another record: I'll Be Seeing You, by Billie Holiday. It was one of her favourites. She held out her hand to me and I smiled

and took it. I held her close as, together, we danced again.
    Forever.

The End

A Life Eternal

Richard Ayre

Did You Enjoy This Book?

If so, you can make a HUGE difference

For any author, the single most important way we have of getting our books noticed is a really simple one—and one which you can help with.

Yes, you.

Us indie authors and publishers don't have the financial muscle of the big guys to take out full-page ads in the newspaper or put posters on the subway.

But we do have something much more powerful and effective than that, and it's something that those big publishers would kill to get their hands on.

A committed and loyal bunch of readers.

Honest reviews of our books help bring them to the attention of other readers.

If you've enjoyed this book I would be really grateful if you could spend just a couple of minutes leaving a review (it can be as short as you like) on this book's page on your favourite store and website.

Thank you so much—you're awesome, each and every one of you!

Warm regards

Richard

Acknowledgements

I would like to say a huge thank you to my beta readers, whose comments and feedback were invaluable in helping us to turn this story into the finished product you have in your hands. So thank you to: Andreas Rauch, Fi Phillips, Joyce and David Oxley, Chris Tetreault-Blay, Keith Lemmon, Phillip, Cynthia Jenson, Alison Belding, and Roger Owen.

A special mention for Pete and Simon at Burning Chair. Thank you for your belief in my work.

Richard Ayre
May 2020

About the Author

Richard Ayre was born in Northumberland, too many years ago now to remember. He has had a variety of jobs including roofer, milkman and factory worker. Tiring of this, Richard studied for a degree with the Open University and now teaches History for a living.

At an impressionable age he fell in love with new wave Heavy Metal and rock music and at about the same time read his first James Herbert novel. The combination of these two magnificent things led him to write his first novel, Minstrel's Bargain, a tale of music and horror. He now lives in Newcastle upon Tyne where he continues to write whenever he can. When not writing, or putting children on detention, he can be found pottering around the Northumberland landscape on his motorcycle, Tanya.

You can contact Richard via FaceBook, Twitter, or through his website: https://richardayre1.wixsite.com/richard-ayre-author

About Burning Chair

Burning Chair is an independent publishing company based in the UK, but covering readers and authors around the globe. We are passionate about both writing and reading books and, at our core, we just want to get great books out to the world.

Our aim is to offer something exciting; something innovative; something that puts the author and their book first. From first class editing to cutting edge marketing and promotion, we provide the care and attention that makes sure that every book fulfils its potential.

We are:

- Different
- Passionate
- Nimble and cutting edge
- Invested in our authors' success

If you're an **author** and would like to know more, visit www.burningchairpublishing.com for our submissions requirements and our free guide to book publishing.

If you're a **reader** and are interested in becoming a beta reader for us, helping us to create yet more awesome books (and getting to read them for free in the process!), please visit www.burningchairpublishing.com/beta-readers.

Other Books by Burning Chair Publishing

Going Dark (Tom Novak Book 1), by Neil Lancaster

Going Rogue (Tom Novak Book 2), by Neil Lancaster

Haven Wakes, by Fi Phillips

Beyond, by Georgia Springate

Burning: An Anthology of Thriller Shorts, edited by Simon Finnie and Peter Oxley

The Infernal Aether Series, by Peter Oxley
*   The Infernal Aether
*   A Christmas Aether
*   The Demon Inside
*   Beyond the Aether
*   The Old Lady of the Skies: 1: Plague

The Wedding Speech Manual: The Complete Guide to Preparing, Writing and Performing Your Wedding Speech, by Peter Oxley

www.burningchairpublishing.com

Richard Ayre

Printed in Great Britain
by Amazon

66630739R00163